A DAUGHTER FORGED IN FIRE

CHRONICLES OF THE TUATHA

BOOK ONE

JESSICA LEIGH

Cover art by © Krafigs Design

Proofreading, developmental, and copy editing services provided by Sarah Giblin

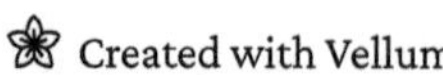
Created with Vellum

For Justin

DEAR READER

Thank you for choosing to read my debut novel, *A Daughter Forged in Fire*. I am so excited to share the characters and world within this novel with you all. As a courtesy to my readers, I would like to disclose the following trigger warnings for the book. Your mental health matters and I always seek to ensure my readers are aware of any sensitive themes explored within my written work.

A Daughter Forged in Fire contains sensitive and mature themes and is intended for an adult 18+ audience. **The following sensitive topics are contained within the work**: fantasy violence (swords, bows, and arrows, warfare, genocide), abuse (NOT by the MMC), misogyny (NOT by the MMC), loss of a parent, infant loss (mention of miscarriage, not graphic in nature), sexual content, suicidal thoughts, and language.

There is also a link on my website listed below that you can use to submit a content warning that you felt should have been included based on your interpretation of the book.

https://linktr.ee/authorjessicaleigh

I am humbled and grateful to have you as my reader and I hope you enjoy this world I have come to love so very much. Welcome to the world of Eire!

Always,

Jessica Leigh

Éire

Ulaid

Uí Néill

Dál Fiatach

Tír fo Thionn

Maigh Tuireadh

Lia Fáil

Connacht

Hill of Tara

Osraige

gan mhíniú

Hedrek's Estate

Rhia's cottage

Baile

Muir Éireann

PRONUNCIATION GUIDE

Éire - ay-RUH

Rhiannon - ree-ANN-uhn

Rhia - ree-UH

Beatha - BA-huh

Draíocht - dree-AH-ck-t

Ecna - eck-NUH

Rowan - row-UHN

Alistair - ah-LI-stare

Murdag - mur-DAH-g

Baile - BAL-yuh

Nichnevin - nick-NUH-vin

Aine - ahn-YUH

Hedrek - head-RICK

Hectre - HEC-ter

Brenainn - BREN-an

Dagda - dahg-DUH

Imogen - EHM-o-gen

Lugh - looh

Balor - bah-LORE

Famorians - fah-MOR-ee-uhns

Tír fo Thuinn - chier-FO-hun

Maigh Tuireadh - mwee-TU-rah

Dál Fiatach - DUHL-fee-YA-tuck

Lia Fáil - lee-UH-fall

CHAPTER ONE

RHIANNON

Rhiannon ran barefoot through the lush forest floor, covered with moss and leaves. Spring had settled over the land, and she could hear laughter from a nearby celebration echoing on the wind. The breeze swept over her, the setting sun's rays warming her skin. Her people would be celebrating Beltane, the midway mark between the spring equinox and the summer solstice. The ceremonial fires would be lit, and the children of Danu would dance until the sunrise of the following day.

Peculiar, Rhiannon thought to herself. *I do not recall Beatha mentioning that any of our people would be joining us to celebrate this year . . . I wonder, has Elder Ecna brought company?*

Her thoughts were interrupted by a flutter of dark wings that flew before her eyes as a striking raven perched on a branch of a nearby yew tree. She paused to admire the regal beauty of the creature for a moment.

Rhia's heart began to race as she smelled a slight tinge of

smoke wafting in the air. The scent of burning trees and something *else* that she could not quite place.

All at once, a deafening scream pierced the silence of the forest as a dagger seemed to come out of nowhere, impaling through the center of the raven's chest. The bird fell from the branch into a lifeless mass of blood and feathers on the ground.

Rhiannon immediately leapt forward as she cried out, scooping up the bird into her arms and attempting to remove the dagger. She pressed the hem of her tunic into the bird's chest in an effort to stop the bleeding. She felt an icy cold chill climb her spine as the raven opened its eyes, meeting her gaze. The creature's eyes were the most piercing gold color she had ever seen. She broke into a cold sweat as panic began to set in, she could now hear screams and cries all around her as the forest became engulfed in flames.

Rhiannon opened her eyes with a jolt, her breathing was labored, her linen bedclothes soaked in cold sweat. She focused on the warm sunlight pouring into the house as she turned away from the window by her bed, flinging an arm over her eyes to delay the start of the day.

As if she could prevent the sun's imminent rise, and with it, today's task. She huffed a breath as she slowly sat up and felt the coolness of the wooden floor against her bare feet.

This was reality.

Here and now. Each breath settled her as she attempted to quiet her mind and reorient herself to her surroundings.

It was only a dream.

Each creak of the wood was familiar as she collected her linen robe and followed the smell of brewing tea into the kitchen. "I thought you'd sleep all day, child—you'd best prepare for Elder Ecna." Beatha greeted her with a half-smile and a gleam in her eye.

"Oh Beatha, I've done nothing *but* prepare . . . for *weeks*. Do I not have the marks to prove it?" Rhiannon replied in an exasperated tone as she held up the pale skin of her fore-arms, displaying an array of small burns in various places. Rhiannon had tried her best to perfect her fire magic over the last year.

Each year nearing Beltane, the first fire festival of the warm months, Elder Ecna would make his way deep into the forest to where she and her grandmother resided in their small dwelling to take inventory of Rhiannon's progress in her training. Beatha had served as Rhiannon's guide in developing her draíocht, or magic. Each year, Rhiannon underwent a set of tests and trials conducted by the elder of her people's tribe, to determine the effectiveness of Beatha's guidance and decide if the girl would be able to advance in her training. If not, she must repeat her previous series of lessons for the next round of seasons.

She still remembered the season she almost failed, last year, the year she began to work with fire—her most difficult lesson yet. She knew that Elder Ecna was only performing his duties as the councilman of their people, but she dreaded his presence every season.

Rhiannon could now boast of the ability to bend water into various shapes and strengths, call forth stems and shoots of plant life from the earth, and use her very breath to manipulate the breeze into a strong gust of wind. However, last year when she began her first fire trial, the test that would determine her ability to call forth flame from her fingers, she almost fell short.

She would never forget the look of concern on Beatha's face as she could barely create heat friction from the earth into her palms. Rhiannon did not know if it was pity in Elder Ecna's heart, or if Beatha had somehow pleaded with him for her advancement, but he passed her to the next year of lessons without an assessment of her final task—palpable heat from her fingertips.

"Rhia, you know what he will want to see. You possess all that you need inside of you, never forget that." Beatha said gently, calling her by the nickname she had given her as a young girl, breaking Rhiannon free from her spiraling thoughts as her stomach tensed into a ball of anxiety.

"I know Beatha, I have prepared as best I can," she replied, although her face told another story.

Beatha raised a single wild gray eyebrow as she huffed a remark into her teacup. Rhia could slip nothing by her. "Fear will stalemate your success if you ever let it catch up to you," the old woman remarked with a smack of her lips as she tied a strip of leather around the base of her wild grey locks.

Beatha was wise—irritatingly so.

Rhia picked up a clay cup of warm tea from the table that Beatha had prepared for her and brought it to her lips. The aroma of the herbs and spices within brought warmth to her bones and calmness to her heart as her smile reached her eyes, "Thank you."

During her last several days of training, she had managed to create enough friction within two ribbons of veiled wind energy to bring about a spark of light, each one extinguishing almost as fast as she had created it by the wind gust that followed.

Never had she brought forth fire from her fingertips. Always by an outside effort of her air draíocht—hence the burn marks on her arms. She secretly hoped that a sleight of hand could fool Elder Ecna into seeing the flames appear from her fingertips rather than from air.

She had foolheartedly practiced this illusion instead of the fire draíocht exercises that Beatha had left her alone to practice. Beatha's instructed method of bringing about the fire seemed more tiresome, more difficult for Rhia to perform. She instructed the girl to call the fire forth from her center, from her heart space, to feel it flow down her arms to her fingertips. Try as she might, Rhia had not yet proved able to do this. It was this shortcoming that had her the most uneasy about Elder Ecna's evaluation.

It's not like Beatha could perform this task either, she only dully read the words from the old leatherbound book she had taught her from since childhood. Beatha could manipulate earth and stone with a skill that made Rhia's bones shudder but that seemed the only element she had dominion over. She often wondered why she was held to a standard that even her tutor did not possess. She wondered if Elder Ecna even possessed all four elemental abilities, or did he just find satisfaction in appraising skills in others?

He's how many centuries old now? How good could his vision still be? she thought to herself with a roll of her eyes as she sat her mug down on the table and rose to make her way back to her room to dress.

She breathed in the dusty air from her wardrobe as she pulled free a soft moss-dyed wrap to bind her breasts and midsection in a crisscross pattern, a pair of soft deer hide leggings, and her worn leather boots that laced up to her knees. She pulled on and wrapped the clothing until it was securely in place, donning a silver-encased oval charm that she tied around her neck with a thin strip of hide. The silver bezel of the charm showcased a pearlescent pale blue stone in its center—the color of the stone matching the shade of her own eyes. Her necklace was a twin to the one worn by Beatha.

She braided the long, loose red curls that flowed down her back into a single plait, tied with a strip of leather to avoid any mishaps with her fire draíocht. As the stone rested on her chest, she felt the weight of what she suspected to be its magic. Beatha told her that she had been gifted this stone by her parents when she was left with her as an infant. She was told that her parents had been enslaved and sent to a faraway land against their will. Their departure forced them to leave Rhia in the care of her grandmother.

Beatha had hidden Rhia deep within the forest, lest she grow up a slave as well.

She knew the intention was for a better life for their child, but she often wondered what her parents were like, what it would have been like to be brought up by a mother and a father. Often, she couldn't shake the feeling that she had a sibling as well. Out of nowhere, she would be accosted with memories that came flooding back—red braided hair, strong but graceful footsteps crunching the leaves of the forest floor, the scent of morning dew on the grass.

She wondered if any of them were still alive at all. Everyone knew the fate of the Tuatha people, if they were discovered by the race of men that seemed to be closing in around them. Trapped like animals by the Milesians. Enslaved.

Subjugated to torture and pain to extract their draíocht against their will and use it for the advancement of Milesians —of mortal men.

It was only by the wards placed around the forest and the home that Beatha and Rhia shared, only by the enchantments cast by the old woman that she had been protected from the suspicious eyes of the race of men these last 126 years. How Beatha had managed to stay protected and hidden for the 537 years before even she had been alive, Rhia wasn't sure she wanted to know. She shuddered with the breeze blowing in her window.

Every other new moon, when the sky was at its darkest, Beatha and Rhia would don their heavy hooded cloaks and make their way to the nearby village of Baile near the border of Éire to replenish their supplies.

The women would pull their hoods tightly over their heads to hide their faces, and *gods-help* anyone see the blue-tinged band of flesh encircling their left forearms.

Tuatha were born with narrow bands of raised flesh on their left forearms that turned a darker hue of blue with each passing season of age. Some say the old gods placed these bands upon their children so that they will know those who call upon their names, even those who do not use draíocht, when they return to the land and reclaim the throne of their people.

In any village or township within Éire, the land of men, the band meant a death sentence. A life of forced servitude or an instant beheading—depending on the motives or cruelty of the captor.

Rhia felt a deep sadness sinking into her chest at the thought of the state of her people. She had been told of Tuatha ways by Beatha since infancy and had gleaned as much information as her mind could digest through scouring through the old leatherbound volumes of ancient texts that Beatha kept shelved by the front door. If only she could find a text that explained *why in the fates* her fire draíocht refused to work . . . that would be the most useful information at the present time.

The sun painted shadows that cut through the trees as the light shone brightly against Rhia's fiery red hair and milky freckled flesh. Her pale blue eyes glanced upward as she determined from the sun's position that over half the day was already gone. An uneasiness crept up her spine as she looked through the trees carefully for any sight of Elder Ecna. She heard neither footsteps, nor the rustling of a cloak against the leaves on the ground. She was met with only the silent stillness of the forest and the occasional whisper of the wind through the trees.

As the sun sank low over the horizon, Rhia slowly pushed open the door to the cottage as Beatha's bright eyes flew up from her book to meet hers. "Well child, how did you fare?" Beatha asked with a hint of apprehension in her voice.

". . . He never arrived."

Rhia's breathy reply had Beatha immediately on her feet and making her way to the closet to fetch cloaks for herself and the girl. "Gather your bow and your wits at once, something is amiss," the old woman commanded with a seriousness that had Rhia scrambling to her room to fetch the bow and quiver of arrows she kept tucked away under her bed.

Beatha tossed the dark wool cloak to Rhia. She slung it on, tucking away the wild stands of her copper mane into the hood. Beatha fastened the ties tightly above Rhia's chest, her bony hands almost trembling as she worked. She did not look into Rhia's eyes—she didn't need to for the girl to feel the gravity of the situation.

"Listen to me carefully. Tonight is unlike any new moon that we have traveled to the village. Elder Ecna has roamed these lands at least three hundred years longer than I, and I have never known him to fail to keep his word. It would take a great deal to keep him from his duty. We do what we must, but we tread carefully. We keep our ears and eyes open for any threats moving our way." Beatha huffed with a tight pull of the cloak fastenings.

Rhia's eyes flashed with something akin to fear as she searched the old woman's face for any hint of what could be awry, fear settling deep into her bones as she slung the quiver of arrows over her shoulder. "What did I tell you about *fear*, girl? Never let it catch you and do not look back."

Rhia pressed a kiss to Beatha's weathered hands as they adjusted the cloak to conceal her weaponry. "We stay close together this night," Rhia said softly as they prepared to leave the cottage under the cover of darkness. There was not even the illumination of the moon to lead them as they departed and made their way to the village of Baile.

Darkness was their friend, and tonight, their protector.

CHAPTER
TWO
ROWAN

A pale horned owl flew overhead and wailed a piercing cry into the silence of the early evening as it dove toward the shaded tree line of the nearby forest. Rowan glanced up at the sinking sunset, using his forearm to wipe beads of sweat and ash from his brow.

The night sky was fast approaching, and with it, the pressing need for him to finish the task at hand. He glanced down at the red-hot piece of iron in his hands, each strike of his hammer hurling tiny sparks of fire upward into the darkening sky. His large forearm tensed with each assault on the piece of metal beneath him. Dark brown tendrils of long hair that escaped the leather tie at the nape of his neck clung to his forehead, trapped in a mixture of sweat and ash as he winced at the increase in the pace of his strikes. He needed to have this blade ready to quench before sundown.

His father had been working on the weapon when he left town for his most recent trip to a distant territory of the Milesian kingdom. Rowan had finished his fair share of blades within his twenty-seven years of life, but added production demands had increased the blacksmithing trade in recent years. King Hectre's army had a need for strong blades for their conquests beyond Milesian borders.

Rowan's father Alistair had been a devoted supplier of blades to the king's forces in recent years. His business often took him to faraway territories to deliver his wares to armies posted in distant encampments. He had packed the scabbards and swords of the most recent order onto his horse Seamus, and began the ten-day journey there and back from a seaward encampment on the continent's northwestern coast at Connacht.

Alistair had instructed Rowan to finish the broadsword he had been working on for Hedrek, the captain of the guard and the king's own brother. In recent years, news of Rowan and Alistair's smithing skills had spread across the region.

Rowan felt the seriousness of his father's request when, a day prior to Alistair's departure, he clamped his only hand on Rowan's shoulder and met the gaze of his piercing green eyes.

"Hedrek's messenger has requested that we sprinkle this vial of powder on the blade before it is quenched," his father stated simply, reaching into his pocket, and discretely placing an iron ampule into Rowan's palm. "I would do this myself, but the king's business takes me elsewhere," he said with a long sigh.

The weariness in his eyes was beginning to show.

Alistair had only his right arm to bring the firm swing of a hammer down to meet metal. He had only spoken briefly of the battle in which he lost his left arm—from the forearm down. Rowan had assumed an enemy had taken it in an attempt at his father's life. He had never known the full tale as his father did not like to speak of past wars.

"I am honored to complete this task for you, and for the kingdom," Rowan replied as he held his father's serious gaze.

"Son, I am not so sure anymore which of the tasks we do are for the kingdom, and which are for the greed that thrives within the hearts of men."

Rowan's fingers traced the wax-sealed rim of the cold iron vial. "What is this father? Some sort of ore to strengthen the integrity of the blade?"

"It is a powder that Hedrek has had concocted that he feels will add *something* to the quality of the steel," Alistair replied with an exasperated tone. "Of what that is, I do not know. I am not privy to that information."

Rowan's brow quirked as he threw his father a suspicious half-smile, "What exactly would he be able to concoct to do that? Does he employ the aid of some mysterious Tuatha spell-worker?"

"That's enough questions for today. Please only do as I ask and keep your discretion about you when it comes to this task," Alistair replied curtly.

His knitted brows softened into a gentle smile as his hand curved around the back of Rowan's head and brought his forehead to his own. "I will return soon. I am confident of your abilities to complete whatever is needed for the kingdom."

"And for our family. You and me, father," Rowan met his smile with his own. For a moment, an ache moved through his chest as he thought of his mother . . . or what he knew of her. He mourned what could have been, more so than the person she was. He had never known her face.

She had passed in childbirth. The day he entered the world.

He mourned the absence he felt in his life, growing up without a mother to lean upon, like many of his boyhood acquaintances. He mourned more than that for his father, as he saw the deep pain in his eyes each time he spoke her name.

Alistair only spoke of her on two occasions: on the anniversary of her death—Rowan's birth—and when the ale cast a glossy distant stare over his eyes as he remembered her fondly. The memories of their time together would escape his lips until the familiar embrace of sleep claimed him.

"Í a aimsiú. Í a chosaint. Tabhair ar ais é a bhfuil caillte." Alistair would mutter before dreams took him. Always the same phrase. Rowan often thought that maybe it was a command from his mother to his father before her passing. Perhaps it was a prayer to the Gods in the ancient tongue, but he knew not what for.

He once told Rowan, after a long night and many pulls of ale, how they had decided on his name—just before he was born. As his mother fought the passing through the veil into the next life, his father always reminded him of her last words upon the earth:

"Name him after the Rowan. For its wood is strong and resilient; I hope this babe will grow to be the same."

Hammer met iron in a mad surge of sparks and heat as Rowan held up the flattened and shaped blade in the light of the setting sun. The sword glowed a deep red as he lowered it over the metal beams of the worktable and withdrew the iron vial from his pocket. A slight sizzling sound could be heard as Rowan gently sprinkled the contents over the iron.

As the powder billowed back into the air from where he had sprinkled it, Rowan felt a nauseous feeling come over him. His legs and arms began to feel heavy, and his movements became slightly clumsy. The sizzling sound slowly faded as the powder bound to the metal. The feeling that came from breathing in the air near the powder quickly passed as it faded into the blade.

Odd, Rowan thought, as he lifted the sword and walked to the barrel of oil and dipped it into its contents, quenching the entirety of the weapon.

CHAPTER THREE

RHIANNON

The occasional rustling of cloaks and light footsteps over crunching leaves were the only sounds heard through the dense cover of night as Beatha and Rhia made their way to Baile. As they neared the border of the wood line and prepared to venture into the border of town, Beatha turned nose-to-nose with Rhia. "I will meet with Murdag at the trading post and make our dealings for supplies. If something is truly amiss nearby, he will tell me of it. If his loyalties still lie with his mother's people, he will not betray our trust. Stay close to me. If the need to flee arises, we will exit the trading post from the back door and leave town opposite the way we entered. I know of a mountain pass at the north end of Baile that will encircle back to our wood. We cannot risk leading an enemy back into our home by using a direct path."

Rhia's eyes widened with each word Beatha spoke. "Do you feel something has changed? Are we ourselves in danger?"

"Danger comes in many forms. As does trust. We know not where a Milesian's loyalties lie. In the past, we have found friends among us in Baile, but I fear that times are changing with the coming age. As I have said, keep your wits about you." Beatha replied as she pulled the hood of her cloak tightly and continued toward Baile with Rhia following closely behind.

Rhia looked to her surroundings, glancing at the remnants of a thatched-roof cottage. She smiled to herself, remembering their past trips to Baile on this very path. She recalled the first time Beatha had allowed her to join in. She was but a young girl, barely on the cusp of womanhood, when she had first journeyed into the village on one of their supply outings. Beatha had spent all morning preaching on about keeping a low profile, only for Rhia to separate from her grandmother at the first interesting thing she saw on their journey.

She had heard the cries of a woman in labor from within that very cottage, thirty years before. Rhiannon had separated from Beatha, moving inside the cottage to aid the woman in the birth. She remembered how her pale face had been stricken with fear as the young redhead approached her. She wasn't progressing in the birth, sweat beading on her forehead as she agonized through the contractions.

Rhia placed a gentle palm on her belly, as the nursemaid beside her shuddered in fear, seeing the blue-tinged band of flesh as she pushed up her sleeves to help.

"Are you here to take my baby? To . . . to steal him away for . . . for a changeling?" the woman asked, through panting breaths.

Rhia smiled a gentle smile, her palms gently pressing into the woman's abdomen, her body relaxing beneath Rhia's touch. "No, no I am here to help you." Rhia had replied. Warm light filled the cottage as Rhia closed her eyes, using her draíocht to ease the woman's pain and comfort her during the transition.

Beatha had burst into the cabin moments later, swinging the door wide as she studied Rhia, sitting behind the Milesian woman, braiding her hair as the mother held a flushed, pink, healthy baby boy nursing at her chest. Beatha simply beckoned Rhia to come, and they silently left the cottage.

They never spoke of the occasion again.

Now, as they exited the wood line and into open land, a foul odor wafted on the air toward them. In the reflective light of the nearby town, Rhia could see a shrouded figure lying on the side of the road leading into Baile. "My child, do not approach," Beatha warned as she placed a hand across Rhia's shoulders.

Rhia looked up to the gate to the entrance of Baile in horror as bile rose to her throat. The pale glazed eyes of Elder Ecna reflected in the light of the guard post lantern—his head impaled upon a sharpened post.

The blue raised band of flesh from his left forearm was carved away and placed upon his dismembered head as it shone as a light and a warning to any who entered Baile. Beatha placed a gentle hand over Rhia's mouth to silence her cry as she crouched their two bodies together as they entered the town, keeping a low profile in the shadows. She knew that the slumped silhouette on the roadside must be Ecna's body.

"Beatha, what is the meaning of all this? Are Milesian forces here tonight?" Rhia whispered, wide-eyed as she followed Beatha into the trading post. Beatha remained silent as they pulled their cloaks around their faces. They made their way through the throng of people to the side of the wooden counter nearing the back of the room. Rhia held a deep tension in her shoulders as she navigated the room with Beatha. *There are so many things that could go wrong this night*, she thought to herself. She struggled to calm the racing of her heart and even her breathing. Rhia didn't miss how Beatha was careful to tuck her own moonstone fragment necklace far down into her tunic, away from watchful eyes.

A Milesian male with a ruddy complexion and graying stringy hair found Beatha's eyes immediately and motioned with his chin for the two to approach the far side of the counter. "It's not a night for an elder woman like yourself to be meandering into town." He said to Beatha with a warning in his dark gaze. Rhia thought it peculiar that he would not look her directly in the eyes. "Hedrek's forces have just made an example of one of the likes of you and my gut tells me they're not done yet."

Hedrek Scrios was the brother of King Hectre. The captain of his armies and a man who made wiping out any remaining Tuatha his personal campaign. The two women had heard through Murdag that his forces had been seen riding across the continent as of late, rounding up any remnants of their people that he could find. Evidence of his conquest this close to home was unsettling, to say the least.

"The old man only confirmed Hedrek's suspicions that

we were harboring Tuatha here." Fear shone in Murdag's eyes as he glanced between Beatha and Rhia. "Best you leave this pretty gem at home next time. If I know Hedrek, he'll be back himself next time, the gods only know how soon that will be." Murdag moved closer to the women. "And I'm sure he'd like nothing more than to take her for his spoils. We have heard rumors of the captain's *appetites*." Murdag's eyes slid unceremoniously down Rhia's cloaked body.

Rhia's magic bubbled to the surface, along with her anger at the man's blatant stares, causing her to shiver with disgust. A slight wind picked up inside of the trading post from the window and wound itself around the bottom of Murdag's cloak, eliciting a puzzled look from the man.

"I am more than capable of defending myself—" Rhia's words were cut off by Beatha turning her shoulders to walk her away to the corner of the room.

"Child, this is not the time to be anything but a peasant woman, here with her grandmother, purchasing supplies. *Nothing* more." The seriousness in Beatha's eyes brought her *draíocht* back to her center and her breathing evened out.

"Is this not the time to prepare to defend ourselves Beatha? Milesian forces are all but on our doorstep. We must use what gifts we have cultivated to shield ourselves if need be."

"Yes . . . and you must learn what deserves your anger and defense and what does not," Beatha replied quietly as she glanced back at Murdag. "As crass and indecorous as he is, he has been a friend of our people for many years. His mother's blood runs deep in his veins. He has not forgotten his Tuatha heritage." Rhia nodded. "Now that we have learned of Elder Ecna's fate, all we have left is to gather supplies and leave this place. The sooner the better."

Beatha walked back over to the counter and exchanged a small pouch of copper for a cloth sack filled with oats and wool that she slung over her left shoulder. Rhia started toward her to offer to carry the bag, "Thank you, Murdag—" Beatha's exchange was cut off by a sudden slamming of the heavy wooden door into the side of the wattle-and-daub wall. Heavy booted feet entered the dwelling, silence settling over the patrons of the establishment.

"MURDAAAAG!" screeched a soldier in leather armor, his hand on a longsword at his side. Beatha and Rhia ducked behind the door at the far end of the room, their bodies pressed against the wall as they sought to quiet their breathing. "I heard some interesting news on our way out of town this evening. Who knew there were this many Tuatha wandering around the same shit-smelling, rat-infested town." The man remarked as he sauntered into the trade post, eyes sweeping left to right, surveying the crowd of people from under large dark brows. Several armed soldiers with blades drawn followed into the dwelling behind the man, herding men and women into the center of the room.

"Hedrek and the king grow tired of deceit. Tired of sympathy for these vermin, whose sharp-tongued words keep this land under a heavy curse." The man bellowed out over the crowd. "You toil in the soil year after year, wondering why your crops grow weaker each season. You *ignorant* peasants call yourselves kinsmen of the king, yet you blatantly betray him by harboring enemies of the crown in plain sight."

He turned, pointing a finger toward the entrance to the town, "The elder was to be an example to you—this is how the crown regards the remaining Tuatha who may be among you, as well as *any* who may be foolish enough to aid them. We will rid the land of their kind once and for all, and any man, woman, or child who sympathizes with them." The man spat as he withdrew his blade and made his way to the back of the room, where a trembling Murdag withered behind the counter. The deadly end of a broadsword met the pulse point of Murdag's throat, sweat glistening as it ran down his temple. "No more games, merchant."

Rhia and Beatha slowly slid the bag of supplies behind the corner of the door and quietly moved to the right, ducking behind the corner of the back door of the dwelling. Beatha's wide eyes met Rhia's as she mouthed "*Run*, run fast. Take the mountain pass."

"Not without you, Beatha. Don't even consider it," Rhia whispered as Beatha placed a finger over the girl's lips and leaned closer.

"I *will* find you again. We will meet down the road; this is not the end of our journey. It is safer if we travel separately for now. I have my reasons Rhia, *please* trust me," the old woman said with a fierce look in her eyes.

"Find the large, forked tree at the wood line. Pass it until you come to a stream. Follow the stream toward the sunrise —it will lead you around the base of the mountain. Use the path to find your way back to the wood. Return home, take the book we use to practice your draíocht. Flip to the end — you will understand where to go from there." Beatha instructed.

Confusion etched Rhia's brow as Beatha angled her body and turned back around the corner where they just had just come from and shoved her out into the town lamplight. "*Run*, girl."

Rhia's eyes widened as she watched Beatha enter back into the trading post. Just as she was preparing to run after her, she heard heavy booted footsteps rounding the corner of the trading post heading in her direction. *Damnit,* she thought as she ground her teeth in anger. She craned her neck, struggling to see Beatha's form in the window of the trading post. Another loud set of footfalls echoed from her left.

Her bow and quiver rattled beneath her cloak as she took off toward the wood line. Her breathing was heavy and ragged as she hid behind the forked tree and looked back between the trunks toward the village.

Shouts of fear echoed in the night. She could see the frightened residents of Baile begin to light lanterns and crowd the streets as the town awoke to shouts of fire and the clanging of swords. Heavy hoofbeats shook the ground as soldiers in leather armor with bronze helmets covering their faces rode into the town center from all sides. A soldier leading the battalion, likely the captain of the guard himself, wore a dark cloak that billowed behind him as he rode out front to face the ranks.

"For the future of the Milesian people! Let it be known, all who stand with the Tuatha stand against the king!" The captain reached down to grasp a torch of fire, handed to him by another soldier standing nearby. "If you will not surrender them to us willingly, we *will* drive them out!"

Murdag appeared from behind the line of soldiers, pushing a cloaked figure in front of him. Rhia's breath caught in her throat. Her heart stopped as she saw Beatha thrown to the ground before the captain. Her grey hair shone brightly in the torchlight as she glared up at him and a guard flung back the hood of her cloak. She was at once apprehended by a nearby guard, the sleeve of her left arm pulled back, revealing to the captain the blue band of raised flesh on her left forearm. "Oh, don't look so surprised, old woman," Murdag spat as he glared down at Beatha, "Hedrek's men could offer more coin than your measly wares could ever hope to garner."

"I knew you'd come to your senses, Murdag," said the man who had entered the trading post earlier. He stepped from behind the line of soldiers and placed a coin pouch in Murdag's hand.

"I do not fear you, false one," Beatha spat as she unabashedly glared into the captain's eyes. A booted foot came down upon her back, knocking the old woman to her hands and knees in the dirt. Rhia felt her body involuntarily lurch forward as she saw Beatha being shoved to the ground. She caught herself and did her best to stay in the cover of the shadows.

"You will speak with respect when addressing the brother of the king."

"I know of no such king. In place of a *man* on the throne, this land is destined to birth a *daughter of fire*. A queen of land, sea, wind, and flame. One to restore all that has been lost. To bring back life to the famished land, the Nichnevin will return our people to their rightful place—" Her words were cut off by the blunt handle of a sword to the back of her head.

NO! Rhia screamed internally. She watched the woman's unconscious body fall to a heap on the ground. Rhia prepared to run to her, to offer herself in Beatha's place. It was all she could do to keep her feet firmly planted on the ground where she stood. Her mind and body were at war.

Why—why didn't she run with me when she had the chance? Surely, she had to know that she would be captured . . .

Rhia's mind flew in a hundred different directions. Maybe she could be a bargaining tool for these Milesians. She shut out every thought of the repulsive life she would live as a young female in their company—should they choose to keep her alive. She must protect Beatha. Beatha was the only family Rhia had ever known, and she would *die* to protect her if need be.

As Rhia prepared to bolt out of the wood line, guards seized Beatha, binding her with ropes to a post at the center of Baile. The captain of the guard held his torch high and then dropped it at the foot of the old woman's cloak. Rhia's heart dropped inside her chest.

No, no, no.

Her breathing ceased for a moment.

She couldn't move, couldn't think. Fear seemed to paralyze every muscle in her body—a horrifying sound escaped her lips before she could stop it.

Her screams were drowned out by the accompanying shouts from the townspeople as guards simultaneously threw torches of fire onto thatched rooftops and into the windows of houses within the village. "There was another!"

a soldier on horseback sounded as he rode hard from around a house, circling the perimeter of the city's guard post at the entrance to town. "You cannot keep them hidden forever!"

Rhia's glance flew back to where Beatha was bound to the post, only to find her cloak hanging loosely from the ropes binding it to the pole. The boots and dagger that the old woman kept on her side were lying on the ground near where her feet would have been. Her entire being had seemingly vanished. The cry of a great horned owl pierced the air as feathers fluttered in the distance.

CHAPTER
FOUR
ROWAN

Rowan awoke to the smell of smoke and the sound of screaming outside the window of the small home he shared with his father. Alistair was due back any day now. Rowan had counted the days carefully, and when his father did not appear by sundown on this day, a knot of tension had begun to develop in his stomach. He quickly rose from the straw mattress and flung open the clouded window. Smoke billowed from homes on either side of his as folk ran through the streets in maniacal panic.

He flung his sword and scabbard over his shoulders and quickly strapped two daggers to his thighs as he ran from the house and weaved through the thongs of people in the streets. Men and women were throwing all manner of liquids on the burning buildings—water from the livestock troughs, even piss-filled chamber pots—to try to extinguish the spreading flames.

The town was slowly being overtaken by fire and panic.

Rowan's eyes desperately searched the crowd for any

sign of his father. He looked to the hill overlooking the town, hoping to see him ride over the horizon. They would attempt to salvage what they could from this mess together. Rowan kept their home in the corner of his vision, tension building in his wide shoulders as the flames inched closer and closer to their humble dwelling. His eyes met those of their young neighbor Cillian. A boy of no more than eighteen years, attempting to aid his aging father in hauling a chest of family heirlooms from their burning home.

"How did this begin? Who is behind this attack?" Rowan shouted to Cillian over the sound of cracking beams and shrill cries.

"Hedrek and his men. They found Tuatha here," the boy replied with something akin to fear in his dark eyes. "They are gone now. They appear to be tracking one of them who has fled to the forest."

Rowan whirled at the sound of a splitting beam behind him. A large beam of wood engulfed in flames fell into the side of his roof. He turned and ran quickly back inside the house as the thick smoke continued to surge in through the windows. He made his way to the room that his father slept in and retrieved a hinged wooden yew box from beneath the bed. He ran to his own room and slid his best hammer into the holster he wore at his waist. He retrieved a cloak from the hook by the door and fled back through the front door of their home.

He sprinted far from the flames to a clearing close to the edge of town, near the entrance to a hidden mountain pass that led deep into the forest. He used his hands to dig a shallow hole in the dirt and placed the wooden box inside of it. He covered it with dirt, and again with loose leaves and sticks to further conceal its presence. His father's grief for their mother had reinforced the thought that Rowan had always carried—to find a way to preserve the box, and her memory with it, if his father were ever unable to do so.

He had lifted the lid just once as a young boy. He was curious, as most young ones are, and his father caught him exploring the contents one day when left to his own devices.

Rowan had discovered a leatherbound book, secured with a deer hide strap with his father's writing inside the fading pages. A lock of what he assumed was his mother's hair, and a rough-cut oval blue stone of the most peculiar color.

The stone seemed to refract the light and resemble the haunting paleness of the moon with a blue hue that glowed bright in the warm sunlight that had poured in through the window. Rowan was holding up the stone to the light and tracing the patterns of color through it when his father had suddenly appeared in the doorway.

"What are you doing, Rowan?" he bellowed as the boy had quickly shut the lid and attempted to slide the box back underneath the bed.

"I only wished to know what was inside," he said with a hint of apprehension, unsure of his father's reaction.

"I will show you more when the time comes. For now, I wish for you to stay away from the contents of *my* box," Alistair replied with a smile and a stern edge to his voice. He held his hand out to Rowan expectantly. "Come now, I know you still hold it." Rowan reluctantly placed the blue stone in Alistair's hand.

"Today, you will learn that which you seek out will become your responsibility. You must learn to treasure what is left in your care, *Dionadair*." Rowan looked puzzled as he pondered over the meaning behind the nickname that his father had never spoken before. "Come, my son. Today we will give my sword a new addition to its hilt."

That was the day that Rowan and his father had welded an encasement to the end of Alistair's sword hilt and placed the blue stone inside of it. "It is a moonstone sapphire. My father passed it to me, and one day it, as well as the sword it sits upon, will be yours," his father had promised.

Rowan stirred from the memory of how the sword had felt in his hands the first time his father had let him wield it. He piled more leaves onto the buried box and stood up to return to Baile. He would help his neighbors mitigate their losses while he continued to vigilantly await Alistair's return.

He could hear screams piercing the night as he turned to see three of Hedrek's guards riding back into the entrance of town. They carried axes high above their heads as they violently rode straight into the center of the panicked throng of townsfolk. Rowan watched in horror as armed soldiers swung their axes low, hacking through men, women, and children as they circled the chaos they had created.

Soldiers bearing the Milesian crest—the emblem of the crown of King Hectre.

The very crown his family had sought to serve all his life. He could not say in confidence if he and his father had not forged the *very* axes that they now used to cut down innocents in their wake.

The sunrise was beginning to slowly creep over the horizon to the East. Soldiers continued to pour into the town in hordes as they brought turmoil and suffering.

Rowan shed the hammer from his holster and laid it on the ground beneath the tree. He pulled his sword from his scabbard to prepare to enter back into the chaos. He would not stand idly by and watch loyal Milesians be slaughtered under the very crown they served.

He spun to look over his left shoulder as he heard the crunching of leaves from within the wood line. He could not smell the scent of another person on the air, he did not feel the vibration of footsteps upon the soil.

Rowan could not explain it, but he had always had unusually heightened senses. His eyes caught flashes of light, his nose wafts of scent, and the soles of his feet could detect vibrations of footsteps from far distances—far better than any of his peers growing up.

His eyes caught the morning light reflecting off a deep shade of copper-red hair that quickly shifted from behind a nearby tree. He moved toward the tree line, attempting to peer around the trunk and find the source of this puzzling sight. His eyes adjusted as a strange sight appeared before him.

A young woman with brazenly bright copper hair and piercing blue eyes slowly rose from a crouching position. As she rose, a breeze began to blow around them, lifting golden bronze leaves from the forest floor to whirl, slowly suspended in air, as they circled around her. She locked eyes with him as she stood to her full height. She was petite, barely as tall as Rowan's shoulders.

Her cloak hung open around her elegant shoulders, revealing smooth curves that were embraced by deer hide leggings and a gauzy wrapping that bound her full breasts in a crisscross pattern. Her milky skin was the color of winter snow, dotted with freckles. Her gaze did not break from Rowan's as he let out the breath he'd been holding and struggled to find the words to speak . . . words that never came.

Her gaze did not falter as she reached behind her back to grasp an arrow from her quiver and retrieve the bow she wore slung over her shoulder. The arrow knocked against the bow as she pulled back and aimed directly at Rowan. He, again, could not find the words to stop her.

All thoughts eddied from his mind.

If this was the manner in which his death took place, he would not resist leaving this realm in the presence of this being. Something about her presence made his entire body feel as if it were effervescent, floating, as he watched her loose the arrow and it found its mark.

The arrow flew over his left shoulder with a hiss and planted directly into the eye of a Milesian soldier—one that had been preparing to bury an axe into Rowan's back.

He had been so distracted, so utterly captivated by this woman that stood before him, that he had become oblivious to the solider attempting to cut him down from behind. He spun around to assess the state of the man who was now lying in a heap on the ground. He scanned the direction of the town and did not see any additional members of the guard coming toward him. He turned back around to attempt to thank the woman who had saved his life, to at least learn her name or an idea of where she came from, only to find her gone without a trace.

She left no footprints in her wake and no sign as to which direction she fled to. Rowan felt a deep ache in her absence. A ridiculous notion, as he knew exactly nothing about her.

The only thought he was left with, was that this must have been who the members of Hedrek's guard were looking for.

His chest clenched at the thought. Rowan felt a deep pull to run into the forest. To find this mysterious creature and ensure she would not come to harm. He could not place what fueled this desire. It was not as if he had heard her voice, knew where she came from, or knew if she was even true flesh and bone and not some form of Tuatha draíocht sent to draw Hedrek's forces away from the village. He glanced at the stiffening corpse lying on the ground behind him.

No, she was definitely flesh and bone—and she had saved his mortal life.

Although, he could not be sure that she was mortal herself. He had been told fragments of tales of the Tuatha by his father. He had heard whispers about town of their kind, but to his knowledge, he had never encountered one. Rowan assumed they were all but removed from the borders of Éire, with the onslaught of Milesian forces. Driven away by the king and his brother's desire to see draíocht extinguished from these lands.

Some folk claimed their curse for being driven away was what was slowly causing the land to lose its splendor—for each year, the harvests yielded less and less. The ground grew drier by the season, driving wild game further into the forests to remain even more elusive from desperate hunters and hungry mouths.

Rowan had once been told by his father that the Tuatha that remained in their lands drew their magic from a source deep inside the forest. Their draíocht could obscure the human senses and disorient a person, should they venture too far into the wood.

His boyhood curiosity had often drawn him into Baile's nearby forest to explore the territory that remained so elusive to the rest of the townsfolk. He could not explain why the forest seemed to bring a sense of calm to him and awaken his senses in a way he could not completely understand. His vision, sense of smell, hearing—all of his senses heightened the further he ventured in. His father had not allowed him to venture too far.

Now, his curiosity urged him to continue further into the cover of trees and branches and find out who had come to his aid—and *why*.

Rowan spun around to the echoes of shouts and the pounding of hoofbeats coming from the direction of town. He reached down and pulled the bloody axe from the hands of the fallen soldier. He lifted it to the rising sun to reveal the inscription of his father's imprint on the base of the blade. His stomach tightened in disgust as he threw the weapon down onto the ground.

He had likely forged the very blades used by the Milesian troops to destroy his home and take innocent lives this night. What began as a desire to remain loyal to the crown to ensure the safety of their family and village had turned into an outright betrayal. Rowan seethed at the thought of how hard he and his father had worked to build their forge's reputation, how many miles his father had traveled in service to the crown—only to have his creations used to cut down the very people that had remained loyal all these years.

As the sun fully crested the horizon over the hill leading into town, Rowan saw Alistair riding over the hill and back toward their village. He took off in a mad dash toward his father. He passed by the skeletal remains of their home, the frame falling and partially collapsed beneath what used to be the thatched roof as smoke billowed all around him.

He ripped a shred of his sleeve and tied it around his face to shield his nose and mouth from the thickening smoke.

In the light of the emerging dawn, he saw Alistair secure his horse Seamus's reigns over a fence at the entrance of the guard-post and took off toward the town's center, toward their collapsing home. He ran toward Rowan and grasped his shoulder with his right hand as his worried eyes shone blue in the morning sun. A line of discontent etched between his brows as he frowned, his heartbreak weighing heavily upon his slumped and aging shoulders.

"Please tell me this was not a Milesian attack. Please tell me that the crown isn't biting the hand that feeds them," Alistair craned his neck from left to right, surveying the burning village. Its people sifting through the rubble of their homes, pulling free the limp bodies of battered and broken family members. Alistair walked a few paces away to pull a sword free from the chest of a stiffened body of an elderly man.

His eyes glossed over and became distant as he glanced at the very emblem Rowan had seen in the axe he plucked from the fallen Milesian soldier. He drew a deep breath. “Does the crown care nothing for loyalty anymore?” Alistair softly spoke into the breeze that began to pick up and dust ashes over the crumbling town.

As quickly as Rowan’s next breath, an axe flung through the air, burying itself in the center of his father’s chest. His glance tore to his right where the body of a half-dead Milesian soldier was belly-down, crawling toward them. His arm outstretched toward Alistair, his axe having met its mark.

“You forfeited your loyalty to King Hectre the day you *filth* decided to harbor Tuatha in this gods-forsaken town,” the soldier choked out as dark blood dripped from his left leg and from beneath his right shoulder. He collapsed onto the ground and closed his eyes—unable to move any further.

Rowan shook himself from the initial shock of what was happening. He was at his father’s side in an instant. He cradled Alistair in his arms, careful not to disturb the axe. If he could get him to the next town, perhaps he could find a healer to remove the blade in such a way that they could bind and stop the bleeding. He had learned from many hard-fought battles that disturbing a blade could bring a quick end for the victim.

Alistair attempted to reach behind him, grasping for his blade. Rowan unbuckled his sheath in an attempt to make him more comfortable. He quickly glanced around them to assess for additional threats that may be coming—he could see none. The wafting smoke clouded around them.

“Son, you must take my blade—take Faobhar. *Í a aimsiú. Í a chosaint. Tabhair ar ais é a bhfuil caillte,”* Alistair muttered as his eyelids grew heavy.

"*No*, father. You *must* hold on. If I can get you on the back of Seamus, we can make it to a healer and—". His words were cut off by Alistair's firm grip on Rowan's hand.

"You must find her, protector. Bring back what is lost," he choked out between wet coughs. "Take my book. I have written where to go, what to do. Rowan, you are he, the *Dionadair*. You must find our homeland. You must do what I could not. Our heritage, our lineage, our task in this life is to protect the One who will be the liberator of the Tuatha people . . . of *our* people," Alistair continued, shock painted over Rowan's face. "I have long sought to hide who we are for your protection, and for mine." Alistair lifted the stub of his right arm. "I removed the evidence long ago to ensure you would survive among these mortals until the time had come." he struggled to voice the words as his breathing grew stifled.

It could not be.

Alistair's eyes confirmed what Rowan knew to be true. His left forearm had once borne the mark of the Tuatha. The blue band of flesh that could only be removed by the sword. Rowan had always assumed his father lost his left forearm in battle.

No, Alistair had removed it himself, and with it, the evidence of his very heritage that could endanger his family. "What about mother?" Rowan asked hoarsely, "Was she Tuatha as well?"

"No, she was not. She was Milesian. She was the only c-cause I had to b-bind my loyalty to these people. I wanted to-to be with her. I did not know b-bearing the child of a Tuatha would be too m-much for her body to—" Tears welled in Alistair's eyes and trailed down his ashen cheeks, leaving streaks of grey in their wake.

"Father, please, don't speak." Rowan placed a hand on his father's forehead and felt his flesh growing colder. Alistair grasped the handle of Faobhar and placed it in Rowan's palm.

"When I found your mother, hurting at the hands of her own kind, I only wanted to make her mine. I only wanted to love her."

Rowan pressed a palm to his father's cheek. He wiped the sweat from his brow, "Shhhh, father, please."

"No, Rowan . . . I need you to remove this axe from my chest. I wish to see her again. I wish to pass into the next realm free of any blade wielded by the crown," he pleaded.

"Father, I cannot—" his words were broken as Alistair pressed the handle of Faobhar into Rowan's palm and with the same grasp, reached to the handle of the axe, pulling it free from his own chest as blood gurgled from his mouth, pouring down his chin.

"*NO!*"

A loud ringing began to deafen Rowan's ears as he roared, the world crumbling around him. His shoulders tightened and his broad chest felt as if it were collapsing inward, his breath caught in his throat as tears welled in his eyes.

He felt his father's body grow cold and limp as the light left his eyes.

He gently laid him on the ground as he tore his cloak from his shoulders and gently wrapped it around Alistair's body, watching as the grey fabric darkened with pooling blood.

He threw the discarded axe to his left, hurling it to the ground with a thud. Rage swirled around his body in a way that he had not felt before. The ground seemed to vibrate beneath him as he stood and turned to the man who had taken his father's life.

Rowan reached to the ground. He picked up and unsheathed Faobhar and stalked toward the soldier, his eyes darkening. He used a booted foot to rouse the man and roll him over to his back as he stared into his wincing face. "You will feel the *loyalty* to your king bleeding out of your body as you leave the earth on this day. I will not make this swift. I will not make this easy," Rowan spat. He placed the edge of the sword at the side of the man's face, hacking off each ear with swift movements of his blade. His howling cries pierced the air.

"May your ears forever hear the cries of the children that you have robbed of their mothers and fathers."

He twisted his blade into the opening of the man's nose as cartilage cracked and blood pooled down the side of the soldier's face. Rowan wrenched the appendage from his skull.

"May your nose forever smell the stench of blood from the innocents you have slaughtered."

Finally, Rowan tilted his blade and pressed it firmly into each of the soldier's eye sockets, gouging them from their home and flinging them from his face with a wet-sounding slap.

"And may the last thing you see on this Earth be my face.

May you be tormented by it, in the short remainder of this life, and in the *next* as well."

Rowan walked away from the gurgled sounds of screaming and thrashing as the soldier writhed on the blood-soaked ground beneath him. His cries were no longer discernible. The Dionadair flung his father's sword and scabbard, alongside his own, over his shoulder once again as he made his way back to the edge of the forest. He spied Cillian at the town's border and motioned for the young man to follow him. There was work that needed to be done.

Rowan and Cillian gathered as much wood for the many funeral pyres they could hold, until the sun sank low over the horizon at dusk.

That night, the stars shone brightly overhead under a full moon. Rowan, Cillian, and the few surviving members of the village huddled together in silence as the smoke from the burning bodies of their kin billowed toward the milky moon. Rowan's thoughts drifted to his father. To all the things he had said and the things that he had not.

He crossed his arms, his fingers brushing over the smooth skin of his flexed left forearm and his muscles tensed. He did not bear the raised blue band of flesh that was evident in so many of their kind—a trait he inherited from his mother, he supposed.

He was sure that his father had been grateful for this, as it aided him in keeping the long-held secret of their identity. He wondered what traits of the Tuatha he *did* inherit. He had never felt the pull of any specific type of draíocht, although, he did not know enough about it to truly determine if it lay dormant inside him. He had only ever heard of the Tuatha magic spoken about in hushed voices over late-night fires. Or on the lips of his father after too many pulls of ale had left him with a newfound sense of boldness, but only ever within the walls of their own home.

Rowan lifted his hand and placed it over his heart as he reached into the pocket of his cloak. His fingers brushed over the lock of his mother's hair and the spine of his father's small journal. These objects were the last remaining tangible ties he had to either of them. He silently swore an oath to the stars, and to his father's spirit, that he knew now drifted high among them.

He would find her. He would protect her. He *would* find their homeland—and restore what was lost.

CHAPTER FIVE

RHIANNON

She was lost.

Rhia was frustratingly, despairingly, undoubtedly lost. Anger rose in a red flush to her face. She fumed embarrassment at her inability to navigate the path Beatha had proposed she take home through the other side of the forest.

Her forest.

The place she had spent the last 116 years of her life. The home she had roamed as a child when her view of the world was simple and linear. She had spent most of the night lurking in the shadows around the borders of the town, looking for any sign of where Beatha could have disappeared to, and attempting to avoid capture. She feared the worst. If another Tuatha, perhaps Murdag, had spoken some unknown incantation that had banished Beatha to the after-life—no, she would not think on it. Rhia had fought sleep, forcing her bloodshot eyes to remain open and vigilant while she searched for the woman. Tears carved rivers down the dust covering her face. If there was one thing she was not, it was easily dissuaded.

Once the sun had risen, Rhia calmed her mind and ceased her searching. After much thought, Beatha's instructions to her prior to her capture and her speech preceding her disappearance became a subtle reassurance that this departure was her own choice. She then replayed in her mind each word spoken to her that night, looking for any hidden meaning in the woman's words. She knew she would find the answers she sought in the book Beatha had spoken of. The book instructing her in her draíocht.

She glanced to her left at the moss covering the north side of a large oak tree rising starkly from the forest floor. Her eyes narrowed. She had been traveling east, away from the rising sun. How could she have passed this tree again? The moss was growing in the same direction, yet she had not veered from true east.

Tiny hairs rose on the back of her neck as the leaves beneath her feet cascaded upward into a twirling dance around her. She felt a strong tug on her draíocht. A warm feeling descended on her shoulders—like an embrace. A familiar scent filled her nostrils. It reminded her of the scent of morning dew on the grasses beneath her feet.

A gentle breeze blew the debris of the forest floor in an otherworldly crescendo, surrounding her body as the sunlight cut luminously through the trees. She reached her right hand toward the light, closing her eyes to greet the warm way in which it washed over her skin. She walked toward the rising sun, her footsteps growing more confident as she stilled her mind and welcomed the guidance of the ancient wood. She turned her head at the sound of trickling water and her eyes caught the source, dripping from within the trunk of a nearby tree onto the forest floor.

The reflection of the sunlight cast a silver glow on the water. Rhia crouched down by the spring and filled her water pouch. She brought the cool liquid to her lips and exhaled as she drank deeply. Her eyelids grew heavy and the world around her grew quiet as her head found a home amongst the moss and soft grasses beneath the shade of the tree. An owl perched atop a branch above her and began to croon softly. As she slowly drifted under the surface of sleep, the face of the man she had encountered at the wood line came to the forefront of her mind.

She was somewhat surprised, for she had not given him much thought as she had continued her desperate search for Beatha, but as she calmed her mind, his face filled her thoughts. She did not completely understand the reason for this intrusion into her mind. As she was attempting to evade the watchful eyes of the Milesian soldiers, she had spotted the man looking as if he were attempting to bury something. His broad shoulders beneath his cloak worked in tandem with his strong hands as he milled through dirt and leaves. His eyes held a faraway look. His dark chestnut hair fell loosely around his square jaw, escaping the tie that held the remainder of it at the base of his neck. His jaw, shadowed with stubble, ticked. His brows etched into a line as he seemed to remain deep in thought.

She assumed he was not of the Milesian guard by the threadbare grey tunic and tan breeches he wore. Nevertheless, she could see that he carried weapons on his person, and he was *still* a Milesian, after all. A mortal. She knew better than to let her guard down around his kind—in any circumstance. She had kept her distance.

Rhia had noticed the approaching Milesian guard before the kneeling man had. His eyes flew to hers as she gave away her location by stepping forward from behind a tree trunk. *Why* was she stepping forward? She could not explain the force that compelled her to reach for her bow and quickly knock an arrow against it. She knew this man could bring harm to her, betrayal, or *worse*. Nevertheless, she also knew he had likely lost everything as his village was being burned to the ground by the members of the Milesian guard.

She did not trust him, but her heart compelled her to help him. If she could prevent even one more death at the hands of the soldiers, it is what she had resolved herself to do. The kneeling man rose to his feet. His emerald eyes bore into her, a look of confusion, fear, and something *else*, something she could not quite place. She swiftly loosed her arrow at the guard behind him. Her aim rang true as the arrow pierced through his left eye and the guard fell into a slumped mass of blood and leather armor on the ground. As the man looked over his shoulder in astonishment, she took her opportunity to flee back into the cover of the forest.

The moss covering the trees around her reminded her of the color of the man's eyes—an image that persisted within her mind as she sank deeply into sleep. Beatha's scent surrounded her as she dreamed of a blanket of light being pulled over her shoulders, surrounding her in comfort.

An hour or so later, she awoke to the soft chirping of a bird. This bird sounded oddly similar to the chattering chirps of the wren that disrupted her sleep from outside her bedroom window each morning. She sat upright with a start to see the sun bathing the wooden slats of her home in the early afternoon light. She rubbed her eyes to clear her vision. *How* had she ended up here? She knew the forest around her to be enchanted . . . but this was a new experience entirely. She wondered if Beatha's wards around their home to keep out unwanted guests had somehow *ushered* her back in. Her thoughts traveled to the owl that had perched above her sleeping form and stared at her as she had fallen into sleep. A shudder descended over her shoulders as she brushed off her uneasiness, walking toward her home.

She pushed open the door to the cabin and spent the next couple of hours pulling the leatherbound books from the shelves by the door and arranging them side by side on the table. She bit into an apple, resting her chin on her hand. So many emotions rattled her mind: confusion, worry, despair at Beatha's disappearance. She took a little solace in the fact that although the conflict had taken her from Rhia, the old woman's life had not been taken outright by the Milesians. She felt certain that Beatha had secrets yet to be revealed. If only she knew where those secrets were hiding within the pages of these ancient texts.

The Chronicles of the Tuatha Dé Danann was burned into the leather cover of the largest volume in the collection. In years past, when Beatha was not looking, Rhia had attempted to finger through these very volumes to learn more about what was to be expected of her in her training. Much to her dismay, her prior searches through the texts had been fruitless. Whenever she had opened the chronicles, only blank pages filled with dust and curling at the edges had greeted her. She suspected a strange magic presided over the pages, perhaps placed by Beatha or Elder Ecna to deter her ill-timed curiosity.

Rhia flipped through the first few pages of the dusty manuscript. To her amazement, each volume was filled front to back with text and illustrations. She ran her hands across the paper. There were beautiful figures, bathed in light and drawn in bright shades of gold, blue, and green dancing about the pages of the book. She began the chronicle by studying the origins of how her people had first come to the continent of Éire.

The Tuatha had entered a centuries-long battle with the Fir-Balog, an unforgiving people who had once inhabited their lands. She read of the Battle of Maigh Tuireadh and of the final stand of the Fir-Balog and their great warrior, Balor, as the hours passed. She sat the book down, taking a moment to attend to her aching belly. She had lost track of time and had not eaten anything since returning from Baile.

The sun sank low behind the trees as she sipped a warm cup of herbal tea and chewed on a hunk of oat cake. She walked back to the table and picked up where she had left off toward the center of the book.

Rhia read of the trial of Balor, the giant Fir-Balog warrior who possessed dark magic and wielded a heavy-handed club. It was written that he could dispel his enemies with a single glance from his one giant eye that beamed from the center of his face, swinging an enormous club that leveled entire battlefields. Her sapphire eyes jumped from page to page in anticipation as she read through the saga:

And it was Lugh, with his slingshot and keen wit, that finally found weakness within the giant warrior. As he stood on a cliff of the shores of Maig Tuireadh, he glanced at the giant—directly into his dark and swirling eye. He launched a stone, hitting the center of the giant's eye as he cried: "I shall bring forth the wind and the waves of a sea dark as raven's feathers, earth and fire shall shift to bring you to your knees, giant one."

Balor grasped his eye, but only laughed.

"You cannot hurt me, Lugh of the Tuatha. Your stones are as powerless as the Earth you stand upon. Your words are as weak as the oceans you claim to churn from the depths. Your fire will be extinguished as easily as the last flames of a smoldering fire with the morning dew. My magic will shake the foundations of this Earth."

Lugh smiled. The giant's eye was so weakened, he did not see the magic that he had summoned from the very earth itself. "Oh, how you are mistaken, great one. The one whom I would give my very life to protect. She will be your downfall. For it is she who helped my people to draw the draíocht from the pillars of this land.

This land called to us. We answered her."

Lugh raised up his arms to the sky. Smoke rose from the ground and began to swirl around him, thickening into tendrils of inky-black darkness. A woman's shadowy form emerged from the blackness of Lugh's draíocht—an ominous laugh on the air.

"Balor . . . " the phantom-laced husky voice of a woman cried out. "Your people did not listen to the whispers of the land. Whispers which have now become loud cries of vengeance. You will bow. Bow before the queen who brings showers of fire, swiftness of slicing winds, the raining of stone, and the splitting of lands." The very earth beneath Balor's feet quaked as he lost his footing and one gargantuan leg fell into the chasm forming beneath him. "It is I who calls stone and rock to turn into slicing waves of the sea and the waters of the depths to dry, to form the land on which you stand." The queen laughed darkly as she began to materialize from the hazy inky night into a slender female form. An obsidian spiked crown rose from her tendrils of curls falling to the ground in masses of darkness. Her hands raised high into the air. "By the brightness of the sun, by the illumination of the moon, the waves shall drag you beneath the depths. Your watery tomb shall be the place you remain bound by the power of the Nichnevin."

Water rushed from the chasm beneath Balor as corpse-like hands formed of water clutched greedily around his body and washed him out to sea. A deep bellowing cry could be heard throughout the land as he was dragged beneath the depths. It is said that when the sky cracks loudly under the heaviness of storms and rain, that it is Balor, crying out to be set free from the depths once again.

Rhia rubbed her eyes and flexed her neck from side to side as she sat the teacup on the table. The hour must have been late. She had continued to read of the Nichnevin, a subject that had become the focus of the saga after the fall of Balor and the rise of the Tuatha in the land of Éire.

Rhia learned that the Nichnevin was the spirit of the mysterious Tuatha Queen. She was a power that rose from the collective magic of her people. A magic that had no physical form, only shadow and darkness. Cloaked in a divine feminine rage, the Queen of the *Sidhe*—as she was called, rose to lead the Tuatha in harnessing all four elements of draíocht magic: air, water, earth, and wind. As the anthology continued into the second and third chronicles of her people's legacy, Rhia read on.

The power of the Nichnevin was fiercely protected by Lugh until the end of his days. After summoning the Nichnevin to defeat Balor, the people began to call him the *Dionadair*—protector of the Nichnevin and restorer of what was lost. Centuries passed and the power of the Nichnevin eventually dispersed among the women of the Tuatha people. Their collective feminine energy gave them the power to conjure her draíocht from deep within themselves. Priestesses, witches, or the Sidhe—as they were collectively called. Members of the Unseelie realm. Fae males and females alike that drew their magic from their communion with the land and with nature herself.

They drew their greatest strength from the forest. They were not afraid of feeling the full spectrum of their emotions within their lifetime: joy, bliss, rage, jealousy, passion—it all served to fuel the fire of their draíocht within.

Rhia read of how they learned to cloak themselves in plain sight. She read of how the Tuatha had slowly fled the realm of man and departed into the realm of the Sidhe over time as the arrival of the Milesians forced them from their lands.

The Milesians. Her slender fingers clenched the sides of the book. At this point in the anthology, the Nichnevin, as a source of magic, was all but lost. Although the Tuatha had remained firm in their power, they had lost the ability to utilize all four elements of draíocht, as her name had not been spoken in centuries. The Nichnevin, wherever, or in *whomever* her spirit dwelled, would need to harness all four elements of draíocht—earth, water, wind, *fire.*

How foolish it seemed to her now that Beatha and Elder Ecna had thought that *she* could somehow learn to do this. She could not be the Nichnevin, so why was this expected of her?

Rhia had taken several summers to learn to harness earth and move land with her hands. It took her equally as long to manipulate air and wind, and *twice* as long to bend water. She had not yet mastered the conjuring of fire.

It was her final trial.

One final skill to master.

Now, one she seemed certain to never have access to. Her training came to an end the day she and Beatha had seen Elder Ecna's head on a spike at the entrance to Baile. It was over the moment Beatha had disappeared when Prince Hedrek had tried to burn her at the stake. Flames seemed to take everything in her life that she loved dearly, but never gave anything back. No matter though, clearly Beatha or Elder Ecna did not understand that she could never hope to wield all four elements unless she was the Nichnevin herself. *A foolhardy notion indeed.*

However, it did appear to Rhia that the Nichnevin was the key to renewing the strength of her people. She wondered if the Woman had withdrawn deep into the realm of the Sidhe in an attempt to protect her people from the encroaching Milesian invaders.

She wondered if that is where Beatha might have gone as well.

Her mind was a sponge, absorbing all the information that she could as her eyes once again grew heavy. It had to be late as the sun had been down for a long while. She placed a black raven's feather in between the pages that she had just finished reading. She lay her head down on the faded pages and soft leather of the chronicle as her breathing evened and slowed, and sleep claimed her.

She awoke with a jolt at the sound of a twig snapping outside of the window. As she stirred, she looked down to the pages of the book beneath her in disbelief. The words, images—every mark of writing had vanished. Her chest grew heavy with disappointment and anger. She swallowed the lump in her throat as she doused the candle burning on the table. There was little time to ponder how this had happened. The sound of more crackling underbrush and the crunching of leaves from outside had her eyes flying to the window. She slowly rose from her seat to grab her dagger hanging from the belt by the door. She could hear a set of footsteps surrounding her home. Clumsy, the echo of erratic steps peppered the perimeter of the house as more leaves crunched and twigs snapped under what she assumed to be Milesian boots. *But how?* She crouched low under the window to attempt to see outside while evading the intruder.

She and Beatha had placed strong wards around a large boundary of their homestead in the forest. The draíocht had concealed their home to the naked eye and could not be breached by anyone who was not of Tuatha blood. Rhia was not foolish enough to believe that any remaining Tuatha in the village had tracked her to come to her rescue—nor to offer protection. *No*, she had learned from Beatha not to trust anyone. Even those assumed to be allies of her people.

Just then, as loud as clapping thunder, a heavy boot kicked through the front door of the home. A fiery torch held by the brutish arms of a cloaked figure illuminated the room as he stepped into view.

Murdag.

"There's a pretty gem, just where I thought you'd be." He sneered with a toothy grin. "The old hag got away somehow, but I suspect Captain Hedrek won't be disappointed when I bring *you* to him. We haven't happened upon one as young and fair as you in quite a while." He licked his cracked lips as he tightened a fist around the rope he held in his opposite hand. His eyes darkened. "And I might just enjoy myself a bit before I take you to him. Like I say, we don't see many as young and fair as you 'round these lands."

The torch swung wildly as he lunged toward Rhia.

She released an earth-shattering scream that pierced into the black night around them as the sharp end of a broadsword penetrated through Murdag's back and emerged from his chest. Dark red gore flowed from the tip of the weapon now protruding from beneath his leather chest plate, illuminated by the torch Murdag held as he coughed and sputtered blood down his stubbled chin. Darkness flashed across his features as he pulled his lip into a growl and sneered at Rhia, throwing the burning torch upon the floor of her home. He fell in a heap upon the ground as the flames quickly spread from the torch, enveloping the wooden boards of the floor. A figure cloaked in shadow stood behind Murdag's lifeless body, holding a sword in his hand as he stepped forward from the darkness.

CHAPTER
SIX
ROWAN

Moonlight poured in through the window of the house, illuminating the room as the flames on the floor spread. Rowan's heart was pounding in his chest, his breath heaving as his fist clutched his father's sword. His eyes snapped to the firelight gleam reflected off bright copper curls tumbling from the crown of a young woman's head. She knelt on her hands and knees, drawing great heaving breaths, and appeared frozen in place with fear. Her head slowly tilted upwards as fire and moonlight mirrored her eyes in the most devastating shade of blue that Rowan had ever seen.

It was *her*.

The woman from the forest who had saved his life.

She leapt to her feet with a gasp and ran to the far corner of the home, swiping a cloak and her bow and arrow from the hook on the wall. She quickly slung a full quiver of arrows over her shoulders as she returned to the table and attempted to throw several large leatherbound books into a satchel. She frantically gathered papers from the table, stuffing them in between the pages of the volumes, the size of the satchel unable to accommodate the thickness of the books. The seams of the satchel suddenly split, spilling out the contents of the bag all over the floor. She gasped, flinging her arms in front of her, as she stooped to the ground in a desperate attempt to gather the volumes.

Rowan lunged forward past the flames toward the woman. "*Leave* them! You have to get out of here!" He reached down and gently grasped her forearm to help her stand. She threw him a penetrating gaze as she sharply withdrew from his grasp.

"*You* leave this place! Save yourself and leave me be!" she cried out desperately as tears pricked the corners of her eyes. Rowan ran a hand down his face, grasping his chin and letting his hand fall as he let out an exasperated grunt.

"*Please* Red, there is nothing in that dwelling that is worth your life," he pleaded as he moved closer to her.

"You know *nothing* of my life, except how to take it, Milesian. And *don't* call me that," she spat.

Rowan huffed a sigh as he used the sleeve of his tunic to wipe the blood from his sword and quickly sheathed it into the scabbard strapped on his back. "Have it your way then," he grumbled as he stomped toward her, reaching down, and scooping up her petite form in one fluid motion.

He slung her over his shoulder and made his way to the door as she cried out in protest. She flung her arms, pushing against his broad shoulders in an attempt to escape his grasp —all to no avail. The firm grip of his left arm held her legs to his chest and balanced her body over his shoulder as he stalked from the burning home. By now, the flames had overtaken the small structure, a loud crackling could be heard as the flames licked up the thatched roof.

Rowan placed the woman down on the ground beneath a tree a good distance from the home. Ash lightly dusted her face, and tears had begun to stream freely down her cheeks as she pushed away from his grasp. She bared her teeth and attempted to force past him as she lunged her body back toward the direction of the burning structure.

"Woman, can you not hear?! It's gone. Lost. To run back into a burning house is madness. Keep your wits about you," he shouted as his forearms grasped around her waist, pulling her back to him. His eyes softened as he glanced down at her trembling form. His body buzzed with an otherworldly feeling. Every part of his body that she had touched seemed to light with an unforeseen flame under his skin. Her slender fingers curled into the muscle of his bicep as she began to breathe rapidly. She slowly brought her eyes upward to meet his. Flame danced in her glossy eyes as something akin to fear shone on her face.

"Why did you save me? What do you *want* with me?" she asked, a defeated tone to her melodic voice.

"I was only returning the favor," Rowan replied, as his eyes roved over the soft curves of her porcelain face. His words brought her to silence. Her cerulean eyes were softly set in elegant high cheekbones that were pink and flushed from her recent struggle.

Freckles danced across her delicate nose. Rowan's eyes wandered down to her full lips, softly parted, that matched the rosiness of her cheeks and the suppleness of her milky skin. Her pulse danced from the side of her slender neck as her breathing hitched. His eyes met hers as she slid her grasping hand slowly down his arm, her fingers skittering across his skin, surrendering in defeat as she glanced back over her shoulder at the burning house. His skin danced under the current of her touch. He knitted his brows in confusion as his own heart began to jump to a wild rhythm.

A loud thud came from the burning house as a wooden beam cracked in half under the weight of the crumbling structure. At the same moment as the loud crack, the woman's entire body jerked, throwing her head back and jutting her head upward toward the sky. Her eyes rolled to the back of her head revealing nothing but white in their wake. Her body began to feel as hot as the burning fire itself.

Rowan knew of Tuatha magic, but was she using her draíocht to drive him away? His hands burned against her flesh. He could feel the heat steadily increasing and radiating from beneath her cloak as he released her.

She fell to the ground onto her hands and knees. She rocked back onto her ankles as she flung the top portion of her body upward and looked back up to the sky, the moon reflecting off her now-whitened eyes. Her soft lips parted, and she huffed out a breath. A soft breeze built upon itself and began to blow leaves around the two of them in a cyclical pattern. Her hands and wrists began to fling wildly among the leaves covering the ground. The woman exposed an area of dirt and began to etch shapes and lines into the ground with her hands. Soil and earth lodged beneath her fingernails as her breathing grew more erratic with each shape she carved in the earth.

Rowan stepped toward her slowly, peering at the ground. It appeared to be a map that she was etching, along with various shapes of swirls and whorls. The designs interwove, forming a long banded line in the ground. This design looked familiar to him in some way. He reached into the pocket of his cloak, pulling his father's journal out. He flipped through to the middle of the book to reveal part of a map bordered in an interlaced pattern. His eyes widened in amazement as he held the page of the journal to the ground next to the etching in the dirt.

Rowan's mouth was agape as he knelt by the woman, struggling to see the intricacies of the scribbled map under the glow of the burning house. He walked over to the home and snapped a burning twig from a nearby tree, its end singed and smoking. He used the coal end to etch a rudimentary design of the map onto the blank side of the map's page in the journal. He struggled to replicate the trees, flowing rivers, and mountain passes that seemed to appear under the woman's slender fingers. She scratched and scraped the earth with otherworldly movements. Her hands jerked side to side, as if they were being held on strings.

Suddenly, her hands froze, and her body halted. The breeze blowing in a circular rhythm around them stopped as quickly as it had begun. Rowan quickly replaced the journal into his cloak and threw the twig into the brush. The young woman's eyes clamped shut and reopened as she let out an audible gasp—her sapphire eyes shone again in place of the previous white glaze to her irises. She locked her gaze on Rowan and collapsed to her side. As quickly as she had begun to fall, Rowan extended his arms and caught her in his strong grip as her head lolled against his shoulder.

"Are you alright?" he asked as she struggled to keep her head upright. Confusion etched her brow as she regained her composure and attempted to move away from him.

"What did you do to me?" she demanded. He drew his brows together as he released her shoulders from his grasp and stood.

"Well . . . I saved you from a wretched man bent on capturing you and returning you for ransom, pulled you from a burning home, and prevented you from foolishly returning to it *multiple* times . . . oh, *and* I did not abandon you through whatever magic tried to gain ahold of you as you decided to make some pretty etchings in the dirt," he said through gritted teeth as he pointed at the ground.

"But please, Red, let's see if you can find one more thing to accuse me of while you're at it," he spat as he rose and began to straighten his cloak, adjusting his sword and scabbard on his back. He walked away and into the darkness toward the soft whinnying of a horse. Silence followed in the wake of his absence.

"Rhia. My name is Rhia. Or Rhiannon. Not *Red*," she called out after him, as she looked down at the ground and the etching she had carved in the dirt.

He stopped and turned to face her as the glow of the smoldering embers of the house combined with the soft colors of the rising sun. He regained his composure and suppressed the slightly astonished look that passed across his features as he relaxed his brow and his shoulders lowered. "I'm Rowan," he replied.

"And just so you know, I could have taken care of myself just fine," she added.

". . . And there she is," he huffed with an exasperated tone as he shook his head, turned again, and began to walk away. Rhia was staring at the ground, a puzzled look on her face. She moved to bend down and picked something up from beneath the leaves.

"What is this?! Did you do this?" she demanded as she flipped through the sketches that Rowan had scribbled on the pages of the leatherbound journal. She trailed behind him. The journal had somehow dropped from his cloak pocket and onto the ground. He turned on his heel and moved to grab the journal from her hands, retrieving it in one fluid swoop, holding it above her head.

"Hey!" she exclaimed, as she reached upward in a feeble attempt to regain possession of the book. He was a full head and shoulders taller than her, much to her dismay. "I just want to know why *some etchings* in the dirt are of such interest to a Milesian!" she spat.

Rowan secured the book back into his cloak as he let out a long sigh. "I'm on a journey. The map, or whatever you would call *that*," he pointed at the dirt drawing on the ground, "looked very similar to the map I happen to be following. These etchings that you did . . . they seem to resemble ones made by my father. The pieces match up perfectly."

Rhia's eyes widened as she looked back to the ground with a blank stare. "That's just it though . . . I've never done anything like that before. The only place I've ever seen those types of drawings or maps was within the pages of the chronicles." She let out a huffed sigh. "The chronicles that I thought were lost in the fire. Words that seem to have disappeared from paper and re-appeared inside the confines of my mind." Her tone quieted a bit as her shoulders relaxed and she stared at the rising sun. "The only problem is that I seem to have no control over when they choose to materialize."

Rowan was taken aback by her sudden confession. He could feel the honest bewilderment radiating off her. "So, you're saying that you may have a map, that *may* just so happen to correspond with my father's map . . . but it now dwells within your mind rather than on paper . . . and you have no control over how to access it?" he questioned with a look of genuine amusement on his face as he crossed his arms and shifted his weight to one leg.

"Listen, it makes just as much sense to me. But now we must decide what we do with this. Here's the thing, I have lost my only family, my home, and the only knowledge I have of who I am or where I come from within the last two sunrises. Now, it seems a stranger, a *Milesian* no less, may possess the missing piece of the only map I have to reach my family's homeland and—" She stopped herself as she took a deep breath and attempted to regain her composure. She hardened her features and looked down.

Rowan slowly walked toward her and placed a gentle hand on her forearm. "Listen, Red, if you wanted my help, all you had to do was ask," he teased with a half-smile. Her composure faltered as her cheeks flushed a rosy hue.

"I do not *need* your help. Are you hard of hearing? I *said* —" she grumbled, but Rowan was already turning to walk away. His long strides putting ample distance between the two as he walked back toward his horse. Rhia hurried after him as the bow and arrow upon her back clanked as she bobbed through the tall grasses of the forest floor, struggling to keep up with his hurried pace.

"If you didn't need my help, it would seem that, perhaps, you're chasing after me for another reason entirely," he said over his left shoulder with a wry smile.

"I am not!" she cried out as she picked up her stride, but he was already three paces ahead of her. Rowan stopped in front of Seamus, his stallion, with a sleek coat and mane as black as midnight. He untied the bridle from a nearby tree and slung it over his back as he stroked the horse's soft nose. The stallion nuzzled into his shoulder as he produced an apple from his cloak, Seamus nipping it eagerly from the palm of his hand. Rhia paused where she stood three paces behind.

"It would seem that unless you suddenly gain the ability to finish one of these etchings on your own, instead of sketching incomplete maps in the dirt, you may just have to learn to trust me," Rowan said over his shoulder with a smirk. Rhia snorted a breath at the word *trust*.

"What makes you think that Milesians have ever given me a reason to trust them?"

"Trust is earned, this I understand well, but perhaps I have at least earned your pause. A pause in your incessant firing of insults and accusations at a man you hardly know. For it was your *pause* at the border of the forest that compelled you to fire that arrow into the skull of the soldier attempting to take my life—and the last time I checked, you fired that arrow of your *own* free will," Rowan replied.

"What can *you* speak of free will? For as long as I can remember of the last 126 years, that is all *your* people have sought to take from mine," she spat as she turned away from him and retreated into the shadows of the trees.

Rowan tilted his head toward the morning sky and let out a long exhale. His father's face came to the forefront of his mind. He reflected on the patience his father had demonstrated in forging iron to blade time and time again.

The memories of his father had Rowan feeling more determined than ever to avenge his memory and find his homeland. He followed her deeper into the forest, knowing she was headed back to the smoldering remains of her home. He watched from afar as she knelt to the ground, her small hands sifting through rubble and debris as tears welled in her eyes. She desperately pulled scraps of blank parchment that were singed on the edges, throwing them to the side in defeat.

"I seek nothing from you Rhiannon, that you are not willing to freely give."

Her dewy eyes flew to his as she hesitated in her efforts. His words had brought her to pause at his use of her name. She drew in a deep breath as she rose and walked toward him. Her gaze was the color of a sky dawn as her soft lips drew into a slight smile.

"It seems that you and I both have something of value to the other. We both have missing pieces to this map—both pieces bound together by some ancient draíocht. My people's true homeland has remained hidden for many years, I will not stop until I have found my way to it. It appears as if we are both on a journey to the same place. It appears we *both* have something to give." She spoke with a deeper edge to her voice.

She stepped closer to Rowan as her delicate fingers traced down the opening of his cloak. She slipped a hand just inside the opening, passing the daggers strapped to his side and bringing her hand lower as she brushed slightly against his solid thigh.

Rowan froze. Every muscle in his body tensed as his breath quickened. *What was she doing?*

His jaw flexed as he stared down into the gaze she refused to break. His lips parted slightly as his breathing quickened and his skin heated, a growing warmth in his lower abdomen, ignited by the feather-light touch of her hand. His hand quickly grasped her wrist just before she could grab the journal she was aiming to swipe from his cloak pocket.

"Wicked little thing . . . " he breathed as he brought her hand around between their bodies, his lips tilting into a smirk. She wrenched her hand away as she huffed and spun around to retrieve a satchel that she had left lying on the ground nearby.

"But you mortal men make it so easy," she huffed over her shoulder, reaching down, and slinging on the satchel along with her quiver of arrows.

"Let us make a truce. I plan to journey on, following along the river until I find the first mountain pass on this map." He tapped at the journal in his pocket. "I cannot say how long this journey will take or what will be revealed along the road ahead—but I intend to find this hidden land as well. I know you don't trust me. I know you think I have hidden motives regarding the location of your people because of who *my* people are. If you come with me, I can only offer you my word, my sword, and my protection. You can choose not to take it, but it is yours all the same," Rowan offered.

He could not place why he felt so compelled to keep this woman near to him. He knew they both had something the other needed. He was a good deal larger than her petite frame and, although his conscience would never let him, he could easily take her captive, wait around until she was taken by another vision, and make off with the rest of the map that she would reveal before she regained her composure.

However, something about the way she looked up at him with a spark in her ocean eyes, something about the abysmal flame she elicited from his skin with only a touch of her hands sent his mind spiraling. He felt that something deep inside himself had already surrendered to her. He had already lost before he had a chance to begin the fight.

Rowan had been close to his fair share of women in his lifetime. He had choked down the weight of regret with the dawn on many mornings, as he rolled off the mattress of whatever village girl the ale had compelled him to tangle up with the night before. He had ridden far and wide with his father, delivering blades to distant outposts of the Milesian kingdom, his eyes and hands drinking from the cup of various exotic women of the continent. The bed had always remained as cold with the dawn as it had been when he had fallen asleep the night before. Now, his flesh was aflame from only a touch, from only the closeness in proximity to this creature that stood before him, her oval face peering up from beneath her tumbling copper curls.

"Your words, like all Milesians I'm sure, can hold many meanings. The true value of your *protection* will remain to be seen—if you hadn't noticed, I am quite capable to taking care of myself," Rhia retorted as she pushed past him and headed toward the river. She compelled a strong breeze to ruffle the hood of his cloak over his head as she passed him.

Rowan smiled to himself at her silent agreement. They began to walk toward Seamus, preparing to follow the river and the path to wherever it may lead. "Whatever you say, Red."

Rowan mounted the horse in one fluid movement, his long legs finding their home as he seated himself in the leather saddle. Rhia continued to walk on foot by the riverbed, her hips swaying as she strolled ahead of Seamus.

"Let us hope that we do not run into any more Milesian soldiers." Rowan said with a smirk, "I doubt you will be able to keep up with Seamus's pace if you insist on walking."

"I understand that Milesian eyes are not as keen as those of my people, but do you *see* another horse around here?" she retorted. Rowan replied by halting Seamus and reaching his hand down toward her.

"Absolutely not," she quickly countered. Rhia stalked away, moving forward with her back turned to Rowan as she continued to follow the bend of the river.

"Fine, have it your way," Rowan replied under his breath as he slowed Seamus's pace to follow her, continuing to watch over from his periphery. *This long journey just became even longer,* Rowan thought to himself as the horse found a comfortable pace and his mind calmed with the crunching of the leaves underfoot as they continued forward.

The riverbank path opened to a break in the trees, the sunlight pouring into the clearing and painting a glow on the grass underfoot. Moss covered the rocks lining the riverbed in a patchwork of green hues.

A sharp snap of wood penetrated the silence around them as Rhia halted her steps and moved backward to where Rowan sat atop Seamus. Her eyes met his as she held her breath and they both froze in place to determine the source of the noise.

Rowan continued to swivel his head around them, watching for the emerging threat as he slowly reached down toward her, silently beckoning her to grasp his hand. She obliged and with one swooping motion, his strong arms glided her atop Seamus, mounted in front of him in the saddle.

Her soft legs embraced within her deer hide leggings, clung to Seamus's side as her body tensed. Rowan felt her press her back against him as he instinctively rounded his shoulders and chest toward her, encircling her arms with his own as he grasped tighter on the horse's reigns.

He felt the familiar warmth creep into his tight abdominal muscles and spread throughout his body as she unconsciously pushed her backside between his legs, and she reached for the dagger strapped inside her boot. Her bow and quiver of arrows remained at her side, she had removed them and slung them through the loop of Seamus's saddle just before she had mounted him. Her movements caused the leather of the saddle to groan beneath them as the breeze picked back up again.

Rowan slid his hand atop hers that grasped the dagger, stilling her movements. His lips lightly grazed the shell of her right ear as he craned his head over her shoulder. “Shhhh . . . ” he whispered, eliciting a shudder from Rhia as the stubble on his chin lightly brushed her neck. He couldn’t quite determine exactly why that trembling produced a grin that spread across his face.

Suddenly, a large hare leapt from the brush, producing the familiar snap of twigs as it wildly thumped a path to the river. In one fluid motion, Rowan grasped the bow and an arrow from the side of the saddle. In a matter of seconds, the flying arrow pierced through the air and into the side of the hare, causing it to collapse by the riverbank. Rowan chuckled as they rode forward, his deep tone vibrating against Rhia’s back, a satisfied grin remained on his face.

“What was that about the value of my protection?” He smirked as he dismounted, leaving her sitting on Seamus’s saddle alone. She paused, looking like she was biting her tongue as if she wanted to snap back at him in some way. Rhia huffed a breath, rolling her eyes before staring down at him with a smirk.

“I’ll concede this time, only because I’m hungry,” she retorted, dismounting after him and walking toward their dinner for the evening. Rowan reveled in the small victory of her admission, still smiling to himself as he withdrew his dagger and gathered supplies from the saddlebags to prepare the rabbit for their meal. *This would be a long journey, indeed.*

CHAPTER SEVEN

RHIANNON

It didn't make sense.

Rhia struggled to understand two things:

One, how she had gotten into the situation she found herself in; how her journey to find Beatha and her people's lost land had suddenly gained the company of a moody stallion and one very cynical mountain of a Milesian.

Two, what puzzled her the most, was how he had even made it to her doorstep in the first place. Long before Rhia's time, before their home had become overgrown and entwined with vines and moss, Beatha and Elder Ecna had placed strong wards deep in the forest around the perimeter of their dwelling. Wards that prevented anyone's entrance into their homestead who was not of Tuatha blood. She could easily explain Murdag's sudden intrusion, after all, his mother was Tuatha—a fact that he had unceremoniously disregarded upon betraying her people.

However, this male, this *Milesian* who had a knack for getting under her skin and appearing in her life at the *most* inopportune times, whistled gleefully to himself as he prepared a fire near the riverbank—as if both of their lives hadn't been completely uprooted within the last three sunrises.

He *really* had a knack for getting under her skin—a skill that he excelled at more and more by the hour.

Rhia chanced a glance at Rowan. He now sat with his back facing her, atop a smooth boulder near the riverbank. His broad shoulders worked in tandem as he removed the hide from the rabbit, rinsing it in the water, preparing it for their meal. The sun rose high overhead and spilled into the forest floor through the delicate filter of the tree canopy, painting soft shadows on the sharp planes of Rowan's chiseled cheekbones and jawline.

"Be it a pleasurable view or not, you *could* take up a hobby besides staring and gather some herbs or mushrooms to prepare with this game," he remarked with a smirk over his shoulder.

She did not dignify that comment with a response, but instead, rolled her eyes and huffed a breath as she rose, stalking into the wood line.

Rhia felt a warm blush creek up the back of her neck from beneath her cloak. Her cheeks reddened as she strode between the tall trees. Her body and her mind betrayed her. Before she could put her thoughts in check, she shuddered as she remembered the feeling of Rowan's solid form encircling her body as they sat atop Seamus. The way his muscular arms had tightened around her at the sound of potential danger.

She could not help but feel a deep pull toward this

elusive human. She knew nothing of his village, how he made a living, or his people—other than their collective intent of wiping out the remainder of hers. As she fervently stomped through the foliage of the forest, she gritted her teeth at her recent course of actions.

Beatha would never condone trusting a full-blooded Milesian to lead her alone, deep into the forest, even if he claimed to have knowledge of her homeland. She clenched her fist as she reflected on the events that had occurred since the last sunrise.

Rhia had truly lost *everything*—her home, her family, and the book, the one piece of information that seemed to hold any gravity in directing her to her people's lost land. She grimaced as she knelt and aggressively yanked herbs from the base of a tall oak tree, stuffing them into the linen satchel on her side.

Yet, even in the wake of the chaos and uncertainty of the previous days, this Milesian had been there for her at every turn. Rhia was no fool. She knew that Rowan had more than one opportunity to betray her, to turn her in for the bounty that Murdag had spoken of, to exploit her newfound weakness of uncontrolled visions for the information he sought. His actions had not given her cause to explicitly distrust him—his actions had, after all, prevented Murdag from capturing her and returning her to Hedrek's men.

She could not, however, wrap her mind around why Rowan sought out a path to her homeland as vehemently as she did. If this Milesian truly harbored ill intent toward her people and believed Rhia to be foolish enough to lead him directly to her homeland without a fight, he was the fool.

Beatha always encouraged her to keep her wits about her. However, Rhia could also not help but remember some of the last words the old woman had spoken . . . *You must learn what deserves your anger and defense and what does not.*

Rhia placed her palm on the ground beside the base of the oak. She whispered as the breeze picked up. Small tendrils of sprouts and new growth began to spring from the soft soil beneath her hand, replacing the herbs she had previously plucked. She quietly thanked the earth for its provision as she replaced what she had taken with her draíocht. She secured the satchel with the last of the mushrooms and herbs she had gathered and made her way back to their makeshift camp.

The fire was rolling fiercely under three flat stones that Rowan had fashioned into an improvised cooking surface. The rabbit roasting atop them wafted a delicious scent on the soft breeze. He silently held his palms out to Rhia as she placed the mushrooms and herbs in them, watching him intently as he cleaned and prepared them around the roasting hare. By the time he had made the final turn of the spit the rabbit was skewered on, she was all but salivating.

"Regardless of our surprise dinner guest," she remarked, pointing at the rabbit, "perhaps it is unwise to linger here. Should we not continue on?"

"I realize that it is still early, but we have a long road ahead of us. We have not yet encountered any enemies to run from, save your little friend here." He grinned, pointing at the rabbit. "It would be best to rest while we can, sleep in the peaceful protection of this wood while it remains around us, and wash the ash and dust of the last two nights away," he replied.

Rhia scoffed at his taunt regarding the rabbit but sighed in agreement, looking down as she wiped a finger down her arm, feeling the grit of soot and ash between her fingers. It was not lost on her the way Rowan's eyes followed her finger as it traced over her skin.

"If you think I plan to bathe in this river in front of you in broad daylight, you are sadly mistaken," she grumbled under her breath.

"I do not pretend to know of anything that you *plan* to do, Red. I've learned in our short time together that not only are your actions a bit unpredictable, but *you*, little one, cannot be persuaded to do anything that you do not wish to." He smiled to himself as he removed the hare from the stones.

He cupped the tender bits of rabbit covered in herbs and surrounded by roasted mushrooms in a large leaf and handed it to Rhia, making an improvised plate of his own and settling his back against a nearby tree trunk. He removed his holstered sword and scabbard from around his shoulders, sitting it on the ground nearby and kicking out a leg in front of him while drawing up the other to place a booted foot on the ground.

Rhia ate ravenously. In the mayhem of the last two sunrises of her life, she realized he had only eaten a small bit of stale bread and an apple while rifling through Beatha's books back at their home.

What used to be their home.

Her mind spun with the events that had transpired,

causing a knot to wedge in her stomach. The flames of the campfire grew higher, and with them rose the panic in Rhia's mind. She had somewhat learned to control her earth, water, and wind draíocht, but the one type of magic that offered any type of *real* protection, her fire draíocht, remained elusive to her.

Now, with Beatha, Elder Ecna, and the book gone, what hope did she have to ever master it? Fire had taken everything she had held dear. Her home, her way of life. . . it even threatened to take Beatha.

Her mind continued to worry over how she could protect herself should another threat—including the one sitting before her—present itself. Rhia continued to eat silently. Something deep in her bones told her she could trust him. Something lit a fire deep beneath her skin when he was simply near to her. She was caught in an internal war with herself . . . if she should trust this feeling or not.

She felt that familiar heat creep back up the base of her neck and flush her cheeks as she continued to contemplate what provoked this feeling. She had been around a few men in her lifetime. All of them had been young, mindless Milesian males, sent to meet Beatha at various outposts near the village over the years to deliver traded goods from Murdag and collect their coin.

In years past, when springtime blossomed and her bosom had grown large enough to softly press against the hem of her neckline, she had even managed to steal away with one or two of them. Rolling in the hay behind the storehouse of a trading post and exploring each other's bodies with hurried fingertips and mouths. Nervous panting and rapid heartbeats accompanied the fleeting moments of pleasure as Rhia began to learn what it was to be a woman, and the power it often held over the opposite sex. Never had a male's hands, mouth, or any other part of their body elicited the type of heat that Rhia felt by simply being in the presence of Rowan.

It *infuriated* her.

"I've seen my fair share of ladies enjoy a meal made by my hands, but my cooking has never brought about a look like *that* on anyone's face." Rowan broke the silence with a smirk causing a slight jolt from Rhia as she returned from being lost in thought.

She rolled her eyes as she used her lithe finger to stuff the last bit of rabbit into her mouth and licked it clean, setting down the empty leaf on the ground as she rose. The heat rising from her neck and face was now an inferno. Rowan's throat bobbed as his smile fell and he shifted in his seated position.

"You seem to be quite confident in many of your *abilities*, Milesian," she responded with a saccharine smile as she slowly strode toward him. "Although you don't seem to hold the appearance of having riches from a grand inheritance or faraway lands. I am sure that the ladies lining up for your hand in marriage must be plentiful indeed. Pray tell, what is it that you do? To earn coin?"

His shoulders tightened and he straightened his back, looking up unflinchingly from her gaze. "I'm a blacksmith." He tapped a hand on his left hip where two daggers were strapped. "I forge and fortify metal and iron in all manner of ways, from simple daggers to broadswords," he went on to say as his other hand tapped his sword lying by his side on the ground. His voice lowered an octave as he broke her glance to stare at the ground behind her. "We had the unfortunate privilege to serve King Hectre by arming his legions of soldiers."

He looked down at her feet with something akin to shame shadowing his handsome face.

Rhia's demeanor softened. Her eyes caught the flashing of firelight and the setting sun in the reflection of the fractionated stone sitting atop the handle of the blade. She had failed to notice it until now. The gem closely resembled the one she wore around her neck, hidden beneath the folds of her cloak.

"Where did you get *that*?" she said sharply, pointing at the sword.

"That is Faobhar, my father's sword. He passed it to me upon—"

"*No*, I mean the stone. Where did you get the stone?" she demanded, cutting him off.

"How ironic that someone who had resolved themselves to giving me silence and one-word responses has now become such an inquisitor? If I interest you that much Red, we have quite the journey ahead to learn all about one another," he chided as the corner of his mouth turned up into a half-smile, his stark green eyes meeting hers.

"You're impossible," she huffed as she walked past him, pulling blossoms from the branch of the tree that hung low overhead. She went back to her side of the camp, adding several blooms and herbs to her satchel as Rowan rose and began to clear away the evidence of their meal. Rhia helped to clear the campsite and pulled two blankets and furs that she had spotted from Seamus's saddlebag, laying them on opposite sides of the fire atop the soft grasses and beds of moss.

Her eyes tracked his movements as he provided Seamus with a bag of oats, secured his reigns to a nearby tree, and lay on his side atop his pallet glancing at her curiously. The only sound that could be heard was the rustling of river water and the chirping of crickets. "How does one keep themselves from the receiving end of that fire, Rhia?" he asked, breaking the silence that had settled over them as he smiled to himself, looking down. "I'm afraid I'm at a loss for what it takes to get on your good side."

"What if I told you I don't have a good side?" she responded with a roll of her eyes.

"Then I might have to argue with you, yet again. It seems that quarreling is the one thing that we tend to do well together," he replied. Rhia blushed again as she debated if there was a hidden meaning behind the *good side* he was referring to—literally or figuratively.

Rowan sighed as he turned over on his side facing away from her, pulling a blanket over his shoulders. The rhythm of his breathing slowly evened.

Rhia crushed the now-dried blossom petals and herbs together as she rose, walking down to a sandy portion of the riverbed several paces from their camp. Nightfall had brought the cover of darkness that she desired. She smiled to herself as it settled over the forest.

Moonlight bathed the curves of her milky skin as she left her discarded clothing on the riverbank. Cool rushing water lapped at her ankles, then her knees, then the soft curve of her hips as she descended further into the babbling stream.

She used the previously crushed blend of herbs to scrub away the ash and dirt from her flesh. She sighed as the water eased the tension she carried in her stiff and tired muscles from her calves to her shoulders. She dipped beneath the surface of the babbling stream, water saturating her soft red curls as her hair clung to her back and shoulders when she re-emerged. She spun slowly, extending her palm, and created ripples in the stream of water, illuminated beneath the full moon's light. Her draíocht bent the water in a curved stream that glided slowly around her body, washing the grime from her back, slithering around to her soft breasts as they bounced with her movement in the moonlight. Her nipples formed delicate hardened peaks as her mind flashed to the size and shape of Rowan's hands, imagining them firmly grasping each breast and softly kneading them as the pressure of the rippling water caressed her chest. A soft moan escaped her lips.

She broke the thought with a fervent blush of shame and a sharp inhale as the water draíocht fell with a splash around her. She quickly submerged herself under the cool water again.

After she had finished bathing, Rhia wrapped herself in a large swathe of linen and made her way back to the fire. She sat on her pallet, squeezing the water from her long auburn locks, her fingers working her hair into a single braid down her left shoulder. There was that flame again, that smoldering heat that began as a knot in her low belly, licking its way up the back of her neck and bringing a soft flush to her cheeks.

Her breathing hitched as she became aware of the quiet way that Rowan watched her from beneath his lashes as he lay turned on his side, facing her from the other side of the fire.

CHAPTER EIGHT

ROWAN

Rowan awoke to the absence of the woman across the fire. An owl howling in the distance along with the sound of the babbling river near the camp reoriented him to his surroundings—he was sleeping, albeit soundly, in the forest. He did not recall what pulled him from the throes of sleep, be it her absence or something more. Weariness from the events of the last two days had taken its toll on his body and mind as he fell into slumber much more quickly than he was used to.

Normally, his racing mind prevented him from finding comfort in sleep and he spent many nights either planning his next blade design or flipping through the worn pages of one of his father's books until the sun brought the following morning.

The dead of night surrounded him still as the full moon shone brightly overhead. He could hear splashing sounds in the distance mixing with the breathy moans of a woman as he rose to his knees and peered around the corner of a tree.

His eyes were immediately drawn to the way the moon painted soft planes of light over the soft column of Rhia's neck and shoulders as she bathed in the stream. Her back faced him as the water rose around her, increasing her moans, caressing her full breasts as she turned slightly to reveal the way the moonlight illuminated her peaked nipples. If he were not already on his knees, the sight before him would certainly bring him to them. He exhaled as heat burned up his neck to his ears and face. His cock strained against the seam of his trousers, as it had earlier in the evening, when he had watched her lick the food from her nimble fingertips from across the fire.

He immediately looked away, shame creeping its way into his mind for the unsolicited glance he could not have resisted had he tried. All the honor in the kingdom could not have peeled his eyes away from the devastating beauty that stood before him, water encircling her like a river nymph, pulling his heart from his chest and down into the depths of the water. Anger rose in the back of his mind at his own actions.

Rowan laid back down on his opposite shoulder, facing away from the riverbed, and clamped his eyes shut. He longed for sleep to claim him again, should this creature reappear wearing as much as she had in the river and subject him to a whole other kind of torture entirely.

Moments later, he reopened his eyes slowly as he was greeted with the intoxicating scent of hawthorn blossoms and rosemary as Rhia walked by, wrapped in a swathe of linen, and sat down next to the fire. He watched her hands gracefully plait her copper locks, her fingers working with ease in an intoxicating dance with her curls. How did this woman already have him so utterly at her mercy that every movement of her body was an enchantment, an incantation whispered into the deepest recesses of his mind? Rowan groaned, sitting up and pulling his cloak over his shoulders. He retrieved his sword from its scabbard and withdrew a sharpening stone from his satchel.

"Cant's sleep?" she asked, barely above a whisper as her soft lips parted slowly, steadily keeping her eyes locked with his. Her slender fingers continued making work of her hair. The Tuatha were spell-workers, sorcerers, keepers of magic and mirth to be sure, but now, she *had* to be toying with him.

He looked down at his blade as he grunted, frustration burning his bones. He refused to become distracted, to let anything deter him from the task that his father had left to him. He needed to focus. Rhia could not become an interference in finding his father's homeland and the woman that he was meant to protect. The one his father asked him to protect with his final breath.

Rowan positioned the blade between his legs, the hilt resting on his upper thigh and the tip braced on a rock near the fire. Small sparks illuminated the night air as he brought the sharpening stone down the length of the blade. Working one side at a time, he ground out his frustrations onto the metal, brows furrowed, as the tension in his shoulders melted away with each pass. He had hardly given his role as *Dionadair* any real thought since his father's passing—not that he completely understood what the role event meant.

Find her, protect her, restore what was lost.

He remained focused on the journey that lay ahead of

him. However, he knew his destiny was intertwined with the woman he must protect, and he must work harder to find her in the coming days. Rhia remained an ally that he felt wise to keep close for her draíocht and *visions* of what the journey would bring—but he would not let the long seasons that had passed without the touch of a woman become his undoing or divert him from the path that lay before him.

He decided that he would awake with the first light of the morning, study the fragments of the map within the journal again, and attempt to determine the direction of the next phase of their journey.

Rowan's eyes caught the way the light of the fire danced upon the pale blue stone sitting atop the handle of his blade. He thought back to his father's words when he had passed the sword to him on that cloudy day. The heavy timbre of his voice echoed in his mind as if he still walked within the realm of the living: "*A man is only as strong as the blade he wields.*"

With a tightness in his throat, he remembered the stories his father had told him about this very blade—the weapon passed down from his father, and his father before him. Forged of iron and a darker element—the very bones of their ancestors.

Ground into the iron that they had dug from the peat bogs of the continent.

Peat bogs yielded weak iron that must be fortified with additional elements, lest it buckle under the weight of battle. Many farmers and villagers used whatever they could find within their lands to fortify their iron . . . bronze, or copper. Haughty—albeit foolish—noblemen even thought it elegant to use gold in their blades—any opportunity to flaunt their wealth. It was only an opportunity for an enemy in battle to cut them down as their lives crumbled under the weight of a feeble weapon.

No, Rowan's ancestors had forged Faobhar using the ground bones of their predecessors and it had worked to their benefit. His father swore it was the spirit of their forefathers that provided the power behind each strike of the blade. Although he did not once doubt the protection of his ancestors, he suspected that an element in human bone, or *Tuatha* bone, as it were, had something to do with it. Perhaps in the way it bound with iron and fortified the blade. Iron calls to iron, like unto like.

He could sense the tang of iron on his lips when his blade took the life of an enemy in battle, splattering their last warmth across his face as he cut them down on the killing field. As he continued to gaze at the blade, mesmerized by the way he felt as he held it, he was captivated by the way the weapon glided effortlessly when seated in his hand. He thought again of the moonstone sapphire atop its hilt. The thought ran across his mind unbridled, all at once, of Rhia's eyes—the sparkling lightness of blue, the morning sky after the first light of dawn breaks.

From the first moment those eyes bore into his at the edge of that forest, he knew that there was a unique familiarity to them. They bore the exact shade of the fragmented moonstone sapphire that crested the handle of Faobhar.

Rhia stood and walked back into the shadows, emerging a short time later, wearing the freshly rung clothes that she had washed in the river. Rowan had not even noticed that she had taken his tunic as she handed it back to him. Her hands had scrubbed the remaining stains of Murdag's blood from the cloth.

"Thank you . . . I did not realize—" he attempted, as his calloused hands brushed the delicate skin of her thin fingertips while retrieving the tunic.

"Think nothing of it," she quickly replied as she averted her eyes from where he found them to be lingering on the deeply carved planes of his chest and abdomen. She quickly withdrew her hand, dropping the tunic at his feet. He could have sworn he felt heat radiating from the tips of her fingers with her touch. She returned to her side of the fire, facing away from Rowan as she lay down, pulling a fur over her shoulders.

Rowan returned his blade to the sheath as he did the same, needing to calm his mind and rest for the remainder of the night. His eyes traced the glowing reflection of the firelight off the crescent of her shoulder as her breathing evened and she eventually fell asleep. A short time later, Rowan had almost drifted into slumber himself. He smiled at the rhythmic purring sound emanating from where Rhia slept. He wondered if another man had ever slept close enough to this mesmerizing creature to tell her about how much she snored.

CHAPTER NINE

Six days had passed since Rhia and Rowan began their journey together. Five nights of falling asleep to the crackling of a fire and the rushing river water as they followed each bend of the tributary through the changing terrain with the coming dawn. Six mornings of watercolor sunrises. Six long evenings of perpetual sunsets. Six days that had brought a slight chill with the coming of night as the sun set at the closing of the day.

The first two days had passed slowly as Rhia had, again, insisted on walking beside Seamus instead of riding atop him. Day three of walking on buckskin soles through the increasingly rocky terrain of the forest floor had her grasping Rowan's hand and swinging up onto Seamus' back to ride for the remainder of their journey.

Rowan's sturdy legs instinctively flexed against her body, his arms tightening his grip on the reins to brace her with each rough turn or downhill decline in their path, and the horse ambled forward and down the road. She had begun to feel a small sense of solitude in what their daily routine had come to be. Awaking with the first light of dawn, eating with Rowan by the embers of the previous night's fire before they extinguished it, ridding the site of any traceable evidence of their camp, and packing Seamus' saddlebags, joining together on the saddle for the next day's ride.

This morning as the horse strolled through an ever-thinning forest, Rhia noticed the deep ache in her bones as the journey of the previous days had begun to catch up with her. She started to feel her body relax more and more atop the saddle with each day's ride. Her body had begun to anticipate the movements of Rowan's as Seamus carried them further on their journey. For the first time since Beatha's disappearance, she felt *safe*.

Her eyelids began to feel heavy with the growing stiffness in her muscles as she tried to relax and release the tension in her shoulders. She rolled her head back and forth to each shoulder, eliciting a slight inhale from Rowan as he seemed to hold his breath until she relaxed her shoulders again. He leaned backward slightly, further relaxing into the saddle and encircling her with his arms as Rhia's figure unconsciously reclined into the curved frame of his body.

"Sleep if you wish," he whispered into the shell of her ear with a low voice. It was her turn to hold her breath. She blew it out in a slow exhale. What was the use in fighting sleep? She'd take it while she could get it, as she did not know what lay on the road ahead. There was no guarantee of peaceful slumber in the coming days.

Against her better judgment, she lolled her head against the curved front of his left shoulder. She inhaled his scent deeply, leather and earth and morning dew. Sleep drew her in slowly with her next exhale as her eyes drifted closed. Rowan could feel the warmth of her flushed pink cheeks as her head and shoulders relaxed further into him. Her red curls fell in tumbling waves down her shoulders and onto his chest. He exhaled a contented sigh as he relaxed into the rhythm of Rhia's breathing and the horse's footsteps down the road.

Rowan reached into the pocket of his cloak, pulling out his father's journal and the map he had sketched by firelight the night before. He had attempted to piece together what Rhia had inscribed in the dirt with the fragmented pieces of his own map—an attempt to plot out the road ahead as much as he could.

He had ridden toward the borders of this forest many times with his father while delivering weapons but had not ventured into the wood line or along this road, which remained entirely unfamiliar to him. He flipped past the maps to more of his father's writing. He lowered the book in front of him to reflect again on the words he had read by firelight the last several nights.

Alistair had provided brief but detailed accounts of the origins of the Tuatha people. From their origins when they landed on the continent many years ago and defeated the giant Fir-Balog people, to their gradually dwindling population following the arrival of the Milesians. The Tuatha Dé Danann had been the ruling majority and the race of people who had originally brought magic, or draíocht, to the island. Through the ages, history had given them many names—the Tuatha, the fae, the Aós-Si, the Sidhe . . . each one representing their connection to the land—specifically, the woodlands. As time went on and Milesians grew in number, they began to fear the deep magic held by the Tuatha.

Although draíocht was mostly a benevolent form of magic, beckoning new life from the earth or calming storms at sea, the race of men began to harbor fear and hatred for this force that they could not control—and the people who wielded it. The Tuatha had used magic to drive the Fir-Balog from the land in a long war that had occurred centuries before the arrival of the Milesians. The Fir-Balog wielded an ominous magic of their own. During their time on the continent, they had neglected the earth and molested the land, burning forests to the ground and digging up the earth in deep cavities to strip its resources and wage war with one another.

The Tuatha were said to have arrived on the continent of Éire like mist on the sea, settling over the land and eventually restoring it to a state of lush green forests, babbling rivers, strong standing timber, and fertile soil. While the arrival of the Milesians was met by a strong sense of caution and careful observation, the Tuatha soon realized that as a race, they possessed no magic of their own.

They relied heavily on trading with the Tuatha in their first few decades on the continent and eventually fell into a working relationship with them. The Tuatha were skilled blacksmiths, forging strong blades fortified with the bones of their ancestors. The Tuatha deeply revered their Mother Goddess Danu, who gave them the gift of fire millennia ago, and used their craft to honor her, forging weapons fortified with this magic to protect Her people.

Eventually, the Milesians settled into daily life on Éire, and their race flourished under the direction of the Tuatha, having been taught to forge weapons, work the land, and use the resources of the earth in responsible ways. The Tuatha helped the Milesians to become skilled smiths of the blade, but never revealed the ingredient that made their own blades so strong. The bones of their people were kept in absolute secrecy—a practice that would eventually help to ensure their existence as a race remained.

As the centuries passed, Milesians grew exponentially in number. The Tuatha soon realized that the race of men had lifespans far shorter than their own, and subsequently became ready for childbirth much sooner than Tuatha females. The average lifespan for a Tuatha could easily reach five to six hundred years. The women would often give birth for the first time around their one-hundredth year of life. Although the Tuatha often found their mates early in life and settled into a long life with them in years of peace, they did not betroth females as an act of trade or political gain, unlike their Milesian counterparts. In fact, many mate matches were often initiated by the women within their communities. Like their Mother Goddess, women held seats of power in Tuatha culture. They had a say in the passing of laws and the judgment of trials within their society alongside their male counterparts—another trait deeply distrusted by the Milesians, specifically their men.

Milesian women were often promised in marriage before they reached the age of fifteen years. For reasons unknown to the Tuatha, the culture of man held the practice of the routine use and exploitation of their female members in positions of child-rearing and domestic labor. Rowan had read in his father's journal that this had often puzzled Tuatha males as they did not seem to understand how Milesian men could fail to recognize the divinity of a woman—the very force that brought life into this world, and honor that power.

Alistair had written on more than one occasion in his journal of how he had always sought to make Rowan's mother feel loved and valued in their marriage. They had arrived at the collective decision to have children *together* when Rowan had been born. His father never forgave himself for the tragedy that would result in his birth.

Rowan swallowed a lump in his throat as he read on. He had learned of the accounts of how the Milesian population had exponentially grown in numbers over the centuries, eventually vastly outnumbering the Tuatha. A strange darkness had begun to settle over the land in the last 200 years, bringing with it further conflict between Milesians and Tuatha. That conflict had eventually ignited into a spark as the first accounts of war between the two races were detailed 150 years ago. Over time, the combination of a growing population and further knowledge of weapon-making had caused the Milesians to turn on the Tuatha as hatred, fear, and ignorance grew with each new generation of man.

Eventually, they drove the remaining Tuatha deep into the forests of the continent. The remainder of them, who had attempted to continue life as they knew it alongside Milesians in the villages, were enslaved or killed outright. Along with the dwindling population of the Tuatha, the land had begun to fall under a cover of perpetual darkness. Crops gradually began to produce less yield through the years. The earth became harder to till and more resistant to planting, filled with rocks and defiant soil. Livestock produced tiny, emaciated calves barely able to survive their first month of life. It was as if the earth itself was mourning Her people's gradual disappearance. The Milesians held a widespread belief that the Tuatha had cursed their land and used the coming darkness to fuel their flame of hatred that burned brighter than ever.

Rowan sighed as he reflected on the information he had collected over the last several nights. He had read of a power, an emerging light that burned with righteous indignation at the mistreatment and oppression of the Tuatha people. Their queen, the daughter of Danu, the Nichnevin.

His eyes slowly glazed across the faded piece of parchment he held in his hands within his father's journal. He brushed his thumb over the word *Nichnevin*. The elusive savior of Her people. The one who would bring justice to the Tuatha, healing to the land, and, eventually, peace between her people and the Milesians. Rowan knew she had to be the one. The woman that Alistair had so vehemently pleaded with him to find, to protect. The clues were beginning to make more sense, day by day.

Rowan was jolted from his thoughts by Rhia's voice, breaking the silence around them. Her eyes were glued to the journal he held out in his right hand.

"How do you know of *her*? The Nichnevin. Why is the lore of my people of such sudden interest to you that you write of it in your book?" she asked, slowly glancing up over her shoulder at Rowan with a suspicious look in her eyes before shifting her gaze back to the journal. Her jaw tightened as she clenched a fist at her side, locking her eyes with his.

"You have done nothing but harbor secrets by the firelight with each evening, as you pour over that book in solitude. Am I not on this journey with you as well? Did you not say that we must work together to find the Tuatha homeland? Am I not to know of what is written in its contents?"

He studied her for a moment and could have sworn that he saw a look of hurt flash across her features. It pierced him strangely in the center of his chest, to see her eyes harbor uncertainty towards him after the progress they had made over the last several days.

Progress. He thought to himself. He was becoming distracted again. Pulled in by the deepening sapphire of those damned eyes staring back up at him. The only progress that mattered was finding the Nichnevin, as she was the key to finding this homeland. *Did Rhia know this? Could she perhaps aid him in his search for this elusive queen? Would she even be willing to help him? Did she even trust him at all?*

Rowan's thoughts began to spiral as he cleared his throat and tucked away the journal back into his cloak pocket. "Okay, let's take a moment here. Firstly, I think that's the first time you've used the word *we* in a sentence where you're not talking about just how different we are." He smirked as he glanced down at her. She rolled her eyes but continued staring at him intently.

Damn those eyes.

"Secondly, you never asked." He smiled down at her softly, taking an honest moment for himself. He could not keep a secret from her if he tried. One inadvertent brush of her hand over his, a half-smile dancing across her full blush lips, a toss of her copper curls over her shoulder.

He was ruined.

"Okay, well, I am asking now, Rowan." His body tensed at her use of his name. This may have been the first time she had called him something other than *Milesian*, or *you*.

He had to exhale the tension building in his shoulders. To reveal himself as half-Tuatha would ultimately cause her to question his motives, and his past. It would bring more questions altogether.

Rowan was not sure he was ready for the questions it brought up within his *own* mind. He was not even sure of the full meaning it carried for himself. He had not fully processed what it meant for him as a half-breed in a world where both races were at war with one another.

He refused to reveal this part of himself and risk becoming an additional danger to Rhia. The fact that she was Tuatha would draw suspicious eyes to their traveling party as it was. He was determined to keep her safe, to play the part of the Milesian, if need be.

"Apparently, unlike you have been led to believe, not everyone you meet has intent to harm you or your people," he remarked with a smile down at her. A smile that faded with his next words. "The fate that your people"—*my father's people*, he thought to himself—"have been dealt over these last hundred years has been unfortunate indeed. I can understand how that would cause your people to fear. Cause *you* to fear. However, my father seemed to understand a way to bring our people together. To live in a land once again where

Tuatha and Milesian co-existed peacefully, and life once again blossomed from the earth."

Rhia drew a quick breath and exhaled. She thought of the Nichnevin, of what she had read in Beatha's books before the fire took them. She knew as soon as she had read the words that this beautiful and terrifying woman must be restored to power to once again right the wrongs that had been done to the Tuatha. It suddenly made sense to her. *She* must be found to find their homeland. Wherever *she* was.

"My father was born of a long line of protectors. A long line of warriors, called the *Dionadair*, who kept their role in absolute secrecy for generations. I have only recently learned of it myself. They were sworn to defend and guard the power of the Tuatha Queen. To restore what had been lost. My father passed this task to me when . . . "

"I know of her . . . of the Nichnevin," Rhia suddenly interjected. She clamped her eyes closed. *Why was she telling him this?*

"Before her disappearance, my grandmother led me to a series of books . . . those that I attempted to salvage from the fire. They told of the feared queen. The savior of our magic. The one whose draíocht would bring retribution for the wrongs that my people have suffered." Her eyes met his again. "Your father is right. Perhaps he may be able to help us? He seems very wise."

"He was . . . very wise." Rowan's eyes broke her gaze, staring down at his sword. "He was taken from me by a Milesian sword during the attack on Baile." A blush crept up Rhia's cheeks.

"I am sorry, I did not know . . . " She moved to place her

slender hand over the fist he was making at his side. She drew in another sharp breath as the touch elicited a warmth radiating from her palm at the contact.

Seamus ambled down the path. Rowan drew his other hand slowly to her lips as he placed a single finger over the plush pout of her lips. "Shhh . . . think nothing of it," he repeated her own words back to her with a look on his face that made the warmth spread down her neck, to her chest, and light a fire low in her abdomen.

A tight wire coiled inside Rowan, tensing every muscle in his body with the way her lips softened under his touch. He could feel the warmth of her breath on his fingers as he brushed his thumb over the fullness of her bottom lip. He could feel her heart galloping in her chest against his forearm as he cradled her face in his large palm. She stared up at him from under her full lashes. Her half-lidded gaze was hurling him downward, into a deep chasm he knew he could not escape from, even if he tried.

On fire. I'm on fire. Everything is on fire. Rhia's panicked thoughts raced as she felt herself melting further into Rowan's touch. *Why am I like this? I have been around men before. He is a Milesian. Don't forget that. I am stronger than this. I am . . . oh no.*

He brought his other calloused hand to grasp her left hip, drawing small circles on her thigh with his thumb as he continued to meet her gaze. He was dangerously close to the area where she needed him most. *Oh gods.* She felt herself involuntarily flex her hips backward against his, drawing a slight low groan from Rowan as she closed her eyes and her breathing increased.

Oh fuck.

Just then, the path opened wider, and several sets of hoofbeats could be heard in the distance. Smoke rose from chimneys up ahead. Thatched rooftops of a nearby settlement came into view as Seamus crested a hill in the clearing.

Rowan instinctively flung a portion of his cloak around Rhia's left forearm, hiding the blue-tinged band that would surely identify her as Tuatha to any passers-by. She reached up, pulling her cloak over her red locks as she tucked her curls into the hood and straightened in the saddle. She stared at the path ahead, winding downward into the small village.

"We should take this opportunity to stock up on supplies and find a place to rest before darkness falls. This part of the forest is sure to be more heavily guarded than that of the path that lay behind us," Rowan said, clearing his throat as he pulled Seamus's reigns sharply to follow the winding path downhill.

"Then let's find somewhere inconspicuous to rest for the night," she replied.

CHAPTER TEN

Rhia grumbled under her breath, pulling her cloak further over her head as she and Rowan ducked into a crowded inn, making their way to the innkeeper's corner of the bar.

"Milesian, I know we have not seen eye-to-eye in the past about every detail of this journey but, surely, this cannot be your definition of discreet lodging," she said with a huff as her eyes nervously swept left to right, taking inventory of the room.

"Listen Red, in this town I don't think we have many options to choose from. It's this or the stables we passed on our way in." Rowan jerked his head toward the open door of the crowded room. Horses whinnied in the distance, muffled by the sound of many footsteps and the noisy conversations of the numerous teeming patrons of the inn. He had not taken his eyes off the door, the far corners of the room, or the customers jostling about for a seat at the bar. His guard was up, and his glance locked on Rhia, as she stood a whole head shorter than him, gritting her teeth and nervously fiddling with the ties of her cloak. He clenched his fists. He didn't like the nervous energy he was feeling from her direction. Placing a grounding arm on her shoulder, startling her from her lost train of thought, her eyes shot up to meet his. She needed to breathe. He didn't like seeing her this worked up. She didn't need to be. Not with him here.

"Let's get something to drink, shall we?" He gently smiled down at her with a squeeze of her shoulder. He guided her with his large palm on the small of her back until they were standing at the bar. "Two ales please," Rowan asked of a Milesian male with a ruddy complexion, as he slid two coins across the rough wooden counter to him.

"Aye," the man replied as he pushed forward the frothy golden liquid teeming from two full cups.

The sound of male voices rising in volume drew Rhia's eyes from the cups to the corner of the bar where a tall, bearded Milesian stood. He towered over a young woman who was attempting to collect two dirty cups from a nearby table. She was clearly someone who worked within the tavern, struggling to push past the large form of this man and his friend who crowded her on both sides. "I don't want any trouble," she said, eyes pinned to the ground as she stopped her efforts, standing between them.

"No . . . but maybe we do," the bearded one said with a smirk, leaning closer to her ear. She shuddered and it was all Rhia could do to stand in one place. She stepped forward before she thought better of it, her feet carrying her toward the woman as if of their own volition.

"It would seem the lady would like to be left alone," she

began, standing in complete stillness, as she glanced between them. The bearded one was a full head and shoulders taller than the shorter one. Of course, that didn't stop him from attempting to straighten his spine and intimidate the redhead as he looked her up and down with a voracious glare. Rhia could hear Rowan's footfalls from across the room as he attempted to reach her, pushing through the growing crowd.

She flicked her right wrist slightly from beneath her cloak and a vine quietly splintered from the legs of one of the oak chairs behind the shorter male. The vine quickly wrapped around his ankle, and with a subtle jerk of her hand, he was pulled to the floor, landing flat on his back with a thud. The room erupted with laughter. His tall friend abandoned his efforts of harassing the poor woman to attempt to help him from the ground, just as a puddle of water on the floor behind him seemed to triple in size, causing him to trip and land right alongside him.

Rhia stepped over them, grinning down at the ground as she felt Rowan's strong arms grasp her shoulders and whirl her toward him. "Are you quite mad?" he asked frantically, looking her over from her head to her toes, as if to ensure these men did not harm her.

"I'm fine, I'm just fascinated by the peculiar events that have transpired in this tavern. This is an interesting place indeed." She gave him a knowing smile as she let him lead her back to the wooden bar counter.

Rowan lowered his voice, "Do you know how risky that was, Rhia? Part of our understanding is for us to remain as inconspicuous as possible."

"Is that worry I detect in your voice?" she teased, eliciting a half smile from him as he seemed to regard her with wonder.

Rowan couldn't understand how she seemed to remain so brave. Albeit a bit foolish in their current circumstances, but he admired how she never hesitated to help someone in need. Rhia would be the first one to run out to battle for anyone, especially women, who happened to be in a vulnerable situation. She protected others even when she could not protect herself. She'd take an arrow for another soul when she herself was the hunted.

"Rowan . . . " Her words pulled him from his thoughts, "Stop looking at me like that," she said under her breath, her face blushing slightly as she averted her eyes and attempted to busy her hands by grabbing her untouched cup of ale from the bar. Just as Rhia reached to grab the cup, the shorter of the two men from earlier appeared on her left and grasped her arm, forcing the sleeve of her cloak down and yanking her wrist upward—exposing the blue-tinged raised band of flesh encircling her left forearm.

"I knew there was something off about this one!" the man spat.

As quickly as he had touched her flesh, Rowan's sword was drawn and pointed at the center of the man's neck. The room fell into silence. His gaze was lethal as he pressed the tip of the sword further into his bobbing throat. "If you'd like to keep that hand and everything attached to it, I suggest you stop touching what is mine," he growled.

Sweat beaded on the man's grimy forehead as his eyes shifted to Rhia. "How is it that a Milesian walks into a crowded room, with a pretty thing like *this* in tow, and doesn't think every man with a mind for what kind of bounty she'll bring, wouldn't be bitin' for a chance to take her for himself."

"If you have a mind for what it takes to survive until *morning*, you'll remove your hands from *my* bounty, good man," Rowan replied as his eyes searched Rhia's for a mutual understanding of his spur-of-the-moment plan. "She's already been accounted for, and we're headed to Prince Hedrek's estate now to exchange her for the gold she'll surely bring." Rowan's eyes were like steel, never breaking his stare, "As I said," he growled, keeping his sword drawn and lethally aimed at his windpipe, he stepped nose to nose as the Milesian male released Rhia's wrist, "She's *mine*."

Rhia could have sworn she felt the ground shake in response to Rowan's palpable anger. She glanced to her left as the contents of ale in her cup vibrated beneath the surface and the coins on the bar top rattled slightly.

"Have it your way then, mate. But old Doniall here, isn't gonna go for Tuatha filth like this sleeping under his roof." He smirked, thumbing toward the bar keep wiping ale from a cup at the counter.

"I'm sorry friend, but he's right. We can't risk the patrons feeling threatened by whatever heathenry follows her kind." Doniall sheepishly glanced toward Rhia. "She'll have to stay in the iron cell out back. My Da made it a few years back for when bounty hunters like you come through town with the likes of *them*."

Rhia instinctively stepped backward against Rowan's

sturdy form, and it made a hard lump involuntarily form in his throat. "There is *no* way I am . . . " she began in a whisper.

He swallowed the knot, as he placed a gentle hand on her shoulder and leaned toward her ear as she glanced up at him, a pleading expression on his face, "*Please* just listen to me, just this once . . . trust me," he spoke in a low clipped voice.

"Very well," Rowan bellowed across the bar to Doniall, "put her out back, but *I* will be the one to lock her in myself and *only I* will hold the key." The barkeep tossed a large ring of iron keys to Rowan overhead.

"It's the largest one." He hummed with a smug-toothed grin aimed at Rhia.

Rhia stepped into the alleyway behind the inn, shouts slowly fading into murmuring voices as Rowan's hand gently guided her into the darkness, lantern light fading behind them. "I cannot believe you. I mean, *really*? First, you choose the *most* conspicuous place in the entire town." She began with a huff as she stomped the path ahead.

Rowan brought his lips to the shell of her right ear with a low voice, eliciting a shudder from her and her silence that followed. "Trust me, this is better than the alternative."

He opened the creaking door of the cell as Rhia stepped forward. The bottom of the chamber was filled with straw and gods-only-knew what else and reeked of horse.

Just then, the man who had grabbed Rhia in the tavern stepped from the shadows. "Better make sure to lock it up tight." He hiccupped with a crooked grin, stumbling into the connecting alley, and ambled down the road ahead. Rowan cast an apologetic glance at Rhia as he locked the cell and stepped back toward the entrance of the inn.

He turned over his left shoulder to see her bright blue eyes boring a hole into his chest. She turned with a huff, flipping her long braid over her shoulder, and disappeared into the dark corner of the cell. Rowan walked away with a deep sinking feeling in his chest that he could not seem to shake.

Before dusk had completely taken over the horizon, the straw-haired young woman from the tavern peeked her head around the corner of the alleyway near Rhia's cell. Her grey eyes met Rhia's as she glanced quickly to her left and then right, tiptoeing her way toward the door to the cage.

She extended two small, calloused hands inside the cage as her palms opened and she offered Rhia a large chunk of bread. "Here, I am sorry it is not more," she began, looking down with a slight look of shame on her face. "I know what you did, in the tavern. I know you're one of *them*," she whispered, "but I want to say thank you."

Rhia simply smiled as she softly wrapped her palms around the young woman's, replacing the bread in her hands. “Please, keep it,” she replied. “I appreciate it, but I am sure that the famine in these lands has not been easy on your family. You may one day need it more than I.” The woman gave a small nod in response, her face warming as she sighed.

“Be safe, daughter of magic,” she said softly before she hurried into the alleyway and back around the dark corner.

The night grew darker as the patrons of the pub slowly filed out of the doors below. Rowan had barely been able to swallow the remaining ale in his cup as he had covered the bowl of stew provided by the innkeeper and returned to the bedchamber upstairs. He paid for his stay, for the ale and food, and informed Doniall that he planned to take his bounty and leave by sunrise. This seemed to somewhat placate the man for the disruption to his patrons earlier in the evening. He had not been able to eat a bite of the stew. He sat on the ledge of the windowsill in the bedchambers above, like a hawk on a perch. His stomach was in knots as his eyes remained glued to the alleyway below where darkness had settled over Rhia's cell.

Rowan waited until he saw the last customer leave the bar room, as Doniall locked up for the evening and retreated to a small home near to the inn. Rowan wasted no time. He flew down the stairs, silent as he could be, and made his way out of the side door of the inn, toward Rhia.

He slipped the key in quietly as he turned the lock until he heard the soft click. In the faint moonlight pouring through the bars of the cell, he could see her chest rising and falling with sleep as she lay on the pile of straw. He slowly blew out a breath he hadn't realized he'd been holding, as he leaned down and placed his hands under her knees and behind her shoulders, gently lifting her.

She started to stir as Rowan's hand moved to gently cover her mouth. "Shhh." He leaned toward her face, "It's me". Her eyes adjusted to the light filtering in from the moonlight as she relaxed slightly in his arms. He chuckled to himself, "Did you really think I wouldn't come back for you?" He searched her face, lending his own to a slight look of astonishment. "You did, didn't you?" He smirked, while a hard knot formed in the pit of his stomach. She gave him only her silence as her mouth flattened into a line and she looked left, exposing the column of her neck as she tilted her chin away from him, causing his own heart rate to increase. *Ah*. The silent treatment.

"Do you really think I would leave something so valuable in the darkness of a cell, this far away from my sight?" he teased as he grazed the side of her soft cheek with his nose.

He gripped her closer to his body, making his way toward the inn in silence. Her eyes followed his as he motioned upward toward the window where he had been watching her cell from his room. As they returned to the bedchamber and he closed the door to the room, Rhia's face registered with surprise. Her eyes shifted from Rowan to the narrow bed in the corner of the room and back to him.

"Of all the *terrible* ideas you've had today . . . you cannot presume to think that I am sharing a bed with—" she stammered as she glanced back at the entrance.

"I assumed that you'd prefer the comforts of this room to the straw poking your back in that cell." He smirked as he sat her down on the ground, her legs wobbling as she stood. He stalked to the window, quickly pulling the curtain tightly.

Rowan removed the cloth covering the still-warm stew sitting on the small, rickety side table. "I thought you might be hungry." He pointed to the chair, motioning her to sit.

"Since when do innkeepers prepare meals for Milesian bounty hunters *and* their captives?" she asked sarcastically, as she arched a suspicious brow at him.

"They don't," he replied, clearing his throat, breaking her stare. He pulled the chair out for her. "Nevertheless, you should eat. We leave with the dawn, and you'll need a good meal for the journey ahead."

As she devoured the stew faster than she thought she would, her eyes darted back upward to meet his own from over the top of the bowl. "Thank you," she said quietly in between bites. The tension in her shoulders and in the room was palpable, even as she placed the dish by the door and walked to the hook to remove and hang her cloak.

Her milky shoulders peeked from the side of her neckline, tugged down with the weight of her tunic. She quickly pulled it up, nervously ambling toward the bed and sitting on the side with a creak as she began to undo her braid.

Rowan stole a glance at her nimble fingers as they worked to free her loose copper curls. He shifted uncomfortably in his seat by the fire. He did not like the thoughts that were now hastening across his mind. He could feel her discomfort, her hesitation, her *fear*. His brows furrowed at the thought that it could be *he* who caused her to feel this way. Her fear of the unknown. Her close proximity to what she believed to be the race of men who had almost single-handedly destroyed her people and everything she loved.

He stood and began to pull the furs he had brought into the inn before bedding down Seamus for the night in the stables out back. He lay them down on the ground on the opposite corner of the room, removing his daggers and sword and placing them on the table. He removed his leather boots and sat on the pallet. He grunted as he adjusted his large frame to lie on his left side, facing the wall and pulling the furs over his shoulders.

"What are you doing?" she asked playfully, breaking the silence.

"What does it look like I am doing, Rhia? I'm going to sleep." His sudden use of her name was sobering.

Not Red. *Rhia.*

"Yes, I gathered that, *Milesian*," she replied with a sudden air of venom in her voice, "but you seem to forget that your coin is what paid for this room, and it happens to come with a perfectly good bed," she remarked as she threw him a half-smile.

She was most *certainly* trying to kill him. Or maybe just confuse the hell out of him. Either way, Rowan wasn't giving up on getting to the heart of why she appeared so uncomfortable. He sat up and faced her from across the room.

"You're a paradox, woman." He chuckled, looking at the ground as he draped his forearm over his bent knee. He glanced up to meet her gaze. "What troubles you?"

She stilled and pursed her lips into a line, breaking her playful stare to study the ground again. "I'm afraid."

He tensed, clenching his fist. He would not be responsible for her distress—

She continued, as if sensing his concern, "I am afraid that I will fail. I am afraid that I will never have another vision. Almost a week we have been traveling on the road and I have yet to discover another piece of the map we can use to navigate the road ahead."

"We have a large portion of the map—"

"And the portion that we *do* have will lead us to the borderlands of the Milesian territory in two days' time and *then* what?" she snapped, her frustrations building as her blue eyes flashed to his. "Beatha tasked me with finding my homeland. Finding my path. Finding my way back to *her*. I must believe that she is out there. I must find her. If I can't even do that . . . " she trailed off. Rowan could see the reflection of tears building in the corners of her blue eyes.

He quickly crossed the room before he could think better of it and sat beside her on the bed. He tucked her slender arms under his large ones and pulled her into his chest, using his free hand to softly stroke her long curls. He could feel the dampness of her silent tears on the front of his tunic, permeating a hole in his chest.

"Rhia . . . " he soothed. "You must trust that your grandmother had your best interests at heart. I did not know her, but I cannot believe that she would have tasked you with something she felt you were incapable of completing."

Her breathing stilled. She took in her surroundings, her arms coiled around his sturdy frame. His scent of cedar and leather mixed with rain was intoxicating. She drew a deep breath again. "From what I have learned of you so far, I am convinced that you can do *anything* your stubborn mind sets out to do," he observed with a grin.

What had she gotten herself into? Here she was, completely vulnerable in the arms of a Milesian. A mortal. An enemy of her people. A man whose race had almost completely wiped hers from the continent. But was *he* her enemy? In place of the loathing and judgment that most Milesians harbored toward the Tuatha, he had met her with understanding, with patience, with *kindness*.

He met her distrusting glances with a smile, her malicious remarks with soft words. Whether she wanted to admit it to herself or not, she had judged him far more harshly than he had judged her. For he had *not* judged her at all. For the first time in many moons, she felt safe. She felt protected. She felt heard. In a world where she had been in hiding all her life, she felt *seen*.

She slowly raised her head to glance up at the man who cupped her face with calloused hands. His brown hair fell forward in waves down his broad shoulders, framing his chiseled chin. His thumb gently brushed the dampness from the corner of her eye, trailing down her cheek and then gently pressing into the fullness of her bottom lip, his fingers tilting her chin upward.

He could feel the warmth of her breath on his fingertips as the heat of her skin kindled sparks under his own.

Thunder bellowed outside the window as lightning flashed, illuminating the dim candle-lit room in blazes of white light. Rhia's body seemed to tremble with the walls as the storm raged outside the inn. Her eyelids held at half-mast as Rowan softly pressed his lips to hers, capturing her bottom lip tenderly with his own. It was as if she had fallen flat onto her back, all air escaping from her lungs. Every rational thought eddied from her mind.

Rhia opened to him, slowly sliding her tongue past his own, exploring his mouth as her breathing increased and her heart raced ahead. His deep moan in response only served to spur her onward as her desperate fingers pulled him closer by his tunic.

Gods, she tastes like the heavens, he thought.

She moved to slide one leg over his, as she shifted to straddle his lap. Her hands tangled in his hair as a moan escaped her own lips and she pulled him even closer. *What had she gotten herself into, indeed? She could hardly breathe.*

"As I have said, Little One, you are a paradox. One that is surely to be my demise if you continue to press that delicious mouth into mine and torture me with those perfect thighs," he said between labored breaths. Her lips curved into a devious smile as she pressed forward, deepening their kiss, her curved thighs tightening around his body in a delicious dance.

His hands moved desperately upward to grasp the arc of her bottom, groaning again into her open mouth. She began to unconsciously rock her full hips slowly forward and back, bringing her hands down to his stubbled jaw and neck. Heat emanated from her palms, causing redness to build on Rowan's skin as she touched a burning path downward, her fingers shaking as they fumbled with the ties at the neck of his tunic.

He hissed at the contact, reluctantly breaking their kiss to glance down at the red trail of flesh extending from his neck down to his chest. His skin felt as if it were on fire, the flames spreading everywhere on his body in a trail where she had touched. His left forearm, just below the bend of his elbow began to burn far worse. His eyes met hers in a searching gaze. *What was she doing to him?* "It feels as if I am on fire, Rhia," he panted.

"I know. I feel the same," she replied as she locked eyes with him. She looked like a woman depraved. She had never felt heat move from her fingertips in this way. Even after all the past lessons in an attempt to call forth her fire draíocht, she had never felt this much warmth.

No, this was something *more.*

What was happening?

He glanced to his left arm, just as a narrow band of skin began to rise in a twisted pattern of swirls. The flesh twisted and knotted further, raising from his arm to form a band that was a deep shade of blue-tinged flesh.

It could not be.

Rhia's eyes locked on the band of flesh, unblinking. Her eyes slowly moved to meet his as he watched her with a knowing expression on his face. Now, he would have no choice but to tell her.

"*Rowan . . .*"

"Rhia, there is something I must tell you."

CHAPTER
ELEVEN

Rowan felt his chest tighten once again, the knots returning to his stomach as Rhia broke contact and rose, moving to sit in the chair by the fire. Her eyes followed the dancing flames as she stared blankly into the hearth as he divulged what he knew of his heritage. What he knew of his mother and how she had lost her life delivering a half-Tuatha infant, of his father and the life lived missing an arm, to protect his family and conceal his heritage.

She closed her eyes as he told her of his father's recent passing. He could see her jaw clenching as he detailed his father's last moments, prior to being cut down by the Milesian guard. He had even revealed his own wrath in the moments that followed Alistair's death as he had unleashed his rage upon the soldier.

He released a deep breath as he disclosed his father's final wishes. His guidance, his direction to find the Nichnevin, the expectations of his role as the Dionadair. To restore the honor and the sovereignty of the Tuatha people.

Truthfully, it was still a lot for Rowan to process, reality sinking in even more as he spoke aloud of the events following his father's death. He glanced at the band on his left forearm with a puzzled expression, the flesh glowing a deeper shade of blue in the firelight. It didn't make sense . . . Rhia had later told Rowan of Murdag's Tuatha heritage . . . He was half-Tuatha as well, and *yet*, he did not have this characteristic marking.

He rose and walked to his cloak that was thrown over the chair beside Rhia's. He withdrew the worn journal from the pocket, flipping through the pages, his fingers once again danced over the words *Nichnevin*. The fragmented maps, instructions, symbols . . . they seemed to almost taunt him. Encrypted with meaning that he struggled to understand more each day. The only clarity afforded to him was brought by the woman sitting by the fire. Her symbols and map scribbled in the dirt paired with the sketches within these pages were the only ones that made any sense at all. The world that Rowan now found himself living in only made sense because *she* was in it.

"You are the only thing that has seemed to bring any meaning at all to what was given to me." Rowan glanced down at the journal to find Rhia's eyes focused on it as well, "Were it not for you, I'm not sure we would have even made it this far." He smiled to himself, "And you feel as if *you're* the failure?"

"I see . . . " was all she replied, glancing back down at the fire with a blank expression.

"Please, Rhia, understand that—"

"What I understand is crystal clear to me now, Rowan. I

understand that unlike I had previously presumed, you are *not* seeking out my people's homeland to bring them harm." She eyed the blue-tinged band of flesh upon his arm, "You have a duty to fulfill. You have a path to follow. You have a *queen* to protect."

A look of pain flashed across her face. She schooled her features to dispel it as quickly as it appeared. "I understand now. I am of *use* to you."

"Rhia, no, that is not why—"

"Now I understand why you were able to get through Beatha's wards," she cut her eyes at him. "You sought out my home in the forest . . . *why?* Did your father's texts also instruct you to seek out the Tuatha chronicles that Beatha had kept hidden all these years? Is that why you followed me?"

"I did not *follow* you," he replied tightly. "I was tracking another half-Tuatha male that I had seen fleeing the village during the burnings. Murdag had been a friend of my father many moons ago, but in recent years, his love of silver had turned his eyes toward King Hectre's court and the promise of more riches should he do as he was told."

"I knew that he had a hand in the destruction of Baile and the betrayal of its people to the Milesian guard," he continued through gritted teeth. "He could only be going one of two places—to betray another of my father's kin or back to Hedrek's estate. I had a keen interest in both of those, for I knew that his life was mine either way." She locked eyes with him, an element of surprise painting her features in the firelight. "When I realized he was coming for *you* . . . When he entered your home . . . I didn't think, I didn't even breathe

. . . I *acted*. I refused to allow another loss of Tuatha life at the hands of his betrayal, least of all yours," he spat. "Not after you spared my own."

Rhia could feel her heart betraying her, pounding against the inside walls of her chest with each word that flowed from his lips. She knew that finding the lost queen, the Nichnevin, was the key to restoring the sovereignty of her people, of *their* people. However, it did not quell the fire of jealousy that had begun to burn deep inside of her, knowing that Rowan's destiny was now interwoven with another.

As if almost reading her thoughts, he moved to stand in front of her. As he gazed down at her, he marveled at how the firelight glow painted hypnotizing shadows over her features. No matter how many times he had stolen glances at her over the last several days, the flush of her freckled milky skin, the delicate shape of her face, the cerulean blue of her eyes never ceased to take his breath away.

Her copper curls cascaded over her shoulders, her hands aimlessly played with the hem of her tunic, eyes cast downward as she stubbornly fought not to meet his glance with her own. Her battle was short-lived as she slowly lifted her gaze. Her rosy lips parted slightly as he swiftly knelt before her, taking her slender palm into his own.

"I must confess. You have been my undoing since the moment you aimed that arrow in my direction. You've rendered me more spellbound each day that I have known you." His voice was barely above a deep whisper, "Every word from those perfect lips is my new gospel. Every movement of your body is a song I want to sing for the rest of my days. I've even begun to look forward to the way your clever tongue bites back when we quarrel." He smiled to himself as he shook his head slightly. "I never had a chance, Rhia. My sword may belong to the Nichnevin, but my heart belongs to you . . ."

Rhia drew in a breath, tears threatening the corners of her eyes, as she grasped the front of Rowan's tunic from her seated position. She pulled him down to her, wrapping her thighs around his middle, and planting her lips firmly on his. He opened to her as she explored his mouth, and he met her tongue stroke for stroke. The warmth of her soft lips and tongue grew into a smoldering flame as their kisses became fervent and hungry. Her desperate hands grasped his tunic, pulling him ever closer, roving over his shoulders, his neck, grasping his hair as her legs squeezed around him. Rowan felt his heart tightening in his chest until he thought it might burst. His mouth trailed kisses down her jaw as he nuzzled and nipped at her ear, eliciting a soft moan from her.

"Woman, your mouth has awakened a hunger in me that I'm not sure I will ever satisfy." He groaned, "What enchantment is this? Tell me so that I may never awaken from it."

They stayed like that for a good long while, in no hurry to waste the delicious moment they found themselves in. His mouth consumed her lips, her jaw, roaming down her neck and collarbone, peppering kisses as he went. His breathing hitched as her lithe fingers pulled his tunic loose from his trousers and over his head. Her own breathing was ragged as she beheld the most beautiful man she had ever seen.

Her hands explored the grooves of his muscled chest, abdomen, and his broad shoulders. She thought to herself, *can a person perish with desire? Gods help me, I have never felt this way . . . and there's that burning, burning again.* Her fingers began to feel warm as she slowly guided her hands away from his chest and wrapped around his shoulders to attempt to quench the flames she felt rising within her palms.

Rowan scooped his hands under her thighs, eliciting a giggle from Rhia as he picked her up, moving them over to the bed, and sitting them down with a flop that caused her to fall forward slightly. She placed her palms on his chest, gently pushing him further back onto the creaking bed. His eyes darkened and his pupils widened, eyes locked on hers. Her hips began to instinctively twirl, grinding against his hardening length as she smiled down at him.

He growled, reaching up and capturing her mouth again with his own. His large palms grasped her hips again, dragging her back and forth across his length, his pace quickened, and she rolled her hips along with him in cadence. Their rhythm drew soft pants from her perfect lips. Her full breasts bounced with the increased movement, making him harder by the minute.

Her thoughts were no more than a stream of consciousness between them, a silver thread that connected her heart to his, she felt a tugging of her chest in its wake. The headiness of his scent, his hands, his movements, his very being overtook all her senses as she chased the warmth blooming in her lower stomach.

The coiling, delicious warmth in her lower belly was now a full flame. She could feel herself becoming more undone by the moment. She felt the heat rising in her palms again, unsure of what was eliciting this new and very *unwelcome* change in her magic. Her brows furrowed as she sought to concentrate on the luscious feeling this man was drawing from within her. Rowan's movements stilled for a moment as he sensed the slight hesitation in her body. "Tell me you want this, Rhia. One word from you and this stops—"

She placed a finger over his lips and smiled down at him, her mind hazy with need, "Rowan, up until this moment, I don't think I have ever wanted anything *more* in this life." His shoulders softened as he quietly exhaled against her mouth and seized her lips again. As she nibbled his bottom lip, he felt himself approaching the edge of his own restraint.

Their movements increased as he squeezed her hips, rocking her back and forth, back, and forth. She relished in the feeling of her breasts rubbing against his bare chest from beneath her tunic. She needed to feel *more* of him, she needed more of him on her, inside of her. She was wavering treacherously close to the edge of her own pleasure.

Rowan was in danger of losing complete control himself, as he began to groan with the painful tightness within his trousers. He glanced into her eyes like a man starved. He needed her body like a man needs water beneath a scorching sun. She grasped his hand, guiding it beneath her own tunic as he palmed her round breast. He squeezed a peaked nipple, drawing a loud moan from her lips. She increased the pace of her hips as she began to pant against his mouth.

Their movements had begun to cause a repetitive *thud* of the bedframe against the wall behind them. Rowan heard the scrape of the door downstairs slamming against the wall of the hallway as hushed voices danced on the air from an open door.

Dionall.

Rowan quickly moved Rhia to a sitting position with a groan, pulling the curtain aside to see the innkeeper and his wife curiously moving about the alley below in front of the door to the tavern. He blew out the candle on the windowsill and lay back on the bed, pulling Rhia's body flush against his own and throwing the blanket over them, as he turned them to face away from the door and worked to slow his breathing. She was all but panting in his arms.

He closed his eyes as his heart rate lowered, and placed a finger gently over her lips, "If we ever hope to move on from this place together, we must remain quiet until sunrise. It was a close call earlier this evening, but now, they *cannot* know you are here. Let us pray to the gods that this man doesn't get the notion to check the cell . . . " he said with a smirk. He glanced back out the window to see the innkeeper exiting the tavern, shaking his head. Dionall blew out a tallow candle with a sigh and returned to his own home.

Just then, Rowan felt something cold fall forward onto his chest from the front of Rhia's tunic. An oval pendant that dangled from her neck had jostled free from their movement. Her proximity had caused it to fall onto his chest from the delicate chain that remained secured around her neck.

The light of the full moon poured into the room and seemed to illuminate the stone hanging from the necklace. Rowan traced the oval stone and the silver setting that it was encased in, his fingers ghosting across her neck and chest to grasp the gem between his thumb and forefinger, lifting it up to the moonlight. He met her eyes with curiosity dancing across his features.

It was a moonstone sapphire. A twin fragment to the one

that sat upon the hilt of his father's sword. A relic of the Tuatha people, regarded to hold power from the master stone it was chipped from, sitting upon the Hill of Tara in their homeland. He grinned at her with a look of astonishment, "Well . . . it seems that I am not the only one of us who has been keeping secrets."

CHAPTER TWELVE

The sun was steadily peeking over the horizon of the rolling grassy knoll as Seamus crested the top of the hill. Rowan and Rhia had been riding for close to three hours already, leaving the village far behind them as they wandered further down the path.

Before they had left the inn, Rhia had awoken, while the moon still lit the dark sky, to Rowan's lean body curled behind hers. Even in the throes of sleep, his arms arched protectively around her.

She turned over to glance at him, his bare chest lifting with even breaths, solid, shifting with the movement of the muscles under the surface of his lean shoulders. His strong jawline was clenched in sleep, his brows slightly furrowed, accentuating the lines of his handsome face. He seemed to carry the burdens of a thousand days, refusing to set them down, even in rest. Everything about this man was steady and true. No matter how many strikes she threw, no matter how many insults she hurled, no matter how cold she sought to make her exterior . . . he was simply there. To catch her, to warm her, to weather every storm she summoned. She shook her head, stirring from her deepening thoughts.

After having almost been discovered by the innkeeper, she had refused to speak further about the moonstone sapphire. They had shared too much already. Too many secrets now laid bare between them, complicating the path they found themselves on. Rhia knew, with a strange aching in her chest, that at the end of this journey, his duty was entwined with another. All roads led to differing destinations for the both of them. She knew that she had already proved to be a distraction enough to the journey he had found himself on. The journey they *both* were on. She would find their homeland, and find her way back to Beatha. She knew that the old woman could help her learn to quiet her mind again.

Rowan had felt her still, had felt her pull away, withdraw from him. The bright fire that had begun to spark new flames behind those mesmerizing eyes after they shared a kiss, had now quelled to a slowly burning ember beneath the surface. He began to feel a distinct pulling within his chest the further he parted from her, even to simply walk across the room and stoke the fireplace as her sleeping form lay peacefully on the bed. Before they had fallen asleep, he had glanced sidelong at the pendant around her neck and had begun to ask her about it. She merely leaned forward, stealing his breath with a soft touch of her mouth to his, capturing his lips for a single brief moment, before turning to face the wall and pulling the blanket over her shoulders. "Goodnight, Rowan."

As Rhia continued to notice the ever-growing lines and shadows of his sleeping face, she allowed a fleeting moment to let her eyes wander down to the planes of his broad chest and shoulders. His defined pectorals dipped down into the ridges of his abdominal muscles. His skin was slightly bronzed by the sun, his arms strong from the wielding of his hammer and the nature of his craft.

"It's not polite to stare." Rowan had hummed with a smirk, his eyes still closed as Rhia jerked her own eyes away from him and up toward the ceiling. His strong hand gave her hip a playful squeeze.

"You flatter yourself Mil—"

"Uh-uh-uh." He grinned. "Looks like you're going to have to come up with a new insult," he chided as he turned to rise from the bed and part the curtain to glance at the night sky. Her body turned strangely cold with his sudden absence.

"If we hope to leave this place undetected, we don't have much time." He motioned to Rhia's cloak on the wall. He began to gather supplies and stuff them into his leather satchel, strapping on his scabbard and daggers. "Let's be on our way."

Rhia rubbed the sleep from her eyes as she relaxed into Rowan's sturdy form in the saddle. His right thumb began to aimlessly trace circles over the raised band of flesh on her left forearm. The mark of her heritage, of *their* heritage. Rhia could feel that all too familiar heat creeping back up the nape of her neck and flaring at her palms. Her pulse quickened and she felt his response as he instinctively flexed his thighs against her body. She slowly withdrew her arm away from his, and back into her cloak as she sat up straighter in the saddle, attempting to put a bit of distance between them. A few long minutes passed.

"Are you cross with me? Because I did not tell you of my heritage?" Rowan asked, breaking their silence, at last. "If it's of any consequence, I made no effort to hide it from you. I simply allowed you the convenience of your own opinions," he teased, glancing down at her stoic face. Her features remained neutral as she fought to continue to look ahead at the path.

"To be honest, I only discovered it myself a few weeks ago, at the time of my father's death," he admitted, his voice trailing off slightly. “I guess he was only trying to protect me, but all he left me to piece together the origins of who I am, who my people are, lies within the journal.” He glanced down at his left arm, “I surely didn’t expect for both of us to find out the gravity of my truth in *this* way.” He grinned, nodding to his left arm, “Although I must say, I quite enjoyed how that interaction played out.” She rolled her eyes as he continued, his gaze moved ahead to the path before them, “Besides, I could not risk potentially exposing both of us as Tuatha . . . not when I needed to protect you.”

His last statement brought her to pause, further avoiding his gaze. She softened her shoulders, “To be fair, the only other Tuatha I have ever met are Beatha and Elder Ecna. We remained isolated out of fear for most of my life, with the occasional journey to Baile to trade for goods at times that were deemed safe.”

“You mean that *you* came to Baile?” Rowan asked with a hint of astonishment. “All my life I have lived there. I feel that I would have definitely remembered seeing someone like you,” he teased.

“You would not have seen us unless we *wanted* to be seen.” She smirked, “We only had an interest in being seen by traders, those who were trustworthy. Every contact had its purpose for me . . . for trade, for information, amusement—”

“What *kind* of amusement?” he interrupted. A beat of silence passed between them as she averted her gaze with an eye roll and flushed cheeks.

“Surely you don’t think I’ve spent 116 years on this land and not known what it means to find pleasure in the arms of another?" she replied. Rowan straightened in the saddle as a muscle tightened in his jaw.

"Fair enough. We do not need to discuss the past. We have plenty enough to discuss about the future. Like where we are headed. The land of our people. Finding the entrance to the *Sidhe*."

Rhia exhaled slowly. Each time they discussed the impending future of their respective paths, she found herself holding more and more tension in her shoulders and neck. She flexed her neck as she rolled her head slowly back and forth, releasing stiffness with a sigh.

Rowan could feel the exhaustion of the events of the previous days weighing on her, he could sense the tension in her, the retreat, the need for distance. He slowed Seamus to a stop and swung his legs over, stepping down to the ground below as he grasped the horse's bridle and began to lead him down the path as Rhia remained seated in the saddle. She remained silent as they ambled along the path. The information available to them between the map and Rhia's vision had begun to lessen as the days went on. An unspoken fear of the future, the fear of aimless wandering with no clear path forward loomed between them. They would reach the edge of the scribbled section of the incomplete map in Rowan's journal within two days' time.

Almost reading the worry of the silence between them, Rowan broke the stillness. "After we make camp tonight, I plan to study my father's map again. To see if there are any clues we may have missed, anything we could use to determine our next steps."

"Perhaps if I had saved the books from my home, I could

have more information on the location of where my people may be in hiding," she replied stoically, looking forward.

"*Our* people, Rhia. Or do you not yet feel that I am worthy of the title? Are we back to that, yet again?" he spat.

"How convenient they are called *your* people when you are looking for something. How are you to be sure that the Nichnevin is among them at this moment in time? Besides avenging your father's honor, what reason do you possess to want to identify with us? With *my* people?" she retorted.

Silence passed between them for several moments. She knew she had pushed too far. She regretted the words as soon as she spoke them. Rowan slowed Seamus to a stop and slowly glanced up to meet her gaze, his lips a tight line and his jaw taut. A sharp breeze cut through the trees, lifting leaves around them as it pierced Rhia with a cold chill that crawled up her spine.

"Perhaps it is that very reason that *our* people have not found peace after all these years. Do not forget that I have both Milesian *and* Tuatha blood coursing through my veins," he spat.

"This is exactly why they could not maintain the peace they once shared. Because they were too concerned with how they were *different* as opposed to learning of their likenesses. You and I, Rhia, we both have dreams, faces we miss, people we love who have been lost to us. We are on a mutual path, whether we like it or not, and we are headed toward our destinies, whatever those are for each of us. If you do not wish to continue down this path alongside me, by all means, do as you wish." He flung an arm toward the path ahead. "But just remember, we are far more alike than we are different." He broke his stare with a grumble and began again, walking Seamus down the path ahead.

"Our *likeness* does not change our destinies," she snapped at his back, "Our race, our *people* may be the same, but our paths remain different." She took a deep breath, "I will continue on with you, so long as we have the means to find the Tuatha people. I think you will come to find that I am rather resilient." Over his shoulder, she thought she detected a slight grin on Rowan's face.

She took another deep breath and attempted to calm and quiet her mind. As she closed her eyes, a familiar scent wafted through the air. The smell of rosemary, dusty pages of a book, and burning incense . . . Beatha. All at once, the old woman's face flashed across her mind. As she clamped her eyes shut, she could see the piercing blue of her eyes and the weather-worn lines of her face as clear as day.

The shrill cry of a horned owl broke the silence of the glen surrounding them. Rhia's eyes flew open to see the tawny owl perched on a branch of the tree that lay directly ahead. It showed no fear as its piercing eyes burrowed a hole into Rhia's consciousness and stirred something deep within her spirit. Beatha's scent grew stronger as the owl suddenly lifted into flight in a rustle of feathers against the wind. It sailed into the air in a circle above where Rhia sat atop Seamus and glided ahead down the path.

Rhia glanced up at Rowan, eyes wide. "We have to follow her." But Rowan was already swinging onto the saddle, his legs tightening around Rhia's own, arms circling around her as he leaned forward, spurring Seamus onward. They took off in a gallop toward a clearing in the tree line up ahead.

SEAMUS SLOWED to a steady trot as the clearing gave way to evidence of a sprawling estate, visible from their view atop the knoll. As they descended the hill, a chill settled over the air as the owl descended to perch on one of two large gateposts at the entrance of the grounds. An oval crest depicting a serpent entwined around a bird had been carved in bronze and nailed to each post at the entrance's gate. The bird was intricately carved into the bronze insignia, the portrayal of a short-lived struggle, as the serpent strangled its body of life.

Rowan had seen the same insignia, bore on the chest of the Milesian guard that had burned down his village, on the armor of the man who had taken his father's life—the guard he had cut down in a final blow of frustration and revenge as the events of that day caused a burning anger to radiate up his neck. Perhaps the tale he had spun at the inn, as to where they were headed, hadn't been too far from the truth. This *had* to be the manor of none other than the captain of the Milesian guard.

Prince Hedrek.

The estate was eerily quiet. Devoid of guards, servants, or any signs of life walking about the surroundings. Even the wind seemed to hold its breath as Rhia cast a hesitant glance up at Rowan as they rode forward, carefully. Rowan explained who the home belonged to as he led Seamus down a winding path, past several small cottages that seemed to also be deserted. They rode past an area where the trees once again tightly covered the entrance to the main house. He guided the horse over to a break in the trees where the shadow of the wood cast darkness over a portion of the grassy clearing.

He dismounted, helping Rhia down, and tying Seamus's bridle to a sturdy tree trunk. "Stay quiet old man," Rowan whispered to the horse, bringing the animal nose to nose with him and gently stroking his muzzle. He secured his sword and daggers to his waist and the bandolier he wore about his chest, as well as a deer hide flask of water to his side. "We can't risk the noise of hoofbeats when we aren't sure what lies up ahead," he replied to the worried expression on Rhia's face.

"I understand," she replied quietly as she pulled her cloak over her shoulders and secured her bow and quiver of arrows around her back. They began their descent down the path to the house, staying beneath the cover of the tree line and on the lookout for anyone who may happen upon them.

"I don't trust this silence," Rowan said under his breath, his head swiveling, surveying the area.

"Why did she lead us here?" Rhia asked, more to herself than anyone.

"I do not know, but my father always told me 'The gods will show you signs; know them, follow them, they will not lead you astray.' That is not the first time I have seen that owl," Rowan replied, his eyes scanning the trees above.

Rhia stopped walking. "I think it was Beatha. I saw her, in my mind's eye. Right before the owl descended upon us, I felt her presence so strongly. It is not the first time I have seen her either. It gives me hope that, perhaps, she is not gone forever."

Rowan placed a hand in hers. "Then let us listen to her guidance and pray that there is some sort of Tuatha draíocht at work here. We must move ahead. If I know one thing the captain of the guard has in his possession, it's maps. In the very limited experiences my father and I have had with the man, he seemed hells-bent on forging out some new expedition, in search of some uncharted land for himself and his gluttonous brother to claim."

"He is the brother of the king, then?" she asked.

"Yes, King Hectre, self-proclaimed leader of the Milesians and lord of these lands. Or so he has declared for the last thirty years," Rowan replied. "He claims to have descended from the first Milesian to set foot on the shores of Éire centuries ago. He, of course, has no way of proving it, apart from flaunting the wealth he has garnered from the copper and silver he has taxed from the starving people of these lands."

"All while watching his own people starve as the land withdraws into herself? Each time we trekked into Baile, we were told of worsening yields year after year, with each new harvest season. Does the greed of man know no end?" Rhia asked, a look of astonishment on her face as she glanced down at the ground. They passed an abandoned garden sitting behind a deserted gatehouse on the property. Dried brambles and snarled vines climbed a hand-fashioned trellis over the remains of the garden bed.

Rhia strode over to the chaotic heap of dried plants and placed her palms on the ground. She could feel Rowan's eyes on her. As she smiled to herself at the thought, warmth bloomed from her hands, causing a slight vibration in the earth that Rowan could feel beneath his boots. He continued to look at her with astonishment as she closed her eyes, beckoning life from the dried soil and decayed plants. Bright green sprigs of leaves and tendrils of delicate vines broke free from the soil and wrapped around the trellis, leaving blooms of soft white-petaled flowers in their wake. Luscious dark berries sprung to life and hung heavily on the vines that slowly wound around the once-devoid garden bed. Rhia plucked a juicy blackberry and brought it to her lips, the juices tinting her lips rosy as she took a bite.

Rowan was nothing less than captivated each time he witnessed her magic. She did not use her draíocht in the presence of others very often, for obvious reasons. Somehow, he felt that this was a sign of her trust. Something warmed deep within his chest as his glance caught the light reflecting from the juice upon her lips.

"What?" She feigned innocence as her mouth quirked into a half-smile and she gently bit the fullness of her bottom lip.

He grumbled something under his breath as he turned from her and beckoned her to follow him onward, toward the estate.

They continued to scale the perimeter of the large stone manor that stood ominously in the center of the estate. A slight chill spider walked up Rhia's spine as she craned her head back to stare up at the largest home she had ever seen. It was no castle, to be sure, but it far outsized any dwelling she had previously seen in Baile.

Rowan spied an opening in the wooden fence ahead, a piece of timber had crumbled under dry rot and exposed an area of weakness in the home's fortress. They slipped through one at a time. He reached back to grasp her palm and guide her through the opening, pulling her close to him.

Rhia could feel the warmth of his breath on her lips, prompting a quickening of her heartbeat as she locked her eyes on his. His eyes lingered on her berry-stained lips for a moment before slowly meeting her gaze. "We must be prepared. It is uncertain that we will meet the same quiet welcome that we have outside the gates. If this place is truly deserted, I cannot imagine why." He removed a dagger from the bandolier strapped across his chest, kneeling before her.

"May I?" he asked, with a slight smile as he motioned for her to lift her cloak, granting him access to her thigh. Heat crawled up the back of her neck, flushing her chest and coloring her cheeks rosy. Her breathing hitched, "Y-yes . . . but why—"

His hands gently grasped her knee, pulling it from beneath her cloak and resting her foot on his own knee. Both of his palms roved from her knee, up to her thigh, gently as flowing water, leaving warmth in their wake as a tightness grew in her chest and her breathing increased. He retrieved a holster strap from his cloak pocket and fastened it to her thigh, slipping the dagger into the holder.

Rowan exhaled, and leaned his head down, placing a gentle kiss on her knee as he looked up at her through half-lidded eyes. His hands lingered on her thigh, and she did not make an effort to move. "I trust that you know how to use this. Should you end up in close proximity to someone within these walls and I am not beside you."

"Are you planning on being somewhere else, Rowan?" she teased with a playful smile.

"The only thing that could separate me from you is my grave, Rhia. That is the *only* condition in which I will not be beside you," he replied solemnly.

A sharp pain registered through her chest at his sentiment. "Nonsense," she replied as she rested her booted foot on the ground again, reaching down to help him to his feet. "Clearly the Milesian guard is away on business or some other undertaking, so we will enter, locate Hedrek's command center, find the maps we need, and leave," she stated, "while attempting to remain as hidden as possible." She brushed past him, tightening the holster on her thigh, striding forward toward the manor.

Rhia felt another cold chill suddenly work up her spine, slowing her pace. The icy feeling increased the closer she got to the side entrance of the home. Large, grey, and reminiscent of a sky threatening rain, the manor loomed before her, casting dismal shadows on the ground. Dried vines crawled up the aged walls of the fortress, narrow windows dotted the outside walls, interrupted by the occasional arrow slit designed to house an archer to defend the home from intruders. She shook away the hint of fear threatening to crawl inside her mind at the undetermined fate they walked toward.

The chill around her body turned to a sudden blast of cold that settled down into her bones. She could have sworn she felt a pulse coming from the center of the home. From the depths, deep under the surface of the manor, she felt a pulling, a tugging on her draíocht. Her knees slammed into the ground as she flung her head skyward, eyes rolling back once again to leave white pupils in their place as her hands involuntarily planted in the dirt, feverishly inscribing symbols and shapes.

Rowan was at her side in an instant, his arm flung behind the small of her back to brace her small frame. He knelt, his lips coasting near her ear. "Rhia, Rhia stay with me . . . " he whispered, attempting to keep a low profile. The last thing he wanted was for them to draw unexpected attention to themselves with her in this state.

Her body remained rigid as her arms lingered out in front of her, fanatically tracing whorls and paths on the ground. She audibly gasped, as if the air was being drawn from her lungs. Rowan's chest constricted, and he caught her as she was thrust backward by an unseen force. She was shaking slightly, cold sweat breaking out on her forehead. Her eyes flew up to meet Rowan's.

"How long was I out for?" she whispered, as she stared at the ground.

"Only a moment or two. We may have another piece of our map." He motioned at the dirt before her.

"Well, what are you waiting for? Let's record it so that we can move on. Where is your journal—" she began.

"To *hells* with the damn journal, I will see that you are alright first," he ground out. His arms did not budge from where they still grasped her shoulders and lower back firmly.

Her eyes softened, a smile gracing her lips, "Rowan, I am fine." She moved to stand, brushing off her hands on her breeches, "Now if we're done feeling our feelings, let's record this so that we can get out of plain sight," she teased, as she scanned her eyes around the perimeter, ensuring they remained alone.

Rowan cleared his throat as he retrieved the journal from his cloak pocket, quickly sketched the symbols and map remnants from the soil, and scuffed the dirt with his boot to remove the evidence of her efforts.

Rowan's eyes scanned the walls of the manor, looking for any clues that may lead them to the entrance to Hedrek's command center.

When he was a young man, barely sixteen, he had been recruited to fight in the local battalion of the Milesian army in a skirmish to the north of Baile. There were whispers of strange tides along the North shore, bringing unexpected ships carrying men who were robbing several fishing outposts along the coast. The men aboard the ships brought with them whispers of giants, descendants of the Fir-Balog who had been banished and driven from the lands of Éire. The rumors were enough to spur King Hectre to order additional companies of soldiers stationed in the North for the entirety of the winter months.

Rowan and his company had engaged in battle with a few bands of rowdy sea merchants bent on thievery here and there, but no giants. He was convinced that Hectre had simply placed extra manpower in one of his strategic ports to protect his pockets—and the countless pieces of copper and silver that came through the trading ports. He and his men never saw a single coin. They were simply sent home with a pat on the back and the knowledge that they had served their King.

He flexed his jaw as he reflected on those wasted months. At least he could say he had walked away that spring with a few more fighting skills and a familiarity with the operations of the Milesian guard.

Rowan knew that Hedrek's estate must be home to the headquarters of the guard, as Hedrek was their captain and commanding officer. He looked for an indication of where the soldiers might enter the manor, for he knew, that must be where plans are made.

Where plans are made, where strategies are laid out, there are maps . . . and maps mean information. He knew that with Hedrek's keen interest in the inner workings of the Tuatha people and his mission of exterminating them, he would likely take just as eager an interest in locating their elusive homeland.

His eyes caught the sun's reflection on a bronze handle of a wooden door on the west side of the home. As they approached closer, he could see that in front of the door, there was a well-trodden path leading from a hitching post to the entrance. Soldiers would enter here . . . exactly where he wanted to be.

Rowan couldn't explain how, but he felt a change in the air and sensed Rhia tense as she followed close behind him. "I believe that one of my people is near," she whispered as they neared the doorway. Rowan reached out and pushed the heavy wooden door. To their surprise, it opened easily, the hinges creaking slightly as they both winced with the sound.

"I don't know where or how, but I can feel it. I think the visions come when my people are close by." They neared the opening of a large iron staircase that spiraled downward to a dark room with no signs of light. Rhia turned to Rowan, her gaze not quite meeting his as she stared at his shoulder, "I believe that is why my first vision came when you touched me for the first time, the night that the fire took my home."

He turned to look at her as she continued, "I had never experienced that before, but then again, I had never been touched by another of *my* people, save for Beatha and Ecna," she added with a faraway smile.

"Then let us find them, Rhia. You know as well as I do, that if they are inside this home, they are not here as a guest," he added with a somber note in his voice.

They descended the staircase together, Rowan's right hand glued to the hilt of his sword as they trekked further into what looked like a holding cell, of sorts. His boots landed on the stone floor at last, as they fumbled around in the darkness of the room.

"I do not like this. I do not like this," Rhia chanted as she absentmindedly clutched the moonstone sapphire pendant she wore. Her eyes caught a hint of light as she glanced down at it, noticing an iridescent glow that pierced the darkness.

"Well, that's new . . . " she remarked. Rowan was already staring at the necklace as well. As the faint glow illuminated the room slightly, Rowan's eye caught a lantern sconce on the far wall of the chamber where a thick tallow candle sat. He retrieved a flint from a nearby worktable that held iron and bronze tools of all shapes and sizes, although, his eyes could not make out what these tools might be used for.

He and Rhia walked forward as he struck the flint, lighting the candle, further illuminating the room. Just then, a sharp creak of an iron hinge pierced the silence, as Rowan and Rhia spun around in unison to face the source of the sound from the far side of the room.

A large iron cage hung from the ceiling by a thick chain, causing the structure to swing left to right, creaking and groaning with each swaying movement. The cage was dome-shaped and looked almost as if it were meant for a bird—a very large bird indeed, if this were the case.

The shadows from the corner of the room concealed the contents of the iron structure. Rhia moved slowly toward the enclosure, her heart racing with each step she took. Rowan moved to follow, attempting to stop her. She let out an audible gasp as her eyes adjusted to the darkness.

A thin, frail frame of a woman lay crouched against the far side of the cage. She lay with her legs drawn up to her chest, her clothing in tatters around her emaciated body. Her ribs protruded prominently from her sunken chest, peeking out from the garment that was no longer adequately covering her midsection. Her hair was as black as ravens' wings and hung in long, unkempt strands that clung to her shoulders and back. Piercing hazel eyes rimmed in gold stared back at Rhia as she remained utterly speechless in the presence of this silent soul. Her skin was as pale as alabaster, save for the blue-tinged band of flesh encircling her left forearm.

CHAPTER
THIRTEEN
AINE

Ten years ago

The forest floor was covered in lush white-petaled flowers and bathed in the soft light of the setting sun. A rosy hue tinted the leaves bronze, looking as if it were October, instead of late Spring. Laughter echoed through the trees as the merry-making dwindled from the day's Beltane celebrations. In their small, secluded settlement deep within the forest, a remaining tribe of Tuatha had gathered to herald the beginning of the growth season as a community.

A young and spritely raven-haired Tuatha female ran unabashedly through the tall trees, spinning and rounding each trunk, weaving this way and that as her long locks twisted about her shoulders and down her back. Laughter echoed through the fragrant forest air, escaping her soft pink lips and dancing in her eyes of piercing golden hazel. She was running faster and faster to evade the capture of a young Tuatha male, who had begun to follow her beckoning call, away from the day's festivities. The young woman would pause after rounding another corner of the forest and lock eyes with the young male, causing a flush of pink to color his handsome face with frustration as his breathing quickened.

Letting him almost catch her, all at once, a rustle of feathers broke the silence of the wood as she surged upward on the gust of a breeze. Black feathers and dried leaves rained down on him as he glanced upward to see a beautiful raven perched on a branch.

"Aine, that's hardly fair," he said wearily as he leaned against the trunk to catch his breath. A slight smile etched the corner of his mouth. He glanced upward, "It's almost as if you didn't intentionally lead me away from the others . . . now what reason would you have to do something like that?"

"As I recall, you didn't seem to be too sad about leaving the others, Finnin." She glanced down at the young man below, his golden hair glistening in the setting sun, soft curls brushing the tops of his bronzed shoulders. The raised, blue-tinged band of flesh twisted slightly as he flexed his left forearm, his fingers combing back his hair from his handsome face.

Finnin had been in her life since before she could remember. They had grown up side by side in their village. The same village that they had fled as children when their families sought refuge further into the forest and away from Milesian cruelty.

He was the first Tuatha boy she had fought; she punched him square in the nose when she caught him trying to shoot a rabbit with his bow and arrow for sport. He was the first boy she had kissed, the first young man that she had lain with the summer that her body had seemingly grown wings and beckoned the touch of another. It was only natural that she would choose to betroth herself to him, to choose him as her mate, as females often did in her culture. He was strong, a skilled archer, trustworthy . . . and kind.

A giggle escaped her lips as Aine shifted back into her maiden form, pale legs peeking out from beneath a rose-colored gown that danced up around her thighs, feet dangling from the branch she now sat on. "In fact, I think I detected a look of excitement in your eyes when you began to follow me." She grinned.

"Ah, yes, you know all too well how to excite me." His eyes darkened, then locked on hers, "Don't you, Aine?"

She descended to the ground with a crunch of leaves as she prowled toward him. "I'm not sure I know what you mean . . . " she teased.

"Then why don't I show you," Finnin growled, closing the distance between them, grasping a strong hand around the curve of her waist and pulling her closer to him. "After all, if we are to be betrothed, I can at least learn what makes your heart race the way mine does." His lips ghosted the shell of her ear as he ground his hips into hers. Her breathing quickened at the feel of his hardening length against her thigh.

"Tell me, Aine," he reached up with his other hand, softly placing his palm on her chest, as his lips kissed down her neck, "what makes this heart beat faster—faster as mine does? Tell me, whatever it is, and it's yours."

"Well, that mouth for a start," she began, bringing her fingertips up to touch his lips, heat coiling in her lower belly and radiating through her body. The nipples of her full breasts grew taut beneath his hands. Featherlight touches turned into desperate grasping.

"Would you like to see just what this mouth can do, my love?" he teased, kissing her fingers, then nipping down her neck and shoulder.

She pulled the collar of his tunic until he descended atop her onto a soft patch of grass and moss beneath the shade of the tree. "Yes, I think I might need a demonstration . . . " she said breathlessly as she grasped beneath his chin, bringing his mouth to hers and slanting her lips to close over his. She kissed him hungrily as his touch became more fervent, more desperate to bring them even closer together.

He grasped her hip, lifting her thigh and hooking his right arm under her knee. Finnin peppered kisses down her calf, the inside of her knee, and steadily up her inner thigh as she let out a soft moan in anticipation. "Don't worry . . . as with most things with you, I intend to take my time." He smirked, bunching up her gown around her hips, exposing her sex to him. "Damn woman, I will never tire of how beautiful you are . . . every single curve, every dimple."

She could feel the gravel in his voice vibrating inside her body as she reached up, tangling her lithe fingers in his golden curls as his kisses grew more fervent and closer to the area where she needed him the most. The warmth in her core had turned into an inferno.

Suddenly, the smell of smoke wafting on the air heightened her senses and broke her focus. This was not the burning of the ceremonial fires nor the flames of the cooking spit.

The forest was burning.

Hoofbeats pierced the peaceful silence of the forest, sounding closer by the second. "*Finnin!*", she squeezed his shoulder, his glossy eyes flew up to meet hers, his lips reddened from his ministrations as he pulled the hem of her dress down to cover her.

Finnin cried out, a hauntingly sharp inhale escaped his lips, followed by a gurgling cough as the sharp end of a sword impaled from his back through the front of his chest, his dark crimson blood spattering over Aine's face from the impact.

She opened her mouth to scream but no sound would come out. She could only stare in horror as the body of her betrothed slumped into a lifeless form over her legs. A brawny Milesian male with bronzed skin and dark tousled hair, holding his sword standing behind him simply stared at Aine with an unreadable scowl.

He used the toe of his boot to kick Finnin's body to the side, reaching down to grab Aine's wrist. "Now, daughter of *magic*, you can make this easy or you can make this difficult for yourself. You will come with me—"

A blood-curdling scream erupted from Aine that shook the forest floor and sent birds skyward from the treetops. As the male's hand reached for hers, flames erupted from her palms, her eyes pinched shut in anguish, casting forth all the rage she could muster.

"*FUCK!*" he screamed, pulling back his arm to reveal a linear burn that singed across his left palm. His face turned somber as his glance slowly rose from his hand to meet her eyes with a look of slight wonder that quickly darkened. He angled his head to the side.

"*You*. I have been looking for *you* for quite a long time. This was a fortuitous mission, indeed." He reached into his cloak pocket, pulled out a vial of powder, and poured a small amount of it into his uninjured palm. Before she could crawl away or make a move to escape, he quickly blew a puff of air, propelling the powder directly into Aine's face.

She could wield her fire magic with her hands tied, move rocks of the earth with her eyes closed, and manipulate the wind on an especially gusty day. However, when she tried in desperation to call forth again the fire draíocht within her, she felt as if her magic was being thrown against an iron wall. The fine powder settled into her nose, on her lips, and gritted into her eyes. She felt a metallic taste form in the back of her mouth and knew that whatever this substance was, it was intended to snuff out Tuatha magic. Aine could sense her arms and legs beginning to feel heavy, her eyes growing tired.

The metallic tang settled into her nose, but she could still smell the forest burning all around her. The powder stung the corners of her eyes, but she could still see the smoke blurring her vision. Her arms and legs felt weak, but she could still feel brawny arms reaching down to pick her up. The Milesian who had killed Finnin slung her over his shoulder, her body too drained to fight back. For the first time in a long time, she *feared.* Feared for her people and their safety, for her village, for her mother.

The last image she saw through half-lidded eyes was another Milesian soldier dragging Finnin's body away, leaving a trail of blood across the moss-covered ground in his path. She could hear the desperate screams of the other Tuatha in the distance. Slowly, the screaming faded.

Then, everything went dark.

When Aine awakened, she was lying on her side, her body was sore from her neck and shoulders to her hips. She felt as if she had ridden hundreds of miles on horseback, but from a quick glance around her, she had not left the forest where her village had been.

Where her village, her community, her family *had* been. She could no longer hear screams or cries as an eerie silence had fallen over the woods, save for the occasional snap of the fire before her. The smell of smoke had dissipated somewhat, giving rise to another burning stench. *Flesh*. Burning. Tuatha. Flesh.

Aine jolted fully into consciousness. A tightness seized her chest as her eyes adjusted to the light. A quiet sob escaped her lips as she glanced just a short distance in front of her to see a Milesian soldier hauling another Tuatha body and throwing it onto the pile that was already burning.

No, no, no, no, was the only thought circling in her mind as her eyes detected a light blonde braid peeking out from under the slumped form of another lifeless body. Her mother's pale blue eyes stared motionless, boring a hole in Aine's heart, as her bloodied body was slowly being consumed by the flames.

Aine jumped to her feet, springing forward toward the fire, emitting a weak wail, no hint of draíocht to be conjured up as her magic remained blunted by the powder. She had nothing left to live for on this continent. She would throw herself on that fire. Leave this world with her mother, with Finnin, with her *people*.

A pair of rough hands clamped down on her shoulders from behind, restraining her arms as his grip moved to her elbows, tightening as she jerked and fought against him. He drew her close to his broad chest, the stubble on his jawline brushing against her tear-stained cheek. The Milesian guard who had killed Finnin now held complete control over her.

"I told you, sweet. You could make this as easy or as hard as it had to be. You seemed to think fire was a good idea, *hmm?*" he mocked, a dark edge to his voice.

"You had planned to kill my people no matter what I chose to do, you Milesian *filth*," she spat, turning to face him with fire in her eyes. "The race of men knows nothing but murder, theft, and bloodshed—"

Her words were cut off by the swift motion of his hand as he brought the back of it across her face with a forceful slap. She stumbled back as he caught her shoulder with a bruising grip.

"You will learn to exercise respect when you speak to the *prince* of Éire, the brother of the king, and captain of the Milesian guard."

Aine tasted blood from a split lip as she felt her cheek swelling. Her head slowly turning to meet his gaze as he continued to speak, hooking a finger beneath her jaw, and drawing her face closer to his own. "And it seems that the race of men is all that you have left, sweet."

He gazed at her for a long moment. "As you seem to have a fire about you, I fear I'll have to think of another name to call you besides *sweet*. I heard that fortunate soul buried between your legs calling you *Aine*." He glanced at the fire and the pile of burning bodies, "Or maybe he wasn't so fortunate after all, was he?" He smirked, his gaze darkening as he leaned in closer, voice lowered, "I would keep that in mind the next time you think about doing anything foolish. There are some things worse than death."

CHAPTER FOURTEEN

AINE

One Month Later

The sun was setting through a wide window that framed the sitting room in swathes of amber light. Aine sat silently in a high-backed chair, rhythmically smoothing the seams of her gown with her fingertips. Her blank stare stayed plastered to the wall in front of her, eyes not deviating, barely even blinking. Her hands and face had been scrubbed clean by a chambermaid earlier in the evening before she had been dressed in a fine velvet gown of deep burgundy and lace—with long sleeves, of course.

Long sleeves to thoroughly cover her forearms—specifically her left one, bearing the mark of her people. Her people, who were only a memory to her. It had only been a month, but to her, it had felt like a lifetime since she had been dragged from that forest, the smell of smoke and burning flesh surrounding her as her mind reeled at what her new reality would become.

Yet here she sat, firmly planted in that reality and all the fresh hell it afforded her with each new morning. A new gown to be shoved into, a new smiling face to put on, a new courtier to be introduced to, led by Hedrek's firm grasp on her arm.

The captain of the Milesian guard had taken great pleasure in parading her around his brother's palace and court, introducing her to the refined members of their society, all while pretending he was among the civilized. Gowns and jewels were placed on her body to strategically hide the marks of his *civility*.

From the first moment he had brought Aine into his large manor estate miles away from the enchanted wood, it was made perfectly clear just how refined he was, and just what he wanted.

When she first entered through the gilded doors of his large home, Aine had noticed a corner desk tucked into an office of sorts. Papers with symbols of the Tuatha people were inscribed across the sheets that littered the top of the desk. Her eyes grew wild with curiosity, just in time for Hedrek to notice.

"Ah, I see, perhaps it is beginning to make sense to you now, Aine," he began, grasping her chin and turning her nose to nose with him. "Your people have laid claim to these lands, cursed these lands, done what they will with them for far too long," he said through gritted teeth. "Now, it is our turn. Milesians will one day harness the draíocht that your kind uses to summon magic from the earth, the wind, the water, from the very fiery core of the continent." His eyes grew wild with each maniacal word that fell from his mouth.

"And *you* . . . you will be the one to help me. *Nichnevin*."

"No, no, I think you have me confused with someone else, I am not her. I am no one—"

"Oh no, sweet, you are someone now. You are *mine*," he growled, moving to press her body against the wood paneling of the wall as his men hastily exited the room. "And you are right where I want you . . . and you must know that Aine . . . that I want you." His voice lowered as he began to trace his fingers from her chin, down her neck, and to the swell of her breasts above the tattered dress she wore. His eyes met hers, filled with lust and something darker.

"Surely you do not think there could be anything to persuade me to accept the man who has taken everything that I love," she replied through her teeth, barely above a whisper as tears of anger streamed down her face. She extended her head back, spitting directly into his face.

She braced herself for the impact of his hand. Instead, he simply raised his palm to wipe the saliva from his brow and brought it down to his lips.

"*Oh sweet*, I think you underestimate my methods of persuasion," he ground out, his mouth above the shell of her ear. His hands grasped her raven hair at the nape of her neck, yanking her toward the staircase ahead of him. She wouldn't give him the satisfaction of crying out. Tears continued to silently stream from her golden hazel eyes.

"*Imogen*!" he shouted, as an older handmaiden flew down the stairs, dipping into a quick curtsy before Hedrek.

Her curly greying bangs were peeking out from beneath a peasant's cap, plastered to her forehead with sweat.

"Pardon my absence, sir, I was just readying the lady's chambers," she replied hurriedly.

"Firstly, this *creature* is no lady." He glared down at Aine with a look of disgust, "Not yet . . . secondly, she needs a bath and a fresh change of clothes. Her own chambers won't be necessary. She will sleep in mine."

A chill crawled up her spine. Aine drew in a sharp breath as Hedrek pushed her forward onto the floor. She landed on her hands and knees, using the banister of the stairs to pull her weak body upright, to stand.

She tried desperately to call forth her magic, to conjure even a small amount of fire from her palms. The powdered substance that Hedrek had used in the forest had long since passed from her system, as she could detect no more of the metal tang that came with it. However, she had learned long ago that the further her people were from the heart of the forest, the weaker their magic became. When her people began to dwindle in number, they had returned to the wood, to magic, to where they were the strongest.

Aine tasted defeat on her tongue as she ambled up the staircase, Imogen at her side. The handmaiden placed her in a warm tub, scrubbed the dirt and ash from her body, and applied perfumed oils to her pale skin. She drew her long raven locks into braids, and wrapped and secured them atop the crown of her head.

Aine sat in the sitting room, lost in her thoughts, eyes still glued to the blank wall ahead. The sun had sunk far below the horizon. The room was lit only by candlelight and the lantern sconces upon the wall.

All those mornings of sitting in tepid water, being rubbed with oils, her skin being scrubbed over and over. But nothing could scrub away, could remove the layer of filth she felt in the wake of Hedrek's hands on her.

The first night she was brought to the manor, after being stripped, scrubbed, brushed, perfumed, and dressed, she was escorted to a small room off the main bedroom of Hedrek's chambers. A small table set for two awaited her, with Hedrek sitting before a plate of roasted wild boar and vegetables.

He rose, pulling her chair out as she sat. She stared blankly down at the plate of food before her. Hedrek and his men had left her without food for the entirety of the journey back to the estate.

Aine had feared that these men might not even know that Tuatha *had* to eat. Did they understand what they withheld from her with each meal the soldiers ate by the fire each night, or was this just another facet of Milesian cruelty?

She knew the answer as her stomach growled in response to the food before her as she stared down at it. *Curse this body*, she thought, as Hedrek smiled at the noise her hungry belly had made, breaking their silence.

"Eat." He gestured to her plate, as he began to greedily eat from his own.

Even as she stared at the food, even with her body's physical response to hunger, she could not bring herself to eat. As she stared at the crisp skin of the roasted boar, all she could think of was the burning flesh of her mother, her people, as their bodies laid waste on that pyre.

"*Gods damnit*, Aine!" he bellowed, slamming his fists on the table and shaking the dishes on the surface. He quickly rose from his chair, and rounded the table, pinning her against the high-backed chair as he grasped her by the neck. He snatched a piece of boar and shoved it between her teeth. The food felt like ash in her mouth.

"You are of use to me, witch. I have told you . . . You are *mine*," he spat, angling his head closer to hers. "If I command you to eat, you *will* eat."

But Aine was a quick learner. She brought her full lips around his fingers, sucking the oils of the meat from his thumb and forefinger as she met his gaze. Her tongue began to playfully tease his thumb as he let out a long exhale.

"I knew you'd come to your senses eventually, sweet." He leaned closer, her breathing quickening at his proximity. He quickly yanked her body atop his own, swapping seats and leaning back into the chair with her straddling his lap.

Hedrek grasped the curve of her hips, pulling her closer as he angled her head back, reaching onto the plate behind her and bringing another piece of meat to her lips. She ate greedily, eyes remaining locked with his. She tried not to draw attention to how she was eyeing the dagger that lay strapped to his side. Her full lips drew the meat between her teeth, giving an occasional moan of pleasure as she could feel Hedrek shifting beneath her thighs.

"If only I knew this was all it took, just a little bit of food and coaxing for the little beast to come out and play . . . " he mocked. His eyes darkened as he grasped the inside of her cheek with his thumb, bringing his finger into her mouth.

Aine locked her lips around it, watching the lust fill Hedrek's eyes.

Then she bit down. *Hard.*

She quickly moved to grasp the dagger at his side with her right hand. Blood dribbled down her mouth from his finger as she fought to gain control of the weapon. But Hedrek was too fast for her and overpowered her weakened form. He grasped her wrist and wrenched the dagger free, the back of his bloody hand swatting her face forcefully and knocking her from his lap onto the floor.

"So, you want to get bloody, do you, little beast?' he growled. He yanked her from the ground by her arm, as she let out a horrific scream. "We can play dirty if that's what you like. Don't worry, no one will disturb us, so you can scream as much as you like, my love."

He threw her into the main bedchamber and onto his bed. Hedrek was on her in an instant, the dagger's blade pressed up against her throat. "You should know this Aine . . . your escape is never going to happen. *No one* is coming for you. You still exist *only* because it is my will."

"Then will for me to die, Hedrek," she sobbed as she pushed forward against the dagger, pressing her throat into it of her own volition. "*End it!* Please end it!"

"What did I tell you? Do something foolish and there are things much worse than death. You will come to your senses. You will learn to submit to me," he ground out as he tugged her arms above her head and yanked off his belt, using it to secure her hands above the headboard. "You will give everything to me eventually Aine, every fragment of your magic, of yourself, belongs to me now."

Aine shuddered each time she recalled the feeling of his hands on her body. Each morning bringing with it a new soreness to her limbs, a new ache in her head, a new bruise to her skin. Hedrek was well-respected by his brother, and by his soldiers. His orders were followed without question, his household running like a well-oiled machine. But behind closed doors, he was a man unhinged.

The dark depravity that ran deep within his blood was enough to cause Aine to venture deep within the confines of her own mind. More so each day, she retreated into a dark corner of what remained of her sanity.

For deep within the recesses of her own psyche, he could not venture. He may ruin her body, strip her magic, steal her hope for escape a little more each day, but she vowed that she would *never* let him break her mind. For the life she had once lived, she *had* given up hope, and with it, the light that had once sparked life behind her golden eyes.

Some nights, in the quiet of her room, as Hedrek lay asleep and satiated beside her, she thought of Finnin's face. She remembered the ridges of his body and the soft heat of his lips. She shuddered with disgust, wanting to claw her skin from her bones at the thought of all the ways that her body had been touched, had been violated, since his death.

Her eyes would affectionately stare at the window of Hedrek's room. A window that she would love nothing more than to fling herself from. Aine could no longer extend her midnight wings, could no longer move her bones and skin to shift into her raven form. In the first week of her time here at the estate, she had tried once to shift in the courtyard. She had silently begged her body to call forth those wings so that she could shoot skyward and away from this nightmare . . . but to no avail.

The longing for rescue, for escape from the four walls of the manor was fading with each passing day. Now, she only longed to allow her body, this body that had already endured so much, to enter that freefall path to destruction. Aine longed for the great forever sleep. She did not know if the old gods still listened, but she petitioned them each night with her prayer.

As Aine sat in the chair, her fingers traced the raised band of flesh on her left forearm from beneath the sleeve of her gown. Tonight, she would be introduced to more members of court at a gathering organized by Hedrek and the king.

So far, Hedrek had conveniently kept her Tuatha identity a secret from everyone in the household—even the king. The first night Imogen had assisted her in bathing, he had insisted on being there as she was undressed, much to Aine's disgust. His eyes bore through Imogen as she had sharply inhaled in shock when she had seen Aine's forearm and her

Tuatha marking for the first time. "I think you know the cost, should you decide to open your *mouth*, Imogen," Hedrek spat. Imogen simply looked down at her own forearms and the small bruises that littered her skin.

"Of course, my prince," she whispered meekly.

He had forced his men to swear their discretion at the end of his sword before leaving the forest with Aine in tow on the day he stole everything that she held dear. Not that he needed to ask them to swear their loyalty. Aine could see it each time she looked into their eyes, could smell it, the *fear* that they too harbored toward prince Hedrek. The captain of the guard clearly had motives *far* beyond his loyal allegiances to feel that she was such a prize to be kept in total secret.

Her thoughts were interrupted as the doors of the sitting room flew open, and Imogen entered. "It's time for dinner, milady," she said politely.

Aine rose in silence, her mouth in a tight line across her thin face. She briefly glanced over her shoulder into the mirror by the door of the room. Her face had begun to hollow out since her departure from the forest. The light in her eyes had all but faded, as had the youthful blush that had once graced her cheeks. She pulled the high collar of her emerald dress to the left a bit, to adequately cover the thumb-shaped bruise peeking out from the side of her neck.

"You look beautiful, dear," Imogen began, reaching up with a swath of linen to dab the tears forming at the corner of Aine's eyes. "Now let's be off, don't want to be late," she added.

No, not when he *is waiting*, were the words that went unsaid.

CHAPTER FIFTEEN

AINE

Eight Months Later

The fire roared in the hearth as the echoes of the after-dinner conversation dwindled in the sitting room. Aine sat stiffly at Hedrek's side with her hands folded neatly in her lap. Her eyes maintained what had become their characteristic lackluster stare, focusing on the flames lapping at the deteriorating pieces of wood in the fireplace. Her mind drifted to the snapping of wood and the black rolling smoke of the violent flames that licked up the trunks of the trees, destroying her former home and all its inhabitants.

"Yes, I feel that if our forces can maintain control of the border villages, we can effectively prevent any Tuatha that have fled from these shores from returning by boat, or otherwise." Hedrek gleamed as he adjusted the tartan wool that lay across his left shoulder and chest, as he lifted his copper cup of whiskey back to his lips.

"Aye," echoed the mumbles of the members of his regiment and the male courtiers sitting about the room.

"Brother, it would seem that the border villages might, themselves, be the problem," King Hectre countered, breaking his silence for the evening. A bronze crown encrusted with rubies and emeralds sat atop his long greying locks that were gathered at the nape of his neck. The wrinkles on his bronzed face from the many summers he had seen were almost outnumbered by the golden flecks in his brown eyes. Eyes that did not miss many details, whether great or small.

"I hear from the scouts that have just returned that there is talk of hidden outposts of those savages all along the rocky coastline of Dál Fiatach." The king continued, "Our warriors in the north have sent word several times now, of how elusive this rouge band of heathens have been. They can't seem to drive them out, yet the captain of *my* guard says our borders are well-protected," he finished, with a pointed look at Hedrek.

"I suppose you believe the Selkies are helping them too, brother?" Hedrek goaded, as he chuckled to himself with a twisted grin, halfway through his whiskey, "Ah yes, the old tales of seals by day, beautiful women by night, aiding in the transport of remaining Tuatha right into our lands." He set the cup down, "You can't believe all the hearsay that makes its way back to the manor, Hectre."

"You forget yourself, brother," the king's tone became solemn, "do not forget, however, that I have tasked our borders' safety to *you.* A task that can be reallocated if the need arises."

Hedrek ground his teeth as he reached to his left, absent-mindedly laying his hand on Aine's knee as she sat next to him. She flinched from her lost thoughts, eyes rising to meet his. She noticed anger beginning to rise within his countenance. It was perhaps a survival mechanism, Aine's acquired ability to predict subtle changes in his mood.

Aine reflected on the talk of people of the sea-faring territories of the north. She remembered hearing as a child, the tales of *Tír fo Thionn*—the land beneath the waves, as her mother had called it. A kingdom of the distant cousins of the Tuatha, of the children of Danu, who had made their home beneath the seas in magnificent dwellings of alabaster coral.

It was said that they set up their kingdom to guard the ocean and her inhabitants against Balor who remained imprisoned at the bottom of the sea by the Nichnevin's power. Aine wondered, *Could the people of Tír fo Thionn be helping their distant relatives in the north escape to safety?* Her shoulders had become tight from the last few hours of listening to the men around her discussing the slaughter of her people—like they were animals. Of course, no one in the room knew they were *her* people, save for Hedrek—a secret he would never reveal, not even to his own brother.

Aine shifted away from Hedrek's touch, moving to rise from her seat. "I am tired, Hedrek, I should like to retire for the night."

His frustration at his brother's remarks was already palpable as he firmly grasped her thigh, subtly pushing her body back down beside him. "I am not quite ready for bed, *wife*." He shot a pointed glare at her, his voice a low growl, "And I should like you to wait for me."

A wave of nausea rolled through Aine's body. Just as the tension in the room was rising to a head, eliciting the stares of the other men, the doors flew open and an energetic young Milesian boy burst in, heading straight for King Hectre.

"*Brenainn!*" called a nursemaid from the doorway, trailing behind him with a flushed face.

The boy made a beeline for the king, running up and jumping atop his lap as he threw his arms around his neck. "Papa! Papa! How I missed you!"

The King chuckled as he waved off the apologies from the nursemaid as she walked into the room. "My boy, how big you've grown!" King Hectre laughed as he pulled him into his embrace and placed a kiss on the top of his head. "I have only just returned late this evening, but I thought you'd be long since gone to bed."

"Apologies, your highness, he was—" the flustered nursemaid began. The King raised a palm.

"Ah, it's alright. Let him stay. If Brenainn is to be king one day, let him listen to matters of state. It's never too early to learn, is it, my boy?"

The dark-haired boy beamed up at King Hectre, his bright brown eyes dancing in the firelight. Hedrek stiffened in his seat next to Aine, clearing his throat. Aine was glad for the distraction, as Hedrek seemed to be dangerously close to the bottom of his drink. She knew from her unfortunate experience that, like most men, his anger became more difficult to control the more liquor found its way past his lips.

Brenainn's eyes shyly scanned the room and finally settled on Aine. His face was full of childlike wonder as he pointed at her from his father's lap. "Papa . . . what is she?" he asked. The boy had seen Aine in passing several times since she had arrived at the manor, always conveying the most curious glances, as children often do.

"What kind of question is that son? She is your uncle's wife, princess Aine," Hectre replied, rather perplexed by his son's question.

Aine froze at Hedrek's side. *Surely, he could not have seen the blue band of flesh. He is a child; he would have no reason to know of my identity.* The panicked thoughts began to enter her mind. The boy of nine years had only been in her presence a handful of times at the most since she had arrived at the estate.

"But how can she be a wife or a princess, when her hair is as black as a raven's?" The child continued, "I think she is a bird."

Aine released a silent breath, her eyes softening into a smile for the first time in weeks. "Princess Aine, can you fly?" the boy asked.

Hectre bellowed a laugh as the other men in the room followed suit, she even felt Hedrek begin to relax at her side. The captain of the guard grumbled as she caught a subtle eye roll from his direction.

She glanced at the window to her left as the men slowly resumed their conversation, ignoring the nonsensical notion from Brenainn.

How I wish I still could, child, how I wish . . .

Brenainn had become quite the little companion as Aine's days inside the manor dragged on. Hedrek would be called away on distant raiding parties, or perhaps worse, much to Aine's relief and disappointment. She never knew if he was off slaughtering her people, or simply driving them from the land in the name of protecting the king's lands. She discovered it was easier on her mind if she did not put too much thought into it. She attempted to keep her mind occupied with the day-to-day, the here and now. All she could focus on was the immediate future, it was the only thing keeping her motivated to wake up with each new day. Although some nights she prayed for the alternative.

She was glad for the reprieve that his absence afforded her. She began to treasure the time she had to herself. Although her mind would often wander to think of her people, she tried to avoid thinking of the torment that they may be suffering at her captor's hand.

One sunny morning, the laughter of the young son of the king echoed across the courtyard as Aine was sitting in silence, staring at the way the breeze blew the tall grasses across the knoll ahead.

She glanced over to see Brenainn running across the meadow, playing with a group of young boys as they fought with wooden swords and shields. "I banish you! For I am Prince Brenainn of the Milesian lands!" the young prince shouted as he chased another boy of about his age.

"These aren't your lands! They belong to the Tuatha!" a young Milesian girl with dark brown curls and bright sunny eyes cried as she came behind Brenainn, pushing him onto the ground with a huff.

"Hey!" he countered, moving to chase her with his wooden sword, leaving the other child behind. Aine smiled to herself as she watched the children play for a good long while. She reveled in the innocence of their merrymaking and her thoughts drifted back to her own childhood, running carefree and barefoot through the forest.

As the sun began to sink low over the horizon, Brenainn crested the top of the grassy knoll and spotted Aine sitting on a large stone under the shade of an apple tree. His peers had all gone home and he ran excitedly over to her with a large grin on his face.

"Princess Aine! Did you fly here?" he exclaimed through panted breaths as he flopped down beside her in the shade.

Aine did not know how to respond to the child. It had been a long time since she allowed herself to feel any emotion but regret, sorrow, and shame. Her eyes softened as she glanced down at the beaming innocent face of the young prince. "Maybe I did," she teased with a grin.

"I knew it! I knew you were a raven, sent to visit us!" Aine burst into laughter. “Princess Aine, you’re only teasing me . . . aren’t you?” he questioned with a raised brow.

“You may believe whatever you wish, child. For that is the beauty of childhood, you can believe whatever you choose. The world still appears to you as you imagine it to,” she replied.

They remained quiet for a few moments, as the whip-poorwills called the tune of the setting sun and the coolness of the evening descended on the land.

“Princess Aine, does this land really belong to the Tuatha? Is it as the girl said?” Brenainn asked.

“The land belongs to those who take care of it, Brenainn. It belongs to those who listen to its small voices as well as its loud ones.”

The boy looked up at her with wonder, his eyes full of mirth . . . full of life. Aine felt a sharp twinge in her chest, right where she knew her heart should be. She knew that somewhere, out there, there may still be a reason to live. For the first time in a long time, she knew there may still be a reason to hold onto hope.

Brenainn lay his head down in her lap and soon he began to breathe evenly. She looked down to find the innocent face of the child, fast asleep. The nursemaids came to collect the young prince for bed, and she strode back up to the manor. She placed her hand over her heart and felt the steady rhythm of courage, a feeling she had not felt since before her arrival to her new life.

CHAPTER SIXTEEN

AINE & HEDREK

Five Years Later

The iron rod heated over the open flame as Hedrek stoked the coals below it. He gripped the cool end of the red-hot bar as he brought it back over to the other side of the room, setting it down on the metal grates atop the worktable. The setting sun sliced through the bars in the window, casting an ominous glow on his face.

The grinding of chains broke the silence as the quiet sobs of a woman escaped periodically through the sound of her labored breathing. "Let's not revisit this again and again, you know it pains me to have to do this, Aine."

The light glistened off the sweat coating her pale face. Her chapped lips, parched from days without water, parted as she attempted to form her words. The edges of the iron cuff had caused deep cuts to form in the creases of her wrists as she struggled to hold up her body weight from where she hung from the ceiling. Her legs dragged the ground as she lost the ability to hold herself upright. She grew weaker by the moment. Her last meal was days ago.

"I . . . I do not know how to draw it forth. I have t-told you. I have tried . . . "

"*Nonsense!*" Hedrek roared as he brought the heated end of the iron rod to the outside of her left thigh where her thin linen gown was parted, causing a hiss of burning flesh and eliciting a deafening scream from Aine's lips.

"It has been five years, Aine, *five years* of silence from you. I have given you everything a woman of your position could desire," he spat, "clothes, jewels, a place at my side in my brother's kingdom. All I have asked is for you to help *me* in return."

"When have you ever cared for what I desire, Hedrek?" She asked weakly, through her sobs, "You care only for power. A power that you can never possess. My people's enchantment has all but abandoned this land." Hedrek reached out, grasping her chin between his thumb and fore-finger as he brought her face closer to his own.

"Oh Aine, don't you see? It is only a matter of time before I *do* possess that power. I had hoped that you would be the little dove to land in my hand and give it to me of your own free will." He moved away as he began to pace circles around her. "I should have known when I first beheld you that you were *no* dove."

"For, you see, I *will* have it. Your people have not abandoned this land, I have driven them out. One by one, my men and I have cleansed the land of the filth of your kind. Of their magic. Your draíocht is all but spent—I see that now. Once, I thought you could be Her. The one final hope for the Tuatha people."

Hedrek pointed to a large book lying on the table nearby. "You think I am just a barbarian, don't you? A conqueror. A brute. But I am a man who seeks to learn as well. And I have learned *much* about your people over the years."

Aine's heart began to beat wildly. Long ago, she had been told the legends of her people's long-lost queen, the collective energy that would one day re-emerge from the suffering of her people. The divine goddess that would one day rise again and liberate her kind. He could not know of her. It was *impossible*. Surely, he did not think . . .

"You see, I believed I saw that light in your eyes, Aine. When I saw your *fire*. That day in the woods, I truly believed you to be the Sovereign of flame, the Nichnevin. I believed, at the time, that your ability to manipulate flame indicated that *you* could be the one." He scoffed, glaring at her.

"You *destroyed* any light in my eyes that might have existed, Hedrek . . . Along with so much more. . . " she began.

"Foolish, I was," he interrupted with a sneer. "I soon learned that your power must be tied to something else entirely. We both know how stubborn you can be, my sweet, but I haven't seen a speck of your draíocht since that day we left the forest."

He walked closer to her again. "Do not think me foolish enough to think that magic doesn't still lie dormant inside of you somewhere," he mocked. "Even if it is but a small amount of magic, it is *mine*. If my gold, my jewels, making you my *wife* won't work . . . if making you a *gods-damned princess* won't persuade you," he shouted, "perhaps maybe you are just a wild thing as I had suspected." He grasped the iron rod again. "And wild things only understand punishment. Like an untamed mare, you *can* be broken if need be. However long it takes . . . "

He placed the hot iron to the side of her neck, drawing out another sobbing shriek from Aine. Her body shook with anger and frustration, sweat beading at her temples as she *begged* her draíocht to come forth. She cared not for rational thought anymore. She would give it all away, every last speck of her magic, if she could.

She knew in her rational mind that her magic would continue to lay dormant until she was back in the enchantment of the wood. As with most Tuatha, her draíocht was drawn from deep within the forest, the beating heart of the land of Éire. She would sacrifice her last breath before she betrayed her people by telling Hedrek this. She knew that he would burn the forest down at the first opportunity if he understood its true source of power.

Aine was not sure if the fact that her draíocht refused to appear made her thankful or filled her with even more despair. How much longer would her existence last in this way? She flexed her neck, moving her head to her right shoulder, attempting to ease the pain of the newly singed skin.

"Careful, Hedrek," she scoffed in a low voice, with an edge of laughter, "high-collared gowns and jewelry can only hide so much. Wouldn't want your brother or his courtiers to find out what you like to do in your spare time." She cut her eyes upward in his direction.

"Oh, my sweet . . . do you think you still deserve gowns and jewels?" He laughed darkly, "Gowns and jewels are for ladies of the court. *Wives* of princes and of kings." He glanced down at the ruby ring that he had placed on her finger a year ago. Hedrek had declared her his wife to the kingdom, to his brother, and to all the members of his court.

Curiously, there had not been a ceremony or exchange of vows, much to Aine's bewilderment. She had half expected him to force the vows from her lips by some other form of punishment, but to her surprise, he never did. She still failed to understand why, but a part of her remained thankful for that small fact.

According to his brother, it was only proper that Hedrek wedded her after he had paraded her about the kingdom. There had been too many instances of grasping, touching, and showing that she belonged to him in every way, in the public eye. Particularly after two winters ago, when it was discovered that she was with child.

A child that never came to maturity inside her belly.

That winter, Aine had been intensely ill with each sunrise for a solid month before she began to understand the change that was taking place within her body. She would awaken with the dawn, running to the chamber pot to empty her stomach of last night's dinner before Hedrek would stir from his slumber. When she realized what had occurred, she was horrified, to say the least. Hedrek had seemed somewhat *pleased*, much to her astonishment. He had announced that she was with child at the very next royal dinner with his brother and the soldiers.

She had pondered for days on end, battled with herself

and her conscience for what seemed like an eternity as to what she should do. Aine had tortured her own mind with every possible outcome and no matter which one she envisioned—it was not a life she would ever wish for an innocent child to be a part of. She finally decided that she could not bear to bring another life into the world of abuse that she suffered each and every day. She could endure Hedrek's wrath, she could steel her jaw against his hands, but she would *die* before she gave him the opportunity to inflict harm on an innocent child.

Her child.

She begged the gods for a changeling to be bartered in her child's stead. Aine knew that this was not possible, as the estate was too far from where any of the remaining Tuatha people may reside. She had seen children brought into her colony as a child, Milesian children, rescued from terrible situations or born into cruel families. Cursed members of the Fae, those who had committed terrible crimes, were changed into the likeness of mortal babies or children, and swapped, effectively releasing an innocent life in exchange for a wicked one. Milesians, being the humans that they were, would naturally kill or abandon the changeling once they realized what they were—and that their own child would never be returned to them.

Aine longed to carry her unborn child to term, if her weak body would even withstand another eight months of pregnancy alongside the physical torture she endured so often at the hands of the captain of the guard. She longed to send her child to the Land of Light, the Tuatha homeland, the *Sidhe*—as a changeling, to live in peace with its own people—but this was not a possibility. Not now. Not *ever*.

One morning, before sunrise, as hot tears streamed down her face, she snuck away to an area of the manor where wild herbs and plants grew alongside the edge of the home. She whispered prayers to the goddess Danu as she discreetly gathered in her aprons copious sprigs of bloodroot and clary sage. She would plan to later crush the herbs into a tea and drink it down before anyone in the home would have detected her absence in the course of the morning.

Aine made her way back to the kitchens of the first floor of the manor, retrieved a clay drinking mug from the wooden shelf, and filled it with boiling water from the breakfast stove. She circled back around to the kitchen side door and exited the manor, stealing away around the corner of the stone dwelling. She slid her back down the stone wall and crouched in the tall grass that grew alongside the home and exhaled deeply. Her eyes lifted skyward as she placed one hand on her heart and one on her belly. She whispered a final plea to her people's Mother goddess. "*I commit this child back to the Sidhe, keep them safe, protect their light from the darkness that seeks to overtake us all . . .* "

Just before Aine could deposit the crushed herbs into the cup, a sharp pain struck her lower abdomen, eliciting a wince and a soft cry from her lips. She attempted to stay quiet as pain lanced through her body. The sharpness spread into a dull throb that grew to cover her lower pelvis in agonizing pressure. She dropped the cup, the clay shattering onto a nearby stone and spilling the boiling water onto the grass below. She felt immobilized, with both fear and pain.

Aine knew that her motives for being alone with a pocketful of questionable herbs and a cup of boiling water would immediately prompt interrogation from Hedrek and his household, given her current condition. She pressed through the excruciating ache. She rose and made her way back through the kitchens and up to the chamber she shared with Hedrek. By the hour, she knew he would already be up and preparing for the day, clear of their room. She tossed the herbs into the kitchen fire on her way through the house.

Once she was back safely in the bedchamber, she called Imogen into the room, asking her to draw a bath. The chambermaid looked on in horror as Aine shed her bloody shift and undergarments, depositing them beside the tub. Imogen refused to leave Aine's side. She drew her thin frame into a comforting embrace and helped her into the tub as the warm water was brought up by another servant.

Imogen sent another chambermaid to notify the captain of the guard of his wife's affliction. Upon his summoning, Hedrek had burst into the room with something akin to grief on his features. He had held her hand, and it was the only time she had ever seen anything that resembled sympathy on his face as realization dawned on him. She had sobbed as she let him hold and comfort her for the first time. Her body shook with the fear that he would suspect her to be involved and take out his disappointment on her, although he did not. She felt shame, guilt, defeat, and relief all rolled into one devastating wave of sorrow. Her tears flowed like the rivers that carved through the grassy knolls and rugged mountain peaks.

Only in Aine's mind, these were not tears of mourning.

As much as it pained her, tormented her, and filled her with guilt to realize, they were tears of joy. Danu had heard her plea.

She thought that perhaps there could be a small part of her that still had a connection with her people. It was enough to light a flicker of hope in her heart.

In the darkness of the underground room, as Aine still hung by her wrists in chains, Hedrek reached out and hastily removed the ruby ring from her left finger. "You won't be needing this anymore, Aine. And I won't be needing to keep up this charade anymore either," he spat.

"What do you mean?" her eyes flew up to meet his, her heart rate increasing as fear rose in the back of her mind.

"I mean that you will remain here. You will remain my property for the rest of your gods-forsaken days. Do not think this is the end of our time together. You *will* give me what I want," he sneered, "but your time of being a lady of the court is over. Clearly, it takes a bit more than a life of luxury to soften you, to *encourage* you . . . " He moved closer. "So, now, you will live like the wild beast that you are."

Hedrek motioned behind him to a cage that was hanging from the ceiling by a thick iron chain. "My brother and the rest of court will be told of your unfortunate death. They will comfort me in my time of grief, as I mourn the wife that has been taken from me."

Aine inhaled sharply as he grasped her face in his hands again. "And you may well wish that you had been."

As darkness descended with another sunset, the end of another day that Aine had lost count of, she sank with defeat onto the bottom of the hanging cage like a bird with clipped wings. She adjusted her sore hips against the hard floor as she moved to the left of the cage, grasping a stale piece of bread lying on the ground and taking a bite. An aftertaste of ash tarnished the inside of her mouth. Food had never tasted the same since leaving her home all those years ago.

Months had passed since Hedrek had taken her to her new dwelling, leaving her alone in the darkness for most of the day. He would come and go occasionally, mostly sending his servants to deliver what little food and water he thought she needed to survive. Aine began to feel somewhat thankful for this change in scenery, as it meant that she did not have to share his bed any longer—the cage was a welcome change, in her mind.

Once, around the time of the last full moon, he had visited to question her after his return from another Tuatha raid. Her keen sense of smell had detected perfumed oils on his flesh, mingled with the scent of a woman's sweat. She wondered if Hedrek thought that the ale on his breath would mask the smell of his recent behaviors, but Aine was still Tuatha after all, and there was not much that could evade her sharpened senses.

Of course, Aine cared not. After years of learning of Hedrek's appetites, she knew it was only a matter of time before he found another female, perhaps another Milesian woman, to call his own and serve him in that way. And that evening, she thanked the gods that he had.

The door to the cellar opened with a creak as light illuminated the room, causing Aine to jump in surprise. She winced as her eyes adjusted, bracing herself for whatever mood she may find Hedrek to be in.

Her face froze in shock as Brenainn silently crept into the room, pulling the door closed behind him. She was surprised to see the young man here, as she knew that the underground room in which she was being kept was far behind the manor, its entrance concealed from everyone but Hedrek and his soldiers. He had grown to be a strong lad of twelve years now.

"Princess Aine . . . " Brenainn's face stiffened in disbelief as he beheld her state in the cage. "Did my uncle—"

"Shh, Brenainn, you must leave at once," Aine began, looking frantically from left to right. "Hedrek insists that no one can know I am here."

"But . . . everyone thinks you are *dead*," the young man exclaimed with a look of shock on his features. "Including me. I had given up hope that the scouts would ever find your body after Hedrek told us of how you were captured and killed during his last Tuatha raid. He told us of how those barbaric savages took you—" he stilled and silenced his speaking as Aine rose and walked forward, grasping the rails of the hanging cage.

The blue-tinged raised band of flesh shone against the glowing lamplight that Brenainn held as he looked at her forearm in disbelief.

"It cannot be . . . After all this time . . . "

". . . It is as you suspect. You are old enough now to know the truth. Your uncle kidnapped me from my home years ago. He swore that no one in the kingdom must ever know where I came from," Aine began, "and it is important that they do not know of my existence . . . of my heritage, even now."

"I must help you . . . I must tell my father . . . " the young man turned toward the door as Aine pressed against the bars.

"*No.* No, Brenainn. You will only jeopardize your own future. Do not underestimate the lengths that Hedrek will go to protect his own power."

"I can't simply leave you here to die in this way. I am not afraid of him."

"Hedrek will not let me die. That is a comfort, if you can call it one." Aine looked down as she continued, "I will remain here until it is my time to go free. If that time never comes, do not forget, my sweet child, that I am an ancient. Unless he decides otherwise, I will live far longer than your uncle."

"Princess, this is no way to live. I cannot leave you here. I have to *do* something—" he began.

"I appreciate your kindness . . . I always have. I would only ask you to do this . . . keep your eyes and ears open to the world around you. Learn from those who are unlike you. Live with tolerance instead of ignorance. Learn from the earth—don't destroy it." She looked up to meet his gaze. "And when your time on the throne comes, when you one day take up your father's crown, remember me. Remember the struggles of my people and remember a time when we once lived in peace."

Tears budded from the corners of Brenainn's eyes as a look of shame crossed his face. He reached between the bars, grasping Aine's hand in his. "I vow this to you, aunt, you will always be my family and I will avenge the wrongs that have been done to you. You have been kind to me, you have been there for me, nurtured me when I needed it most. You were a mother to me long after my own had been taken from this world. I will *not* forget this," he replied through gritted teeth.

"You will do great things one day, Brenainn. I have seen it . . . " She squeezed his palm gently, pushing it back from between the bars of the cage, "Now, *go*! Before your uncle knows you are here." The young man pulled his cloak over his head and quickly departed the cellar. Aine heard his footsteps as he ascended the stairs and fled back to the main floor of the manor.

Brenainn began to visit Aine each new moon, when the night was at its darkest. He would bring to her bread, cheese, whatever he could inconspicuously slip into the holding cellar, along with news from the manor. Aine's chest would tighten each time she saw his face in the doorway, a new fear for his life unveiled. She held her breath until he left, hating the risk he took each time he ventured to the cellar.

On his most recent visit, he brought news of an unfortunate turn of events within the kingdom. The king had ventured with his militia to the northern sea border and his caravan was attacked by a band of thieves on their way out of the port village. His guards gave their all to protect King Hectre, even at the cost of one of his soldier's lives. The king, however, did not come out of the skirmish unscathed. Brenainn's face was tight with worry as he described how his father had sustained a wound from a dagger to his left shoulder that was now beginning to look worrisome.

According to the prince, the most skilled healers in the kingdom had already visited the king in the last week, bringing with them their most potent elixirs and remedies. The wound had reopened two days ago, giving way to fevers that racked the king's body in both his waking and sleeping hours.

"Aunt, I cannot think about my father's passing, although I see the light leave his eyes more each day . . . I am not ready. I feel that to even speak of such things is treachery."

"Brenainn, the thing about destiny is that she does not always wait until you are ready," Aine replied with a soft smile, reaching through the bars to grasp his hand.

"The first thing I would do is free you. You must know this. Know that my uncle *will* face punishment for his crimes one day."

Their conversation was interrupted by a stomping pair of boots from the floor above. Brenainn silently squeezed Aine's hand as he quickly made his way toward the door, slipping out again without a word.

Hedrek watched from the shadow of the eves of the manor as Brenainn prowled about the perimeter of the cellar's entrance, noiselessly making his way back toward the main house. He did not open the cellar door or make his way toward Aine's dwelling. Hedrek simply re-sheathed the dagger he had been holding and casually strode back toward the manor.

"Men," Hedrek bellowed over the long tables of soldiers who were eating and drinking within the dining hall of the manor. "I have received word that a band of Tuatha have gained reinforcements from a nearby village and are marching toward the town of Laigain, just a day's ride from this very estate."

A hush of silence passed over the room as the men in attendance turned their attention to the captain of the guard. "We must assemble our forces and meet them where they march, if we are to exterminate this problem before it grows into a larger one," he shouted.

A trusted advisor of the king flanked him on his left side, drawing his attention away from the crowd for a moment. "Do you think it wise, prince, to draw the king's finest men away from the manor at a time when he is at his weakest? What if the manor comes under attack?" he asked meekly.

Hedrek's voice was like cold death as his face darkened and was then replaced by a rehearsed smile. "I do not protect the king, scribe, I protect the kingdom," he spat as he turned on his heel, walking toward the stables. "We ride with the sunset!" he called over his shoulder, to a chorus of ayes from the men.

Brenainn was standing at the stables, brushing his horse as he often did when he needed time to think. His father's condition had weighed heavily on his mind since his health had taken a turn for the worse. The mare shivered under the sable brush as he ran his hands along her coat.

"She'll serve you well on tonight's raid, prince," Hedrek called out from the shadow of the corner of the stable.

Brenainn jumped in surprise and Hedrek strode toward him. The captain of the guard began to brush the horse on the opposite side. "What do you mean raid? I was not aware my father was well enough to commission a raiding party or militia," the young prince replied.

"He is not. But we will be under attack by tomorrow if we do not strike first," Hedrek countered. Brenainn looked at his uncle with wariness in his eyes.

"You have much to learn, young prince. If you are to *one day* wear your father's crown, I suggest you start feeling more comfortable with a sword in your hand," he mocked, as he grabbed Brenainn's sword from where it hung on the post and threw it toward him.

The young prince reluctantly caught the sword and scabbard, staring down at it for a moment before he strapped it to his side, slinging his leg over his mount. "What are you waiting for then, Uncle? Let us assemble."

Hedrek smiled to himself as he saddled his own steed and led him out to the formation of men that was gathering at the gates of the estate.

The rich iron tang of blood hung heavily in the air as the Milesian soldiers moved several other Tuatha corpses to a pile near the border of the forest. The pyre would be piled high with the bodies of each villager of the colony that had been dwelling within this part of the forest.

Brenainn felt a deep pain in his chest, a tugging at his heart as he stared at the faces of those that had been slaughtered by the soldiers within the regiment. *This was wrong. So very wrong.*

He promptly scurried behind a tree, away from the view of the other men, and emptied his stomach onto the ground, retching as tears threatened the corners of his eyes. His vision was blurry with anger toward his uncle for the blatant disregard for the lives he and his men had taken this night.

After arriving at their location on horseback earlier than planned in the night, Brenainn soon discovered that the raid they were on was no more than a surprise attack on an unsuspecting Tuatha colony. There were no marching traitors to the crown, no band of rebels . . . *there never was.*

This, like many of his so-called raids, was simply an

opportunity for his uncle to act on his deep hatred for the Tuatha in the form of more bloodshed.

Brenainn had stayed conveniently locked in combat with a single Tuatha male of around his same age for most of the battle. He dodged strikes and refused to engage with him after finding out the true nature of the venture. The young Tuatha was struck dead by another Milesian soldier who simply scoffed at the young prince as he turned and strode back into the action.

The young prince walked around to survey how much more had to be done before they could pack up and head back to the estate. A stillness had fallen over the scene as the soldiers cleared out from the immediate area, although there appeared to be more cleaning up to do.

Hedrek came up behind Brenainn, placing a large hand on his shoulder. "*Uncle,*" the prince gritted out. "How could you? My father should know, this is not a wise use of his men. These Tuatha were simply—"

"How could I? *How could I?*" Hedrek mocked. "It's either kill or *be killed* when it comes to these savages," he spat. "Brenainn . . . you are so very young . . . You should know one thing in this life. There will always be winners." he moved his lips closer to the young prince's ear. Even beneath his tunic, Brenainn could feel the coldness of sharpened steel press between his shoulder blades.

"And there will always be losers . . . " Hedrek whispered as he swiftly pressed the pointed end of the sword into the young prince's back, bones and tendons cracking obscenely beneath his efforts as he twisted the blade. A dark pool of blood stained the front of Brenainn's tunic, blooming to cover his chest as he choked out a gasp, bright red dribbling from his lips. His breathing ceased as the light left his eyes and he slumped over in a heap on the ground.

Aine let out a sharp inhale as the door to the cellar was suddenly kicked open by a booted shadow. Hedrek strode unceremoniously into the darkened room, his face visible only by the moonlight and the way the lantern he held cast sinister shadows on his face.

"Woman, if you were so hells-bent on conspiring against your prince, *perhaps* you should have chosen someone less conspicuous to do it with," Hedrek spat as he threw a burlap sack onto the ground before Aine's feet with a wet thud.

Nausea lurched forward in Aine's throat as she smelled the stench of rotting flesh permeating through the bag. Dark blood stained the outside of the fabric as a hollow eye peeked out from the opening at the top. She knew those dark curls anywhere.

"Hedrek! He was your *nephew* . . . " she gasped, bringing a hand over her own mouth as her eyes widened in horror.

"He was in my way," he replied with a hiccup, sour-smelling liquor wafted from his breath. It had been at least three days ago that Aine had heard the riders depart the gates and set out as a regiment. She glanced down at the bag.

"When the king—," she began softly. Hedrek unexpectedly kicked the cage in which she sat, spinning the iron enclosure in motion as she gasped.

"The *king*?!" he roared. "The king will soon be standing before you, Aine!" He grasped the bars of the cage in tight fists, reaching through the bars and seizing her by the hair, pulling her face to face with him. "What of this? *Now*, what will you do, witch?"

The members of the royal court and household gathered shoulder to shoulder with their heads bowed in reverence, as the shrouded body of Prince Brenainn was brought in procession down the stone walkway of the manor's main entrance. In the distance, a lyre played a haunting melody as the Milesians bid farewell to their young prince, as a torrent of merciless rain poured from the dark and desolate sky.

The head of the young prince had been placed in an oak box and was carried down the stone steps of the manor, as the procession made its way to the area in which the funeral pyre would be lit. Hedrek had spun an elaborate tale of a Tuatha uprising nearing the end of the battle that resulted in the slaying of young Brenainn and his subsequent beheading by a rogue enemy warrior.

In truth, Hedrek had left Brenainn's limp corpse to rot where it lay slumped in the mud, as he and his men had saddled their horses to head back to the estate. It was only after conversing with one of his most trusted generals on the ride back, that he concluded that the king may require proof of his son's murder to extinguish any suspicion of foul play. Hedrek had turned back alone to ride to the site where Brenainn had fallen, only to find—to his astonishment—that his entire body had disappeared. There was no evidence of a struggle, no trail of blood where he may have been pulled away by someone intent on mending his injury or healing his wound.

A knot formed in the pit of Hedrek's stomach as he dismounted his horse and frantically kicked through the fallen bodies on the forest floor. He callously booted body after body of young Tuatha warriors, searching for any sign of the young prince—but to no avail.

Finally, he withdrew his sword and hacked off the head of a young warrior whose countenance resembled Brenainn's coloring and strong features. He hastily stuffed it in a burlap sack, secured it to his saddle, and swiftly rode ahead to catch up with his men.

As he arrived through the entrance to the large estate, he

bellowed out for all the members of the king's household to hear, "Behold! The barbarity of these savages knows no end! The prince has fallen!" He dismounted, removing his cloak, and wrapping it solemnly around the head inside the burlap sack.

The king's advisor rushed out to meet the captain of the guard, his face twisted in distress. "My prince, please do not take this out of turn, but *please,* the king need not hear of his son's passing in this manner." His eyes held a shade of desperation, "Give it a day or so, perhaps he can recover his strength enough to handle this grave news." But Hedrek was already pushing past the advisor with a hard shove and a scowl that would cut through steel.

Hedrek did not stop until he had ascended the stone column of stairs and was at his brother's bedside in the chambers above. The warm breeze wafted through the open window and through the room of the sick and dying man. The healers were hurriedly darting about the room, attempting to ease the suffering of their king as he lay prostrate in his bed.

"Brother . . . " Hedrek began as he slowly moved toward the king's side and kneeled, "I wish not to place a heavier burden on an already burdened king, but I felt you must be the first to know." He withdrew the burlap sack, stained with blood, and exposed a portion of the young man's head to the king's vision.

As King Hectre slowly turned toward his brother, a deep, aching melancholic sound escaped his lips as his healers rushed to his side, hands busy with nothing to do but look on as King Hectre gasped out a muffled cough. "My *son* . . . "

he began, the effort sending him into yet another coughing fit that seemed to wrench the very air from his lungs.

"My brother, I tried to save him, I truly did . . . " Hedrek watched as the king's face twisted in pain. Hectre's eyes widened as he reached out blindly toward the burlap bag on the ground. Hedrek had hoped that his brother would breathe his last breath before the sun had descended over the horizon that day, the one obstacle in his way to the throne now gone.

However, the fates had other plans, because King Hectre did not slip into that great eternal sleep as the captain of the guard had hoped, only into that night's slumber.

Now, as the members of the royal court and the king's household stood in reverent silence, heads bowed, waiting for the rain to cease and the funeral pyre to be lit, a cold wind sliced through the crowd.

Hedrek descended the stone steps, one booted foot after another, walking with menacing slowness toward the front of the processional. The rain began to slowly cease as the sun peeked over the silver edge of a cloud, reflecting from the shining rubies and emeralds cresting the crown atop his head—a smaller twin to the crown still worn by his brother.

He glanced skyward and a smile curved one side of his mouth. His right hand toyed with the trinket in his cloak pocket, his fingers tracing the roughness of its pointed edges and smooth sides. He withdrew the charm and held it up, the sunlight painting beams of light on the stone path from its reflection. The fragmented piece of the moonstone sapphire seemed to pulse in his grasp as he returned it to his pocket.

CHAPTER SEVENTEEN

Rhia glanced over at Rowan, but his gaze was already locked on hers. He exhaled, understanding perfectly well what Rhia's heart longed to do. He spun to face the table of tools behind him. A table that, upon closer inspection, looked to contain all manner of instruments of torture. Without missing a beat, he grasped a heavy hammer and quickly lunged at the lock that hung on the door of the cage.

His large forearm came down with punishing force in one swift movement. A loud clanging of metal pierced the silence of the room, causing Rhia to jump. Rowan wasn't lost on the way her eyes traced over the sinew of his arms with the motion. Much to their surprise, the woman in the cage didn't even flinch. The worry in Rhia's blue eyes glimmered like pools of water as she observed the way the woman simply stared at the floor of the cage. She glanced over at Rowan, "Well, so much for remaining silent and undetected . . . " she scoffed, smirking.

"What . . . Do you think it would be better for me to hack away at it slowly? Each strike louder than the last?" he countered.

Rhia pulled on the heavy door of the cage until it swung open and crawled inside. She leaned down until she was at eye-level with the dark-haired woman. "We're going to help you," she whispered.

The woman looked as if she was attempting to sit upright. She pressed her palms onto the ground, pushing upwards. As her shoulders rose, the weight of her frail upper body caused her arms to give way beneath her.

Rhia reached out, catching her shoulders, and looking back at Rowan. "I fear that she is too weak to make it out of this place on her own two legs. Gods only know what cruelty she has suffered within these walls." Rowan could have sworn he saw flames dancing behind Rhia's eyes as her anger flared, the woman still clutched to her bosom.

Rowan moved forward without question, leaning into the cage, and placing his arms behind her shoulders and beneath her knees. He lifted her from the iron bars and motioned with his gaze toward the small door to the side of the room, leading to another chamber of the cellar.

"Come, if this is the center of the cellar, that has to be the map room," he stated as he began to walk in that direction with the woman in his arms. Rhia followed closely behind as they beheld the small room that did, indeed, contain walls of shelving with scrolls of maps littering every surface.

Rhia began to rummage through the scattered papers as Rowan moved to a corner of the room to gently sit the raven-haired woman on the ground. Her head lolled as she struggled to part her chapped lips. Rowan reached for the skin of water at his side, pressing it to her lips as she began to drink—slowly at first, and then more steadily.

"How long have you been down here?" he asked, as the light slowly returned to the woman's eyes. Her piercing golden gaze met his. She looked as if she were at war with herself, her stare searching his, deciding if he were trustworthy. The woman looked down at his forearms, left and then right, but his cloak sleeves were long and covered what she sought to find. Her eyes lingered on his as she remained silent, her brow furrowed.

"You can trust him, he is one of us," Rhia spoke softly, stepping forward over Rowan's shoulder. A warmth spread throughout his chest at her admission. It was perhaps the first time that she had acknowledged that he was half-Tuatha.

One of her people.

He glanced down with a soft smile painted on his lips.

The pale woman seemed to relax in Rowan's presence as she exhaled, parting her lips, and wetting them again before replying weakly, "I do not know how long I have been down here, but it has been for many, many moons." Rhia regarded her with a look of deep sorrow on her face. The woman's story was one of many, many tales of the injustices of her people at the hands of the Milesians. From her experience, the typical method of dealing with her people was extermination, so Rhia wondered what motivated the captain of the guard to hold onto a life such as this, for so long.

"I am Aine," the woman said quietly, eyes averted to the ground, staring blankly ahead.

"I'm Rowan and this is Rhiannon. And I promise you . . . we *will* get you out of here," he replied, handing her the water skin and standing to face Rhia. "Now to make sense of this mess and find what we came here for . . . " he grumbled, glancing around the room.

"Two steps ahead of you," she smirked, lifting a stained scroll of paper that she carefully unfurled before him. The map revealed an intricately sketched outline of the surrounding kingdoms, all the way out to the sea to the West. Rowan couldn't hide the slight astonishment on his face. "You found that far too quickly. Are you sure you don't have any other questionable hobbies in your spare time?" he teased.

She rolled her eyes in response as she tossed the scroll into the satchel on her side. "When you live with someone like Beatha, you learn to make sense of chaos. The woman had more scattered books and papers than a learned scholar."

Rowan's entire body tensed as his ears detected movement from the creaking floorboards overhead. Aine's eyes flashed with fear as she grasped her knees with her arms from her seated position on the ground. "Let's go," he barked out as he lifted Aine's body from the ground in one swooping motion. She began to relax in his grasp as Rhia followed closely behind. Rowan didn't like that his eyes could not see her, that her form was in his periphery. He always wanted her in his line of sight. He felt strangely vulnerable in carrying this woman. Aine very obviously needed their help, but it was at the risk of not acting quickly enough if danger befell Rhia.

Almost as if reading his thoughts, she countered, "Rowan, I can feel your tension from back here. I'm *fine*," she said playfully. "Don't forget, I *do* still possess my draíocht and the knowledge of how to use it . . . for the most part."

Aine's eyes shot to hers from over Rowan's shoulders. "But we are miles and miles from the forest . . . how can you still wield your magic?"

Rhia looked almost perplexed as her eyes widened. "I have never put much thought into it, but I have never been to a place inside or outside of the forest where I was *not* able to call it forth," Rhia countered. A look of concern spread across her face. "Why? Have they found some way to drain our magic? Is that why you couldn't fight them off?"

"Daughter of Danu, it is the very essence of nature from which our draíocht originates. Nature herself is the beating heart to each element we wield," she replied. "Separate us from the source and our magic departs with it. That is why these monsters seek to burn and destroy every ounce of land that we dwell in."

Rhia could not hide the look of disbelief as she followed behind Rowan and Aine, too perplexed to speak. *If that is true, then how am I able to call forth my gifts so easily, no matter where I am?* she thought to herself. The footfalls of heavy boots overhead grew louder.

Rowan spun with Aine in his arms, glancing back at Rhia, "When we get to the top of these stairs, we make a run for the tree line to Seamus. There was a mare tied to a post by the front gate that I plan to take once we are close enough, if she is still there."

Rhia nodded in response. Rowan set Aine down at the

base of the stairs, "Do you think you can ascend these stairs on your own?" he asked.

"I don't think we have a choice," Aine replied, setting her jaw. Rhia noticed a wince of pain pass over the woman's features as she spied a recent set of burn marks on her side.

"No matter what happens, just keep running," his gaze shifted from Aine and bore into Rhia. "Promise me, you will keep running." The footsteps sounded almost directly above them now.

"Less talking Rowan, more running, *now*," Rhia hissed as she braced Aine's arm, helping her ascend the first step. The three of them flew up the iron staircase and through the door, out onto the grassy path that ran to the side entrance of the cellar.

Aine's eyes squinted as she adjusted to the sunlight. For the first time in ages, she marveled at the way the sun warmed her skin, soaking in the quiet pleasure of simply breathing fresh air.

"Hey! Who are you?!" a gruff voice shouted from around the corner of the manor's exterior. Rowan pushed Rhia and Aine behind him, jerking his head toward the tree line.

"Remember what I said! *GO!*" he bellowed, shoving them forward, as his hand grasped the hilt of his sword.

He unsheathed Faobhar in one swift movement, the metal glinting in the light of the sun as the moonstone sapphire glowed about its hilt. He remained with his back to the women as he attempted to follow them.

A stocky bearded Milesian came out from around the opposite side of the manor, taking Rowan by surprise. His feet sidestepped, missing the attempted strike to his head, as he brought his sword around and planted the blade in between the man's neck and shoulder. A wet sound emanated from his body as he coughed and clutched his neck, descending to the ground in a heap.

Rowan stalked forward through the tall grasses as the other Milesian guard jumped in front of him, bearing his sword. Rowan's blade met his with a clang of metal as he sparred, strike for strike with the soldier. He countered each move of the trained warrior, calling his father's words to mind from his training as a boy. *Step, strike, block, step . . .* he calculated in his head. He extended his elbow beneath the guard's chin, sending his head backward and off balance as he spun his sword in his hands, plunged it backward, and lanced it directly through the man's abdomen.

"You men are nothing if not predictable," Rowan remarked at the man's slumped form on the ground, the light quickly leaving his eyes. He tore off a corner of the man's cloak and used it to wipe his blade clean. "And if I know your men, there will soon be more of you." Rowan kicked the shoulder of the soldier free from where he lay atop his boot. He turned, taking the grassy path back to Seamus, and away from the estate.

He spotted Rhia in the distance. *Resourceful,* he thought, smiling to himself as he noted the way she had already taken the mare tied to the guard post and was helping Aine into the saddle. She tossed her copper curls over her shoulder as she turned to meet his gaze, giving him a soft smile. The sight was like a punch to the gut, every time this woman looked at him. He almost thought he could see a look of relief wash over her as her eyes met his. *Gods, what is wrong with me?* he thought to himself. He cleared his throat, stepping forward as Rhia's eyes caught the sight of him wiping the remainder of the blood from his blade.

"What of those men?" she asked hesitantly. "Should we worry about more?"

"The men are taken care of, but if I know Milesian guards, there will undoubtedly be more. But we aren't sticking around to find out if there are. We should go," he motioned to Seamus.

Aine glanced back at the manor with a faraway look in her eyes. She clung to the reins of the white mare, attempting to straighten in the saddle as her weak frame began to sway backward. Rhia flung her leg upward, climbing onto the horse in one fluid movement, as she braced Aine against the front of her body.

Rhia's eyes quickly moved from Seamus to Rowan with a solemn look. "I don't think she can ride alone," she said softly. Rowan nodded in agreement.

"Let's be off then," he said as he mounted the chestnut stallion and lead him toward the wood line.

CHAPTER EIGHTEEN

Rowan, Rhia and Aine rode further into the wooded tree line, and eventually, into the heart of the forest. The oak, yew, and ash trees grew more closely together the deeper they journeyed into the wood. Aine's eyes widened the farther they rode, taking in her surroundings in a dreamlike state of disbelief. She had been so far removed from this place, from the elements of nature all around her, that she felt that she had almost forgotten the very fiber of who she was.

Tears threatened the corners of her eyes as she glanced from the dark rich soil of the moss-covered forest floor to the way the branches of the trees twisted skyward, looking as if they were engaged in an ancient dance. The branches reached upward toward the golden-warm rays of the sun that sliced through the breaks in the trees, painting dusk's palette of oranges and pinks.

Aine breathed deeply, feeling a warmth spread from the center of her chest to the tips of her fingers. She never believed that it would happen again for her—that she would return to the heart of the land that gave her life. She had reconciled with her fate to rot away in the balmy darkness of Hedrek's cellar. Yet here she was—she was back. She was *home.* The raven-haired woman felt a primordial, familiar feeling rising within her chest. It was a feeling she had not felt in many years—her draíocht.

Rhia glanced forward, smiling to herself as she felt the magic coursing through Aine as her body relaxed, its strength gradually returning. She did not want to even begin to contemplate the horrors experienced by this woman at the hands of the Milesian army. Aine had not spoken as much as two words since their journey from the estate. Rhia knew that like all forms of healing, hers would likely take time. She did not yet know how this woman's story would weave into their own, but she was glad to have saved her from any further torture by the monsters that lived within the walls of that manor. She shuddered with disgust.

"Rowan, I think we should rest for the night," Rhia called ahead. "Our new friend could use a full night's rest to regain her strength. We have a long journey ahead."

He slowed Seamus to walk beside them as he glanced at Aine, noting how her countenance seemed to be improving already, a slight smile spreading across her face. He nodded to Rhia, "Very well. We'll make camp up ahead. It's another two days ride to the coast anyway."

As the sun sank low over the horizon, Aine helped Rhia to unpack the furs from Seamus's saddle and fill their waterskins from a nearby stream. Rhia used her water draíocht to funnel the water upright and form a spout, pouring effortlessly into the mouth of the waterskin. Rowan had gone out hunting for something to eat and bring back kindling for the fire. He walked back to where they had made camp, looking slightly defeated. He dropped the wood onto the ground and was grumbling to himself as he set to arranging stones and sticks to build a fire. Aine leaned down beside him as he stood to fetch the flint from Seamus's saddlebag. He walked back over to see Aine cupping her palms over the kindling. Moments later, a spark flared from her hands, causing a bright blaze to ignite.

Rhia's eyes widened as she marveled at the fire draíocht that Aine had summoned effortlessly. She met Rowan's gaze to see his eyes looking much the same. *No, it could not be. She could not be . . . Could she?* she thought to herself. She glanced back at the woman crouching before her. She, herself, seemed to marvel at the magic flowing from her own fingertips. She could have sworn she saw the hint of a somber smile cross her face.

Rhia's lips parted slightly as she breathed softly, summoning a slight breeze over Aine's shoulder, aiding her in bringing the flames to a larger burning blaze. "I have never seen someone call forth fire so effortlessly, sister," she said with a smile as she sat down beside Aine, placing a hand gently on her shoulder.

"I thought it had left me forever . . . my magic. I never expected to be able to feel it course through me again," she stared vacantly down at the ground with tears in her eyes.

"I am sorry to ruin a nice moment with not-so-nice news, but something is happening in the forest," Rowan spoke up. Aine and Rhia's eyes flew up to meet his.

"What do you mean? Are they here?" Aine blurted out. Flashbacks of smoke and screams flooded her memory as the image of her mother and Finnin's body engulfed her thoughts.

"No, I mean something is happening *to* the forest," Rowan continued. "I searched for hours and not one deer, rabbit, or even rodent crossed my path. The birds are silent in their nests. I can't explain it, but I have always been able to feel when something is coming within the forest. It helped my hunting abilities as a boy, to be sure, but now I feel that maybe it is more than that." He glanced down above his rolled sleeve, to where the band of blue-tinged flesh encircled his left forearm. His gaze lifted to meet Rhia's with worry in his eyes. "It feels as if the forest is holding her breath. Anticipating."

Later that night, the trio sat around the fire in relative

silence, chewing pieces of dried venison as their meal for the evening. Aine and Rhia had taken turns earlier that night, one by one, washing in the river. The former had spent longer, much longer than she would normally have, scrubbing her skin until it was raw. She dragged her nails across the pale flesh of her arms, clawing at the layer of dirt upon her face. Suddenly, Hedrek's words came washing over her again. *Now, you will live like the wild beast that you are.*

She shuddered as she scoured her flesh harder, as if she could wipe away every touch of his that had marred her skin. Tears stung the corners of her eyes for the second time that evening. However, the tears that flowed were different than those that became her familiar companion over these last eight years. Instead of coming from a deep place of sorrow and defeat, these tears came from a darker place. A chasm of pure, unadulterated *rage.*

The tears turned into drops of silver in her palms. She glanced down at her hands, feeling a sharpness pierce the tips of her fingers as a tingling feeling pulsed through them. As she looked down at her reflection in the water, she noticed how the countenance of her pale, too-thin face began to almost shift into something otherworldly. Her eyes shifted from their usual hazel-gold to black, rimmed in silver. She felt the old familiar pressure forming between her shoulder blades, extending as tension crept down the column of her spine. Aine smiled to herself as she looked skyward, staring into the milky moon. The feeling spread throughout her body as she felt her bones and tendons shift in place, as silky black feathers covered her body, propelling her upward and into flight with a whirl of movement. It felt like her truth, it felt incredible. *It felt like coming home.*

Later that night, as Aine, Rowan, and Rhia sat by the fire, it seemed as if they were being serenaded by a chorus of crickets around them. It seemed almost irreverent to speak aloud when the forest herself was being so very quiet. Aine finally broke the silence.

"Ten years, I think," she said, sitting with her knees drawn to her chest, the firelight illuminating her pale features. Rhia smiled, nodding as she encouraged her to continue speaking at her own pace. "I had been in that place for ten years. Not all were spent in a cage. Well . . . not a cage of iron. It was a different kind of cage entirely, but a cage no less," she continued.

Aine continued, speaking in slow, languid sentences as she detailed the account of how she was taken from her people, how her home was destroyed, and the terrors she suffered within the four walls of Hedrek's estate. She told the pair of her home, of her mother's death, of the loss of Finnin. Rhia's face drew into a twisted grimace as she winced with each event that unfolded in Aine's story. The woman told the tale in such a manner, that no one would ever believe the emotional and physical turmoil that these events had burdened her with. She spoke as if telling the story of a distant relative, as if she were not in her own body. Rhia could see the very burn marks she spoke of and the scars littering the surface of her pale skin.

Rowan could feel his shoulders tensing as his hands fisted at his sides. How had his mother's people taken this path in their dealings with the Tuatha? How had their two races arrived at this place where they had become so barbaric to one another? The Tuatha Dé Danann, the people of the goddess Danu, had welcomed the Milesians all those years ago. They had shared their knowledge of the land, its resources, their strengths, and unfortunately, their weaknesses as well. The people of the Land of Light had given so much, only to be butchered and exiled in return. Their collective magic needed to be strengthened, they needed to unite the people of Éire once again. They needed their *queen.*

"There is nothing that we could do or say to undo what has been done to you, Aine, this I know. But you should know that you are safe with us. We will not abandon one of our own," Rowan said, steeling his gaze. Rhia chanced a look across the fire at him, her own eyes filled with a sense of pride at his admission. This man had lost his entire world, his very identity, yet here he was—defending her people, *their* people with his sword, his life. A sobering realization washed over her . . . his purpose had become hers as well. She knew deep in her soul that the only final hope for the redemption of their people lay in finding what was lost. They must find the Nichnevin. Rhia quickly broke her stare before Rowan noticed, looking down again at the fire.

Rowan began to share with Aine their plan to find the Tuatha homeland, of the maps that they had come to obtain, and how they planned to search for the Nichnevin. Her eyes widened at his declaration as she lifted her eyes to Rhia, who was already looking at her. "I know. I know it seems far-fetched, foolish, risky, all of the above. However, I fear that as our resources and our people's numbers continue to dwindle, we do not have much of a choice," Rhia said.

"I have heard tales of our homeland when I was a child. Many differing accounts of a land of light, a haven where our people can dwell if dangers come," Aine replied quietly. "My mother swore it was not a physical place, but one that must be accessed from within the mind." A beat of silence passed before she continued, "How I wish she and Finnin could have found that place before it was too late for them. I wish that for so many of our people."

Rhia moved closer to Aine, placing her cloak over the woman's rail-thin shoulders. She looked to Rowan and then back to Rhia's blue-eyed gaze, "I will help in any way that I can. My strength is returning. The spirit of Danu is restoring my draíocht, I can feel it simply by being back in the heart of these lands." She smiled, her eyes dancing in the firelight.

Rhia smiled back and laid her head on the woman's shoulder. "Come, let us rest. We have a long ride tomorrow."

CHAPTER NINETEEN

Morning painted slices of light through the treetop canopy and down to the forest floor below, where the three journeying Tuatha lay. Rowan stirred, rising, and made use of the morning light, saddling up Seamus and the white mare. Rhia awakened to his movements, pulling her cloak over her shoulders, and rising to help him gather the supplies.

He smiled over his shoulder at her, eliciting a warmth that spread across her face. She wondered to herself if his presence would always have that effect on her. It was like all the air leaving her lungs at once when he gave her one of his devastating smiles. He probably knew it too. From her experience, men were always smug in that way. She schooled her expression into one of indifference as she gathered the furs and rolled them, securing them atop the horses.

Rowan cleared his throat and looked back to what he was doing. "Well, with another sunrise, it seems we are one day closer. One day closer to finding—"

"Yes, finding the Nichnevin," Rhia interrupted. "I am sure you are quite eager to find the one you are destined to protect." She continued to strap the packs onto Seamus's saddle.

"I was going to say, the homeland. *Our* homeland," he replied quietly, turning to her. His stare was intense, as if somewhat pained. "The Land of Light. I have this unshakable feeling that if we find it, we find her."

"Then let's not waste any time, Rowan," Rhia replied, meeting his gaze, and pushing past him. She grabbed the reigns of the white mare, leading her in the direction of the stream. "I am taking her for a drink before we're off."

As Rowan turned, he saw Aine quietly peering from across the way. She smiled, looking in the direction of the path that Rhia had taken. He slowly shook his head, shrugging his shoulders.

"I will remain here and finish packing up the supplies. *Go*," she said with a grin as he turned Seamus in the direction of the stream.

Rowan approached the stream with Seamus, tying his reins to a nearby tree, allowing him to drink his fill. He noticed that Rhia had done the same for the white mare. He found her sitting atop a large stone next to the flowing water. The morning light was painting the most beautiful glow on her skin, crimson curls tumbling down her back as she sat with her knees drawn to her chest.

"Do you remember what I told you at the inn, Rhia?" he asked softly as he approached. Her shoulders softened as he spoke, announcing his presence.

"The part where you said you had a plan, or the part

where you told me sleeping in a cage was a good idea?" she replied, glancing back at him with a look of cynicism on her face.

"The part where I told you who my sword belonged to," he countered, walking toward her, and sitting down beside her on the stone. "And the next part . . . do you remember that as well?" He grasped her chin, gently guiding her face until he could see her piercing blue eyes.

Her lips parted slightly, taken aback by the closeness of him. His gaze trailed to them, like a moth drawn to a flame.

His scent, the warmth of his hands, his very presence was intoxicating. She fought to keep the evidence of it from her face. His voice was low as he continued, "Have you already forgotten, Rhia? When I told you who my heart belonged to?" He brought his lips down atop hers as she exhaled, opening to him.

Her eyes closed as she responded with her lips, her body. Her hands tangled in his hair. *Gods, she wanted to take him right here and now on the bank of this stream*, she thought to herself. The too-familiar sensation of warmth inside her palms pulsated again.

She placed her hands down by her sides, flat on the stone beneath her, leaning back as he crawled over her body. His hands gripped her thigh, roving upward to caress the curve of her hip and grasp her breast. A moan escaped her lips as she pulled him by the tunic, down to capture his mouth again with hers.

He continued breathlessly, "Woman, you should know by now that nothing will ever make this heart beat the way that you do. Destiny may be what my mind wants," he placed her palm over his chest, feeling the warmth building there. "What my heart wants is another matter entirely." She paused for a moment, smiling at him with a playful expression.

Her finger traced idle circles on the skin of his chest that lay exposed from the collar of his tunic. "What does this heart want, Rowan? What do *you* want? Tell me . . . "

Heavy booted footsteps in the distance interrupted the peaceful sounds of the flowing stream and the morning bird-song. Rowan quickly pulled Rhia to her feet, pushing her toward the horses. His large hands lifted her into the saddle in one fluid movement. They both looked back to the direction of where they had made camp, both thinking immediately of Aine and the danger she could be in. Rhia spurred the white mare ahead as Rowan mounted Seamus.

"They'll already have heard us. Let's go," she called behind to him, already riding ahead. Her heart beating wildly with fear for their new companion.

Aine was silently packing together supplies as her movements halted to a stop at an unwelcomed sound in the distance. She could hear several sets of footsteps that sounded as if they were walking toward her.

Several sets of footsteps, and *no* hoofbeats.

Panic crept up into her throat as the hairs rose on the nape of her neck. She quickly piled the supplies she had packed together and attempted to cover them with a heap of dried leaves. She pulled the cloak Rhia had given her over her head and moved to hide behind the large trunk of a nearby oak tree. The sound of footsteps grew closer and closer as her eyes adjusted to see the figures of two men in the morning light. Two Milesian solders, swords brandished at their sides, were walking in slow strides through the campsite. They were looking for something. *Or someone.*

Aine held her breath as the men used the toe of their boots to pilfer through the dried leaves on the forest floor, no doubt noticing the still-smoking embers of last night's fire. Suddenly, a silent figure appeared behind Ainc. A long arm grasped her waist from behind, his hand coming around to cover her mouth, muffling any sounds she might make. A chill spider walked up her spine as every hair on her body stood straight up. She knew that scent anywhere. Sweat mingled with the smell of old liquor.

"I must say, Aine, I did not expect to see you here. Not on this mission. Not here." Hedrek spat, anger rising in his voice as he pulled her backward, slamming her back into the wide trunk of the tree. Her breathing was heavy as she bared her teeth. "This feels strangely familiar, doesn't it, sweet?" he continued. "It seems like it was only yesterday that you were in a forest such as this, running from me. The day that you came to be mine."

"That is where you are wrong. I am *not* yours, Hedrek. I never was." She writhed in his grip. She knew that this mission was the reason—the reason they were able to escape the manor unscathed, the reason the forest was so eerily quiet.

The very heart of the forest was shrouding itself from the Milesians.

His gaze jerked to the left as his men shouted in the distance. "Two others!" Aine looked over his shoulder to see Rowan and Rhia riding at breakneck speed back toward camp.

No.

They were coming back for her. These two newfound friends who had known her for only a day were here.

Risking their very lives at the hands of these Milesian soldiers.

Headed *toward* her.

Not riding away, as they could have easily done at the first sign of trouble.

Aine would not let this day end like that day ten years ago in the forest.

The day she lost Finnin, lost her mother, her entire *life*.

"Arrows!" Hedrek bellowed out, as the two Milesian guards drew and aimed at the two Tuatha riders. "Incredible, Aine. I have been away from the manor for the past week because I had heard of a band of rogue Tuatha making their way through this forest. I found no one." He leaned closer to her face, whispering in her ear, "But thanks to you, two of your kind were led right to me."

Aine looked on in horror as the arrows fired into the sky. Suddenly, a slicing wind howled from between the trees. She could have sworn that the forest darkened as the temperature dropped suddenly. The arrows were flung backward, falling like kindling to the ground. She looked out to see Rhia's palms held forward. Rowan jumped down from Seamus, running toward the soldiers with his sword drawn. A bright blue stone gleamed from the hilt of the broadsword as he brandished it with precision, slicing this way and that as he met both of the soldiers step for step.

Aine looked back at Hedrek to see him attempting to reach down to his belt and remove a vial from a pouch at his side. But she was, indeed, a quick learner and she would not be fooled again. She did not possess powers of earth and water, such as Rhia's, but her draíocht did give her abilities of wind. And flame.

She focused her thoughts, bringing flame to her palms, pushing Hedrek's shoulders until his cloak and tunic began to singe as the fire reached his skin. He let out a loud howl as he backed away two steps from Aine, dropping the vial to the ground. Aine quickly brought a slice of wind downward, scooping the corked vial into a swirling eddy and depositing it across the way, far out of reach.

Hedrek backed away further as he stared at her in disbelief, glancing down at his singed chest hair. His gaze lingered a moment too long because it was then that Aine acted. Her rage became palpable inside her chest, a flame that burned inside her very blood. She gathered a strong tempest behind her, as she pushed back from the tree trunk, walking forward slowly. A saccharine smile graced her lips as she opened her mouth, emitting an ear-piercing, bloodcurdling scream.

Flames danced on her hands as she cast them wide, the winds from behind her thrusting the flames into a ball of fire that shot forward, driving Hedrek backward onto the ground. Rowan had cut down one of the Milesian guards but was locked in combat with the other.

Rhia ran to Aine's side, her breath heaving as she closed her eyes and attempted to still her mind. She crouched low, placing her palms on the ground. The earth seemed to tremble beneath their feet as sharp pointed shards of earth jutted from the land. "*Ardaigh, talamh,*" she spoke softly, her voice rising with each word. "*Ardaigh, talamh!*" she bellowed over the land as the jutted fragments of earth formed a trench that separated them from where Hedrek lay on the ground.

The sound of wet, splitting flesh flooded the air as Rowan dealt the killing blow to the remaining Milesian soldier. He shoved him down with his boot, turning to run toward the women.

Aine's eyes met Hedrek's as she was pulled under by her rage again. Her anger swelled up from the inside like an ocean tempest, tugging her under the surface as memories flooded her vision. She looked over at Rhia and Rowan, standing to her right. Rowan's shoulders were spattered with blood, heaving as his gaze roved over Rhia, protectiveness permeating his very being.

As Aine looked at his face, the way he beheld Rhiannon, all she could picture was Finnin's eyes doing much of the same. She remembered the way his hands felt, the way his lips touched hers. She remembered fondly the way he always squeezed her hand any time they were about to do something foolish together. For the first time in many years, the memory of Finnin's hands on her body was louder than the nightmare of Hedrek's.

Aine's eyes found Hedrek's again. She closed her eyes and smiled again. And laughed. A laugh that drew higher, growing in pitch until it became an even louder scream. She ran toward him, jumping across the ledge and landing on the jutted piece of earth where he lay crouched on the ground. He attempted to get up, but flames hurled forward toward Hedrek, catching the dried leaves on the ground around them. Fire quickly spread from the kindling, engulfing the trunks of the trees in the clearing. Black smoke rose all around them.

"Aine! No! You must come with us, *now*!" Rhia shouted, staring in disbelief that the woman had run *toward* and not away from the captain of the guard. The raven-haired woman slowly turned, a peaceful look settling over her features.

"Go. You have to go, Rhia. Don't worry about me." Aine called back.

Rhia just shook her head, "*No*, sister! Not without one of my own!" She squared her shoulders.

The flames had begun to engulf all visible parts of the forest floor, the blaze forming a wall between Rhia and Rowan. He launched himself forward through the flames, grasping Rhia's hand. "I don't want to leave her behind any more than you do, but we don't have much longer. She has made her choice and we must honor it." Rhia's mind flashed to the last time Rowan had pulled her from briskly spreading flames. She gritted her teeth. She knew he was right.

Rhia met Aine's gaze with tears in her eyes. Aine smiled, "I will see you again Rhia," she called out to her.

Rowan pulled Rhia's waist until she was pressed up against his body. He held the sleeve of his cloak over her nose and mouth, shielding her further from the smoke as he helped her atop the white mare. He mounted Seamus, who was already whinnying and pawing the ground nervously amidst the smoke and growing flames. Rowan yelled a command, and they rode quickly from the clearing, back to the path up ahead.

Hedrek crawled from his hands and knees, lifting himself upright with a grunt, hobbling toward Aine slowly. "That was rather foolish, don't you think?" he spat as he looked at her with disgust, a smirk on his face. "Your people don't die easily, but today you *will* die here with us. Like dogs. Burned inside the very place you longed to return to for so long," he paused and huffed a laugh. "A bit poetic, isn't it, Aine?"

She sighed, closing her eyes as she smiled pleasantly. An orb of flame blasted from her palms again, this time knocking him a few feet backward onto the ground. The winds circled around her, blasting the fire into a blazing inferno around his body. "It is a bit poetic, Hedrek. Like a ballad for the ages, that my face will be the last thing you see on this earth as *you* die. Like a dog. Inside the very place you so foolishly took me away from. In the place you took *everything*!" She screamed the last word, causing the very ground to shake as birds darted from the trees and leaves fell like rain all around them.

Sinew tore and tendons cracked as Aine shifted into her raven form, catching the gust of wind in an ascent toward the sky. She perched on a high branch of a nearby tree, staring down at Hedrek with her piercing golden eyes.

"Impossible . . . " was all he could say as he stared up at her in disbelief.

In one fluid movement, she lifted her body on a strong gust of wind, sailing high over the smoke and treetops.

CHAPTER
TWENTY

The trees of the forest had thinned, becoming less condensed as the path opened to a hilly landscape of green grassy knolls scattered with large rocks jutting from the earth. The path through the woods had ended several yards back. Rowan and Rhia had halted the horses at the crest of a hill as he peered over the maps. He had spent much of the last night sketching and compiling the maps they had procured from Hedrek's estate with Rhia's recent inscriptions.

"It looks as if we need to head east, toward the sea. From what I can make sense of it, it appears as if the paths leading to the Land of Light converge at an unknown location and it's a straight shot from there," Rowan mused. "So we need to follow the path to the sea, then it curves back around and once we find this mysterious site, we're home free."

"That's an interesting way to say that you have no idea where we're headed," Rhia teased, blinking, and casting a saccharine smile in his direction.

"I guess you'd prefer that I stop and ask someone for directions?" he deadpanned with a pause. "Nope, didn't think so. Guess you'll just have to trust me then. I know how much you love that," he smiled back.

She rolled her eyes, spurring the white mare ahead into a steady trot. They rode along in silence for several minutes before she shrugged her shoulders for the second time in a row, as if shaking a chill.

"What is it?" Rowan asked.

"I know you're going to think I'm just being fearful after the recent attack, but I can't shake the distinct feeling that we're being followed," she said quietly.

He peered over his shoulder, left then right. "What do you sense?" he asked.

"Nothing specific, just a presence. As if someone is watching," she replied.

The sound of beating wings and a flutter from the treetops drew their attention to the small yew tree that sat directly ahead of them. The tree looked to be growing from beneath an immense stone that stood out from the grassy plain. The wood was gnarled and spindly. The branches reached skyward in all directions as a sleek black raven landed, perching atop one of them.

Rhia met its gaze, feeling a distinct sense of familiarity in the way the sunlight glinted off the gold of its eyes. She signaled the horse closer, Rowan remaining close behind her. "Why were you following us, small one?" she asked the raven. Rowan stiffened in his saddle, his hand moving to the hilt of Faobhar.

"I told you, Rhia. I would see you again," the raven

replied. In a flutter of black feathers and a gust of wind, bones cracked, and cartilage gave way to a transformation that left a woman hunched in a sitting position beneath the tree. Her cloak hung about her thin shoulders as she parted her dark hair and slowly looked up at Rhia.

"Aine!" Rhia called out, jumping down from the saddle, and running toward the woman with arms wide. She pulled Aine into an embrace beneath the branches of the yew. Her words resounded with laughter and joy as she spoke, "But *how*? How, sister?" she questioned, brushing Aine's hair from her face.

"I left them. To burn. To die," she replied quietly. "Rhia, I feel nothing. I feel no remorse—"

"Aine, after everything you endured—" Rhia interjected.

"No, Rhia. I destroyed that part of the forest. The trees and the homes of many creatures. But I feel *nothing*," she whispered with tears in the corners of her eyes.

"Shhh . . . " Rhia soothed, holding Aine's head to her chest. "We must ride on. We have an important task at hand, and I would like to put some distance between us and those woods. I don't want to be trapped like that again, in case there are more Milesian solders milling about that were part of that brigade."

Aine nodded as Rhia helped her to stand. She mounted the white mare, albeit much stronger than she was before. Rowan nodded to the women, leading Seamus ahead as Rhia moved to mount behind Aine. Her serious expression ended as she glanced down at Rhia with a playful grin, motioning toward Rowan up ahead with a nod. "You should resume your post. I am strong enough to ride alone in the saddle," she reassured Rhia.

"Are you trying to say I take up too much room?" Rhia teased, her mouth quirking upward.

Aine rolled her eyes, whispering low, "Oh come on, I might have been in a dark cage for years, but I'm not *blind*. I've seen the way he looks at you."

Heat crept up the back of Rhia's neck. She huffed a sigh, her voice raising slightly. "Well, if we're to ever get where we're going, *someone's* going to have to let me ride with them."

Rowan slowed Seamus to a halt, scooting to the back of the saddle and extending a hand down to Rhia with a playful smile. She took it silently, mounting in front of him in the saddle. She settled in, flexing her hips backward, not missing how Rowan held his breath until she was comfortably seated and still.

They rode side by side in silence for several hours, the sun sinking slowly over the horizon that they were headed for. Rowan broke the silence, a look of mischief in his eyes as he spoke to Rhia, "So, can you do that? Shift, I mean. Do you have some hidden form that you plan to surprise us all with?" he teased.

Aine laughed, a beautiful melodic sound that Rhia paused to appreciate. It was a marvel that someone who had suffered so much, should still have reason to possess a laugh so beautiful. In a small way, she didn't mind the joke being at her expense if it brought joy into the eyes of her friend.

"No, I can't say that I do. Although Rowan, you have seen me in the early mornings plenty of times. I'm sure I look like a different creature entirely then," Rhia countered. Rowan stiffened, pausing for a beat of silence. Aine was peering at Rhia with one eyebrow raised.

"No! No, not like that—I didn't mean—" Rhia fumbled, her cheeks blushing.

"Oh, I'm sure. I've known you two for all of three days now, and I can tell that at least *one* of you has some sense of honor," she taunted, nodding towards Rowan. "Even if it's him." Laughter rang through the air as the trio rode on, making light of their happenstance meeting and their troubles thus far.

As the night sky dressed herself in brilliant starlight, the three made camp for the evening. Three jagged boulders jutted out from a grass-covered hill. It was a dolmen that stood out in stark contrast to the surrounding landscape, a shelter of sorts. Aine built a fire in front of it, as they secured the horses nearby and bedded down the furs beneath the rocks. They sat in relative contentment, reclining against the stone, sipping water from their drinking skins, and enjoying the rabbit that Rhia had secured for their dinner.

"It looks as if we should reach the sea in a day's ride, if we can make an early start tomorrow morning," Rowan offered, sitting by the fire, sharpening his sword. "We must remain watchful, Milesian guards are known to patrol the northeast border's villages, as they're most commonly where traders and sailors land, seeking to barter or steal. My father and I used to ride through part of these lands on our way to make deliveries to the northern towns."

"Your father . . . was he? . . . " Aine began.

"Yes. It appears he was, after all, Tuatha. My mother

was a Milesian. Neither are still with us for those very reasons," Rowan replied solemnly. "I came to be in possession of his journal after his death. Of these maps. In the company of this one here, as well," he nodded toward Rhia, grinning as he brought the stone down the sharp end of the blade.

"Oh, is that how it happened? It seems he's forgetting the part where he followed me to my cottage, stood by as it was engulfed in flames, begging me to follow him on this quest—" Rhia began.

"*Begging*? Is that the way of it, now?" Rowan replied, amusement lighting his voice. "I seem to remember a lass who planted an arrow straight through a Milesian guard at the beginning of this whole ordeal when I was in danger," he grinned.

Aine chewed idly at her dinner, amusement dancing across her features as she watched them spar back and forth.

"You're never going to forget that, *are* you?" Rhia said with a roll of her eyes.

His expression sobered slightly with a pause in the conversation. "Never," he said finally, smiling down at his work. He rose, replacing the stone in the saddlebag and setting down on his side atop his pallet.

"I should scout ahead. I can fly faster than we can travel on horseback. If there is, indeed, an increased presence of Milesian guards from here to the shoreline, I will see them first," Aine offered. "It seems a more careful approach than waiting to be ambushed again."

"You've just but freed yourself from danger, and now you want to fly right back into it? . . . Alone?" Rhia asked quietly.

Aine reached out, grasping her slender palm. “As I have said, I will be alright. It is a good plan.”

Rowan simply nodded in agreement, staring down at the fire.

“Very well. But do try to come back in three days’ time, that way we know you’re safe,” Rhia finally agreed.

Aine smiled, “I will.”

Aine and Rowan spent the next few hours scrutinizing the maps and drawings that they had compiled. The path ahead had them scaling the Muir Éireann for three to five days, then riding East, inland toward where several paths converged at an unknown location. When they combined the paths from Hedrek’s maps and Rhia’s drawings, all they could make sense of was what looked to be a cluster of trees forming a large circle in the middle of a field.

Rowan shook his head, rubbing his eyes and pinching the bridge of his nose. “We should rest. Dawn brings another full day’s ride.” Aine nodded as she moved to lie beside Rhia, who looked as if she was already drifting off to sleep.

Rhia swore she could hear the ocean in the distance as silence settled over the campsite with the fading of the flames to embers. Sleep claimed her as the sound of the ocean lulled her into dreams that she did not remember the next day.

CHAPTER
TWENTY-ONE

After a day's ride, the rolling hills of lush grasses eventually gave way to craggy peaks that formed steep ocean cliffs. Rhia felt excitement rising in her chest. She had never seen the ocean. As a girl, she had read of it and the legends of her people's distant cousins that lived beneath the waves. Her imagination had always painted a vibrant picture of deep blues, greys, and white-capped waves as she thought about what it might look like.

As they crested the cliff ahead, she quickly learned that her imaginings had not done it justice—it was magnificent. She marveled at the way the waves crashed against the tightly packed sand of the shoreline below them. Her eyes traced the horizon from left to right, taken aback by how the sunset painted an array of bright hues of rose, orange, and yellows where the sky met the sea. She peered to her left to find Rowan gazing at her silently.

He smiled to himself at her reaction to their surroundings. After all the death, destruction, and pain that they had encountered on their journey thus far, he paused to appreciate this small moment with Rhia.

"Come." He nudged Seamus to the left, beckoning for Rhia to follow, "This path leads down to the shoreline. You can't visit the ocean for the first time and not put your feet in the water."

They followed the winding trail downward, each step they took concealed their path further from the path above. They secured the horses near a stream that was flowing down from the grassy hillside and out to sea. The path became gradually rockier as they walked further down toward the water. The area they were headed to was completely concealed from the path above, as the cliff formed an overhang of land above the secluded cove below.

Rowan instinctively reached out his palm for Rhia's hand as the terrain became harder to traverse. She paused as she grabbed his hand unconsciously, flinching at the warmth she found within her own palms at the contact. She peered out at the ocean to avoid his gaze as they walked toward where the white-capped waves slammed against the shore.

Rhia felt a sudden deep familiar pull within her heart that grew stronger the closer they drew to the water. She felt as if she was being reunited with someone lost to time. Someone she had once loved dearly. Her heartbeat quickened as she broke her grasp with Rowan, running ahead as the rocks gave way to soft sands.

She pulled her boots from her feet, tossing them atop a nearby rock as she ran faster and faster toward the water. The balmy air of late summer warmed her skin. She could feel the contrast of the cold crashing waves all the way down to her bones as she ran into the lapping whitecaps. She drew in a sharp breath as the water consumed her body up to her waist. She held her breath and submersed completely under the surface. As her body emerged again, she slicked back her red locks with her palms, sighing deeply.

Rowan couldn't seem to draw his eyes from the sight of her. He was captivated by the way her body seemed to move in tandem with the ebb and flow of the waves. She looked as if she was always meant to be here. Rhia always seemed that way to him, drawing life from the surface of the earth in every place she visited. She looked just as at home beneath the canopies of ancient trees and moss as she did dancing between the cresting ocean waves.

"Are you going to just stand there and stare all day or are you getting in?" she called from beyond the breaker with a playful expression. She stepped a few feet back toward the shoreline, her gown clinging to the curves of her body.

"But the view is so much better from here," he replied with a smirk, crossing his arms, and leaning against a nearby rock.

She looked behind her to try and follow the line of his gaze, when she realized he was staring directly at her. She quirked a brow, flushing slightly as she called back, "Don't tell me you're afraid of the ocean, Rowan . . . Afraid a merrow or a selkie will make off with your heart?" she teased. But he was already moving to remove his boots. His sword and scabbard dropped to the ground with a heavy thump as he pulled his tunic over his head in one fluid motion.

Rhia glanced back at him, her breath hitching as she

admired the cut contours of his chest and abdominals. *Gods, why did he have to look like that? And why did he have to look at her in that way?* she thought to herself. His breeches hung low around his hips, ridges of muscle leading down in a V-shape that sat just above the hem of his pants. She felt warm even beneath the coolness of the ocean water. She inhaled sharply, dunking herself again beneath the waves.

He walked toward her, traversing the waves with careful calculation, never taking his eyes from hers as she reemerged on the surface. Rhia felt that she might have preferred if it would have been an ocean predator stalking toward her. It would probably make her *less* tense than she felt now, as he prowled to where she stood among the waves.

"Not so smug now, are we?" he teased as he reached her.

She looked back out to the horizon, quickly changing the subject. "How often did you come to the ocean? With your father?"

"Only a handful of times. Our work brought us to the northern coasts where the water is much colder. I have visited the eastern coastline where we are only twice. I prefer it here . . . the water is clearer and much warmer," he smiled down at her.

"It's more beautiful than I thought possible," she said softly.

"It is beautiful," he replied. As Rhia lifted her eyes to meet his gaze, she realized that he wasn't looking at the ocean or the horizon around them, but directly at her. "The way the waves curve over the shoreline," he reached up, grazing his fingertips over the crest of her shoulder. "The way the sun illuminates the blue . . . " He reached up, brushing a wet lock of curls from her eyes, staring down into their blue depths as he continued, "The way the tides pull my feet from under my body until I feel I might completely lose control."

Rhia's breathing quickened as the curve of her full breasts rose and fell. The fabric of her tunic plastered low to her bosom as her nipples peaked beneath the material.

"Something tells me you don't have thoughts as intimate as those about the ocean, Rowan . . . " she said breathlessly with a half-smile. She brought her fingertips to touch the ridges of his lower abdominals, tracing the planes of his muscles up to his chest. His own breathing grew faster with the contact.

"I don't know what you mean, Rhia . . . I am a man who simply knows how to enjoy the wonders around me," he smirked, drawing closer to her. She pressed her chest against his as she stood before him. The smell of the ocean air mingled with the deep scent of leather and cedar that she had so intimately come to know; it was so very *him*.

It was intoxicating.

She closed her eyes, bringing her palms up his chest, resting against the pounding of his heart. She grasped his neck at the nape, bringing his head down so that her lips coasted the shell of his ear, "And how do you like to enjoy them?" she whispered. "As I have asked before, what does this heart want, Rowan?" she motioned toward where her right palm lay across his broad chest.

He was almost trembling beneath her touch, every fiber of his body coiled tight.

"I've always been the kind of man that is better at

showing than telling," he replied, reaching down to gently grasp her hair, angling her mouth upward towards him, his lips grazing the surface of hers. He brought his own palm to rest beneath her full breast, cupping the left side of her chest as he used his other palm to bring their bodies flush against one another. "I am a man who will show you every day what I want. And I want *this*, what's inside here." He pressed his palm into her chest. "I want it all. Everything that you are, Rhia," he covered her mouth with his lips as she opened to him, her tongue roving over his hungrily.

"I want you to never want for anything ever again . . . What I want most is to give you everything that *you* want," he continued, palming her breast, eliciting a moan from her lips as she kissed him fervently in return. He broke the contact suddenly to look into her eyes, drawing a sharp inhale from her.

"You have to tell me, Rhia. You have to use your words," he said breathlessly. "What do you want?"

A grin slowly crept across her features as she guided his hand back up to her breast, capturing his mouth again in a scorching kiss, another soft moan escaping her lips,

"I fear we are too much alike in this way, Rowan . . . I am also much better at showing than telling."

She guided his right palm down to grasp her thigh, lifting weightlessly beneath the sea and wrapping her legs around his waist. She could feel the considerable length of him pressing against her core.

A low groan vibrated from his mouth atop hers as she wrapped her arms around his neck. He brought both arms around to grasp her bottom, moving her body against his beneath the waves as they crashed into their bodies. Her mouth desperately explored his with her swirling tongue as his taste and touch invaded every one of her senses. Rowan strode through the breakers as they made their way back toward the shore.

The spray of the sea clung to their hair as they crossed the waves, the water becoming shallower as they neared the shore. Rowan bent to his knees, gently placing Rhia on her back on the soft sand beneath them, a few feet from where the sea met the shoreline. His palms fervently moved up her thighs as she reached down, guiding his fingers to bring the wet, thin material of her deerskin breeches down her legs.

He thought he might stop breathing as he beheld her soft skin and the curves of her body below him. His hands moved upward as she helped him to lift her drenched tunic from over her head.

Gods help him. He thought to himself as his eyes roved over her perfect full breasts that were laid out like a feast beneath him. It took every ounce of self-control within his body to keep himself leashed inside. He groaned as he drew one of her rosy peaked nipples into his mouth, drawing a deep moan from her own lips.

She arched her body against his, her hips beginning to grind in a desperate movement as she reached down for the buttons of his breeches. He grasped her wrist in his palm, guiding it back up and pressing his lips to her fingers. "Not yet," he said hoarsely, "I fear I'll lose control the first moment I feel those perfect thighs clenching around me . . . " He brought his lips back to her breasts, moving lower as his lips brushed down her abdomen and nipped at the curve of her hipbone, "It is taking every ounce of restraint in my body to control myself right now. And I want to savor every delicious moment with you, Rhia."

She trembled beneath his touch as he trailed kisses down her inner thighs. She felt as if she were going to erupt in flames, already feeling the heat building beneath her palms.

She cried out his name as she felt his tongue lap between her folds, drawing upward until his mouth pressed firmly onto her core. She bucked at the contact, desperate for any bit of friction and more of his tongue. Her pleasure was building to an unbearable intensity within her, coiling deeply within her lower abdomen. She needed him, *now*.

"Please, Rowan," she cried breathlessly, grasping for his shoulders, his hair, for anything to give her purchase. "I need you. You asked me what I want, I want *you*. *Now*. Please." His heart swelled within his chest, feeling as if it might explode as he kissed a trail up her abdomen. His palms grasped her thighs, drawing her core against his length as her hips ground out a movement in tandem with his, desperate for any sort of friction.

Her fingers fumbled clumsily with the buttons of his pants as he helped her slide them down his legs and remove them. He climbed atop her body, covering her form with his own.

She already knew that this was a feeling that she would grow to crave, to be covered by his muscled form, lying beneath the enclosure of his arms. She struggled to slow her rapid breathing as she beheld his sizeable length as he hovered above her. She felt as if her heart would beat out of her chest if she didn't feel him inside of her soon.

He lined himself up with her entrance, slowly entering her, inch by delicious inch, as she moaned beneath him. She felt her body heat rising as she moved her hips upward to accommodate the size of him, desperate for more contact. He gazed at her face, smiling, tracing his finger down the curve of her cheek, and resting his thumb on her bottom lip. "Remember what I said, Rhia, I need your words. Tell me what pleases you," he said in a low voice, bringing his lips to nip her ear and trail soft kisses down her neck, his hips rocking as he pushed deeper inside of her in agonizingly slow strokes, all the way to the hilt.

She gasped in pleasure as he felt her walls clenching tighter around him. "*Fuck*," he ground out, increasing the pace of his strokes.

"I want more of you, Rowan, I don't want your control. I want you unleashed." She moaned beneath him.

It was as if something inside of him had snapped the tether of his restraint as he increased the pace of his movements. His teeth grazed up her neck as he brought his arm down to loop beneath her right knee, hauling it upward as he slammed in and out of her. "*Fuck*, Rhia, you feel so good. It's like you were *made* for me. Look how well you're taking all of me."

Holy hells, she thought to herself as she felt her own control slipping away. She panted as her moans quickened. Every inch of him felt like fire on her skin as her inner walls tightened around him. His own control was long gone as he ravaged her body like a man starved. His strokes were fast and punishing, low groans escaping his lips as he plunged deep into her, again and again.

She tightened her thighs around his waist, pushing his shoulders as he moved to his back to lie beneath her. She straddled him as she pushed his body to the ground, placing her hands on his chest. She moaned with pleasure as her body shifted to accommodate the new position. She could take him so much more deeply this way, and it was enough to drive her mad.

She rocked her hips back and forth as his length filled her with each stroke, her full breasts bouncing in the light of the setting sun. He reached up to grab her hips, moving her up and down on him, his own pleasure climbing higher and higher as he felt her intimate muscles gripping him tighter.

He brought the palm of his hand up to the apex of her thighs, pressing his thumb atop the sensitive bundle of nerves, drawing slow circles as she ground her hips on his.

It was her undoing.

As he moved faster inside of her, her soft moans rose to panting shouts as pleasure ripped through her body in blazes of white light. His hands, his length, his body beneath hers was enough to topple her over the edge of her pleasure. Her eyes blurred as she reached down to place her palms in the sand on either side of his body, rocking up and down as she reached her climax, crying out his name over and over.

His name on her lips was all it took to send Rowan tumbling over the edge of his own desire after her. His strokes became erratic as he gripped her hips tightly, groaning loudly with his climax, spilling into her as he felt every delicious inch of those inner walls, draining every drop of him.

Rhia felt warmth as hot as fire flaring from her palms,

buried in the sand, as they rode out their pleasure. Their mouths explored each other's hungrily as they panted and moaned. As they came down from their heightened state, and their movements slowed, she looked down to the ground to see black scorched sand beneath her palms.

She struggled to even her breathing as Rowan did the same, grasping her thighs and moving them to a seated position. He was still inside her as he rested his forehead against her chest, placing his palms on her back and pulling her into him. He pressed a soft kiss to her clavicle, tucking a curl behind her ear as he looked up at her. She reached down, grasping what looked to be one of many dark obsidian crystals that had formed in the sand beneath her palms. She brought it up to the light of the setting sun, marveling at what had just transpired.

"Rowan . . . " she whispered, drawing his attention to the stone, "I think I finally found my fire."

His eyes widened as he gazed down at the scorched sand on either side of them. A long beat of silence passed between them. "You know what this must mean . . . " he said as he looked into her deep blue eyes. She nodded, as tears streamed down her cheeks, something akin to fear passing across her features. "But how?"

CHAPTER
TWENTY-TWO

Rowan had built a torch of sorts, a flame to guide them as they navigated deeper into the entrance of a cave they had located at the opening of the cove. Water droplets trickled from the top of the rock as they stepped further away from the light of the outside world.

"I think this is likely the best place to sleep for the night. It's the most secluded and it looks as if there are steaming pools ahead." He motioned forward into the darkness. Rhia's eyes adjusted as she stepped forward, peering down into the clear pool of water cut down into the stone floor of the cave. Rowan had brought several large pieces of wood into the grotto, lighting each of them and affixing them between stones of the cave walls. The area was illuminated with a warm glow, softened by the steam wafting into the air.

"I'm going to find something for us to eat. It's best that you remove those wet clothes and get warm." He motioned at the pool, turning to walk toward the mouth of the cave.

Warmth, she thought to herself.

She wondered when they would talk about the stark revelation that had just passed between them. As she had reached down into the sand and grasped the black obsidian forged from the flame within her palms, her mind reeled with a thousand questions. Rowan had searched her face for any sign of doubt, any sign that she may regret what they had done. Rhia had no regrets. Not about the ways they had touched one another, nothing had ever felt more right in her life. She would wait a thousand lifetimes more just to feel his hands on her body again.

However, the discovery of her fire draíocht had left her mind with more questions than answers. She could bend earth, air, and water—she had perfected those gifts long ago under the careful instruction of Beatha and Elder Ecna. But her fire magic had remained elusive to her for her entire life.

Until Rowan.

Rhia thought back to their first moments together. He had always had a way of coaxing warmth from her skin, inside her very blood. She had always attributed it to her growing desire for him, her reluctant attachment to this man who had become steadfast for her, in so many ways. Now she knew it was much more. She smiled to herself, as she stripped off her wet clothing, climbing into the steaming water of the hot spring. Her mind wandered to the feeling of Rowan's warm embrace.

He had touched her like he wanted to claim her, to worship her, to *protect* her.

Her *Dionadair.*

If this was true, it meant that she was much more as well. She breathed deeply as she settled into the water, dipping down until her shoulders were submerged in the water and the sudden heaviness on them lifted a bit.

She was the one they had been in search of. All this time, it was her, the Nichnevin. The one prophesied to possess the elemental abilities to wield earth, water, air, and *fire*. She wondered if, perhaps, that was the reason that she had been kept isolated for so long within Beatha's wards in the forest. Why Elder Ecna had spent so much time on her training. Why she had always felt this deep sense of need to help women around her who were in distress, her sisters, her blood. Why she felt so desperate to help her people. She felt a sense of fear creep into her chest. *But what does this mean for my people? How am I to lead them from darkness?* she thought. *How can I lead them when I, myself, do not know the way?*

Rhia was so deep in thought that she hadn't heard Rowan return, turning to see him a few feet away inside the cave, crouched and building a fire.

"You know, you'll be ill if you don't remove your own wet clothes." She peered at him with a teasing gaze. His back was turned to her.

"Stay as long as you wish, I will warm myself when you are finished," he replied, not taking his eyes from his work. His shoulders were flexed with tension.

Rhia frowned as she turned back, dipping again into the water. Her mind was now filled with another kind of fear. She wondered if he, in fact, regretted lying with *her*. She swallowed the thick lump in her throat as she turned to him again. "What if I don't want you to wait until I am finished?" she said softly.

His shoulders stiffened, "Careful, Rhia."

"Or what? "She pressed.

"Or I'll be submerged in that water with my tongue buried so far inside of you that we'll both forget who we are. And apparently, we don't even know *that*. Not in truth."

She bristled, heat flushing her face, "What is *that* supposed to mean?"

"It means, I had a single job to do. A single task was left to me by my father. Find her. Protect her. Restore what was lost. Well, I *found* her, and I didn't even have the discernment to see her right before my eyes. I could have done *more*." He winced. "I foolishly lead us into a village, let mortal men capture you and put you in a cage." He rose and began to pace, pulling a hand through his damp, brown hair. "What if you had been hurt? What if something worse happened?"

"*Oh!* So, you're only concerned about me being hurt then, because now, we know who I *really* am? Because don't forget, this is news to *me* too!" she spat, rising from the water as she grabbed her damp cloak from the ledge of the spring.

"No, that is *not* what I am saying," he replied, stepping closer to her. "I just can't believe I didn't see it. How could I have been so blind? This is my fault, Rhia. I should have been more focused on protecting you—"

"Instead of *fucking* me? Is that what you want to say?" she shouted. "Because if you regret it, just say that. You seem like a man who takes his oaths seriously, so just pledge your sword like you've been waiting to do and get on with it." She motioned at his sword on the ground nearby.

He huffed a laugh, sending a spark of anger up the back of her neck. She gritted her teeth. He stepped forward, towering over her until she could feel his warm breath on her hair. "I am going to tell you something and I want you to listen to me carefully," he said, bringing his fingers down to hook beneath her chin. He gently tilted her head up until their eyes met. "I regret many things I have done in this lifetime—deeds done, words left unsaid . . . but I will *never* regret you." He brought his lips down to whisper in the shell of her ear with a smile, "Do you know what I find ironic, Rhia?" She shivered beneath his touch, tightening the cloak around her shoulders. "The one I was destined to protect came into my life because she was trying to protect me."

Her eyes lifted to meet his gaze. His pupils were burning blazes, piercing into her flesh, and awakening her fire once again. She dropped the cloak to the ground, grasping the nape of his neck and capturing his mouth with hers. He groaned as he pulled her naked form flush with his body. She reached down and lifted his tunic over his head.

"What have I told you, woman? I never stood a chance. Not when it comes to you." She quickly helped him out of the rest of his clothes as he picked her up. Her legs wrapped around his body as he stepped back toward the hot spring.

He submerged their bodies in the warmth of the water, both sighing in pleasure as the heat enveloped them. Their mouths explored each other in a chorus of soft pants, tongues and teeth roving over skin and flesh. Rowan's mouth traced up the side of her neck as she tightened her thighs around him.

"I think you were lying before," he panted against her mouth, "when you said you didn't have another form." She smiled, leaning back to peer at him curiously as he captured one of her breasts in his mouth, his tongue flicking over her nipple.

"What do you mean?" she asked breathlessly.

"I mean you *do* have another form," he continued, his mouth exploring her body. "You are a *goddess*, Rhia. Look at the way you compel me to kneel before you."

His hands grasped her thighs, moving them to the far side of the pool where a smooth rock formed a small ledge. He placed her bottom on the ledge, lifting a leg and placing one of her ankles atop his shoulder. He left a trail of kisses beginning at her thigh, moving higher and higher until he reached the apex of her thighs. She was breathless beneath him. Every nerve ending on her body was raw and exposed.

Her palms flared with blazing flames, flares of fire hovering over her palms. She submerged them in the water on either side of her, the flames hissing into steam as they encountered the liquid. His mouth hovered over her core, his gaze molten as he peered up at her, "Now let me worship you."

Later that night, as the moonlight passed into the grotto in slits through breaks in the stone above, Rowan and Rhia lay on their sides atop the furs by the fire. He lay behind her, holding her body flush to his, as her head rested on his right arm. He placed a gentle kiss on top of her shoulder, as his fingers traced down the length of her arm, coming to rest on the blue-tinged raised band of flesh. "I realize that I should probably already know this, but how long *did* you live in that forest, anyway?" he asked.

She turned over to face him as he brushed her copper curls back from her eyes. She looked up at him with a knowing expression, one eyebrow raised, "Rowan . . . are you asking me how old I am?"

"It's a valid question—"

"I can't *believe* you'd ask that of a lady," she laughed, both moving to lie on their backs, staring up at the stone ceiling of the cave. "I mean, how old are *you*?" She turned to him.

"Thirty-one" he replied, clearing his throat.

She snorted a laugh, a loud giggle escaping her lips. It was one of the most melodic sounds he had ever heard. He decided his new objective was to make her do that as much as he possibly could. A few beats of silence passed between them.

"I am 126," she replied finally.

He made a choking sound, quickly trying to mask it with a cough. She jabbed him in the side with her elbow. "*Hey!*" she cried out, both descending into laughter. As they lay there, surrounded by a sense of merriment, Rowan reached over and grasped her hand. He brought it to his lips as her eyes met his. His voice deepened. "You know, if you really want me to pledge my sword to you, I will," he chuckled, prompting a roll of her eyes. A moment of silence passed. "I can pledge my blade to you if you'd have it. Just like I pledge my body and my soul to you."

Her expression sobered as she turned, peering back at him curiously through her lashes. He continued, "I don't have much to offer you aside from those three things, but they're yours all the same."

She sighed, smiling at him, feeling as if sunlight itself was beaming from her skin. She felt a gentle warmth envelop her and for the first time since leaving Beatha's house, she felt as if she was finally *home*. She realized for the first time that home was not a place. No, *he* felt like home.

Rhia drew a leg across his body, climbing atop to straddle him. She wove her fingers into his, bringing his hands above his head, and leaning down to softly press her mouth to his, capturing his bottom lip in her own. "What more could I want, Rowan?" she smiled as she began to rock her hips back and forth.

"*Gods*, woman, this is all I am ever going to want. Will I ever stop wanting you this way?" he said hoarsely.

"You don't have to want something that's already yours," she whispered, as they fell into the movements of each other's bodies once again. His chest warmed as he moved her onto her back, gazing down into those deep blue eyes that so resembled the moonstone sapphire they both possessed fragments of. He kissed her again, slowly, and deeply. They danced in the dark throughout the night, worshipping each other's bodies until the moon was far over the horizon and the sun began to peek over the edge of the sea.

CHAPTER
TWENTY-THREE
AINE

The breeze blew a salty mist into Aine's path of flight from where the waves crashed upon the rocks below her. She drew upward, coasting over the slicing wind as the gales from the ocean grew stronger. Heavy rains from the sky began to pelt her coat of feathers. Her wings felt the strain of fatigue worsen with each heavy drop of rain.

She had flown for hours now. The second day of her journey was coming to an end as the light faded over the horizon. She had intended to follow the shoreline all the way to the landmark that would direct her path inland toward Lia Fáil. Rowan had estimated the kingmaker's stone to be just a half-day's ride inland, west from where the Muir Éireann cut a large inlet into the land. She knew she could make it in half of that time if she stayed on course.

The winds were picking up speed and she knew that if she didn't want to chance being pushed out to sea by the worsening squall, she needed to nest down for the night. She spied a forested area down below, several paces from the shoreline. A river cut into the woodland terrain. She could see the mouth of the tributary flowing out to sea. Fresh water and a covered place to sleep—that would do.

Aine landed, and with enough light from the setting sun, managed to construct a makeshift dwelling by stretching her cloak over a parcel of nearby trees. She knew that the deluge around her would surely prevent her from being able to cook anything or make a fire, so she picked some wild berries and nuts to eat. To be honest, she preferred it this way. Sleeping without a fire would lessen the likelihood of being detected.

She had flown for two days straight, the ache in her shoulders telling the tale of the journey thus far. Torrential rains and strong winds had tried and tested her wing strength—the culmination of that exhaustion settled heavily on her now. She could feel grime and sand between her fingers and behind her ears. *Might as well make use of the fresh water*, she thought to herself, as she rose and headed toward the riverbed nearby.

The rains had long since stopped and a peaceful quiet settled over the forest. The evening birds began to call out their ballads, signaling the arrival of dusk as the crickets began their nighttime songs. Aine had shed her clothing, leaving it to hang to dry on a nearby tree branch.

Her pale milky skin was luminous in the emerging moonlight as she dipped a toe in the calm waters. She proceeded, inching her slender body beneath the surface of the water until it reached the curve of her hips. Water lapped at her breasts as she dipped beneath the water completely.

As she emerged her raven hair shone almost blue in the moonlight, clinging to her chest and back as it flowed down to her hips. She ran her fingers over the scars that scattered across her forearms—remnants of fire and pain.

As she reflected on the events of the past weeks, she could not help but feel a deep heaviness in her soul. She was grateful that the wheel of fate had finally seemed to have turned in her favor. She was finally freed from the living hells she had endured for the last eight years. Freed by her people —her friends.

She smiled at the contentment that her newfound friendships had brought to her life. In such a short time, Rowan and Rhia had become her liberators, her traveling companions . . . her family. She would sleep this night outside the iron bars of a cage. Her wings once again knew the feeling of a fresh gust of wind beneath her feathers. She could cry at the thought—tears of joy. Instead, she sang.

The song began low in her belly, a deep haunting melody that seemed to reverberate from her bones. The notes gently climbed in pitch until her lips echoed each syllable in a tone more lovely than the one that came before it. Her breath softly escaped her lips with an utterance of pure, unadulterated elation. Tears began to once again stream down her face as she sang for those that she had lost—for her mother, for Finnan, for her people across the continent of Éire who were still living in hiding.

Her words were a war ballad, a deep cry of woe for her kind. She was determined to help her companions find the Nichnevin, the liberator of her people—to help deliver them unto the Land of Light. As her voice rose to a crescendo, the very forest stilled, as if to listen. A branch cracked in the distance, breaking the stillness.

She quieted as she blinked twice, her head turning to the left, focusing on a rustling sound far in the distance. Tuatha hearing was keener than that of mortal men. Aine knew she had only seconds to flee the water, collect her clothes, and dart to the skies if she was indeed being followed. She stilled, not moving a muscle as she struggled to detect any further movement or noise. She heard neither as she swiveled her head from left to right.

After a few seconds, she settled back down under the surface of the water until the surface touched the tops of her shoulders. The gentle movement of the current was the only sound to be heard. She exhaled slowly in relief.

Aine looked upward to admire the full moon, which was now a splendid light, illuminating the forest and river around her. She hummed to herself again, softly. As she turned around to exit the water, she was surprised to see the most beautiful male she had ever beheld.

A tall, rugged young male was standing on the bank of

the river, staring at her unabashedly. His eyes were bright blue, long coppery red hair framed his face and hung about his shoulders, shining and sleek. He had broad shoulders, a strong jaw, and a handsome clean-shaven face. His sleeves were rolled up around his elbows, revealing a characteristic raised, blue-tinged band of flesh encircling his left forearm. He never broke his stare as his breathing increased. He continued to marvel at Aine as if she were a river nymph or sprite instead of a living, breathing, creature. She remained frozen; her golden gaze locked with his.

CHAPTER TWENTY-FOUR

DAGDA

Where was this song coming from? Dagda thought to himself. As he had been moving through the forest, accompanied by the scouting party he'd recently separated from, he had been accosted by the most beautiful sound his ears had ever heard.

His chest felt a strange tightness from deep within as he had first detected a woman's voice in the air. A dull ache throbbed around where his heart was situated, feeling as if a tight string were tugging him toward the sound. Closer and closer he stepped, moving deeper into the forest with the curve of the river.

Until he finally beheld her.

He felt as if the very air had left his lungs as his eyes adjusted to observe her delicate form in the moonlight. Dagda felt a twinge of shame settle over him as he realized she stood completely naked before him, but judging by the look on her face, she didn't seem to care. She stood with her arms held down by her sides, her shoulders squared, meeting his gaze unabashedly.

Before he realized what his body was doing, his feet were moving toward the riverbank. She made no move to escape as she continued to bore a hole through the essence of his very being with her unforgiving stare. He marveled at the way her raven locks clung to the curves of her body, illuminated and glowing, almost blue in the light of the full moon.

His mind emptied of any rational thought, including the scouting party that he had left behind on the trail, following the sound of the woman's voice deeper into the woods. His legs moved him closer and closer until his body was standing directly in front of her small form. If he did not regard the way her full breasts rose and fell with each breath, he would have sworn she was a figment of his mind. A sorcery of sorts, to deceive his eyes and betray his body.

His mind screamed at him from inside the rational thoughts he had long since left behind, as he slowly raised his palm to trace the curve of her delicate chin. No, she was *very* real indeed. *What a fool you are*, his conscience berated him, *you know better*. For this creature could be a selkie or other manner of dark creature from the other side of the Sidhe. In his years spent sailing around the coast of the continent, he had seen humans and Tuatha alike succumb to all manner of these creatures—selkies, merrow . . . creatures who appeared in the form of beautiful women to lure unsuspecting males to their graves. The warmth of their lust was the last feeling they had before death's cold grip pulled them under. Dagda brushed these thoughts aside, foolishly paying them no mind as he inched closer and closer to this devastatingly beautiful creature before him.

To his amazement, she did not make a move to flee or to even speak. He felt shame settling over him as he wondered if he should begin by introducing himself. *No*, he thought. He would only look like a fool should he try to construct some excuse for watching a woman bathing. Any reason he tried to come up with in his mind was meaningless. All he could do was marvel at the beauty of this woman before him, marvel at how her presence seemed to become more intoxicating each moment he stood before her.

She surprised him once again as she lifted her own hand, tracing the lines of his face with the soft pads of her fingers. She traced over his strong brow, down his chiseled cheek, and came to rest her right hand on his broad chest. His heart was pounding at high speed, his face held an expression of disbelief with each of her movements. She placed her left hand over his that cupped her chin.

She glanced down at his palm as she covered it with her own, bringing it lower and lower until it hovered over her chest, just below her collar bone. He wasn't breathing at all, swallowing hard as she locked her eyes on his and moved his palm to grasp her full breast. Her breathing and heartbeat were even beneath his touch as his body lit into an inferno. He wasn't sure what was happening, but he couldn't look away. Couldn't break her gaze. Lust crept onto every inch of his body, clutching his mind in its grasp as he moved his mouth closer to hers. To his astonishment, her pale pink lips parted slightly, as if to welcome him. *What was he doing?*

He felt a deep ache within his chest, the deep pull

toward this woman growing stronger and stronger. He felt as if he might break beneath the weight of it. His own breathing was ragged as he felt an ominous darkness settle over him. Dagda looked down to see the delicate fingers of the hand upon his chest had sharpened into fine-tipped claws with razor-sharp ends. The woman lifted a single clawed finger, tracing the lines of his face again under its sinister point.

He shuddered. Every rational voice in his mind was screaming at him to run, to flee her grasp. He tried to break her gaze, but he could not. He did not possess the strength to look away. She brought her soft lips closer to his as his hand still rested beneath hers atop her breast. As her lips drifted closer, he felt as if the very air was leaving his lungs.

No, it was being drawn from his lungs.

He noticed the edge of her lips curving slightly into a grin as she drew a razored claw to rest on the pulse point of his neck. Whether he was paralyzed with fear, lust, or surprise . . . he could no longer say. He feared he would die today, by her hand. Somehow, he didn't seem to care.

She pressed her lips to his and his heart leapt violently within his chest. Her warm tongue teased the edges of his lips, his teeth, as he opened to her. He groaned into her open mouth as she responded by bringing her body flush with his. A tether snapped loose within him as he moved to grasp her hips, tugging her body toward his.

Suddenly, a sharp, stabbing sensation pierced his chest. Her mouth slanted against his and he could feel the essence of his very being leaving his lips as she drank him in deeply. He looked down, seeing one of her claws puncture clean through the wall of his rib cage. Dark red blood oozed from his chest as he remained frozen in place.

He couldn't move. Couldn't run. Couldn't even scream or make a single sound.

He broke their kiss as he fought to push away from her embrace. Something kept him pinned beneath her gaze as she continued her work of carving out his heart from his chest.

This was it. This was how he was to die.

No. He could not die. He had work to do.

Dagda used every ounce of strength inside of him and managed to break her gaze, pushing his body back as he stumbled, landing on his back in the water of the shallow part of the riverbank. He was gasping erratically, clutching his chest as he wheezed for air. He slowly brought his gaze from his bloodied chest to the great and terrible beauty standing before him—clutching his beating heart in her hands.

A smile spread across her face as she sighed a deep sigh of contentment, bringing the muscled tissue of his heart to her mouth and taking a bite.

Holy hells.

He broke out in a cold sweat all over his body, looking down to see a gaping hole in his chest wall. How was he still alive? What *was* this creature?

The rain began to fall again as she stood smiling before him, blood running down her chin onto her pale chest as she spoke, "You males all want the same thing, foolish one. One day, you will learn. You will *all* learn."

Her eyes were glazed over in white as she flexed her

talons in the moonlight, leaning her head back and shrieking the most terrible utterance his ears had ever heard. She grabbed shredded pieces of his tunic from the ground below and stalked to the river's edge, leaning over, and dipping them into the water. Red flowed downstream as he blinked his eyes in disbelief.

Could this be? He had heard legends of her, foretold from centuries past. Legends of the re-emergence of a fearsome goddess who would appear when times of war were near. She would materialize when the Nichnevin had returned to deliver her people. One who would foretell death and destruction and foresee who would be the conquerors in a great battle.

The one who would bare her teeth with a smile made for war.

The Banshee.

The *Morrigan*.

He blinked again, rubbing his fists into his eyes to dispel the fearsome sight before him. His wits seemed to return to him as he glanced down to see his skin was once again intact. He placed a hand over his chest to feel his heart beating inside once again. As his gaze shot up to where the raven-haired woman had leaned at the river's edge, there was no one to be found. She had disappeared entirely.

CHAPTER TWENTY-FIVE

AINE

As she walked back to where she had made camp for the evening, Aine slowed to admire the subtle way that the once-lush greens of the forest were slowly fading into yellows, high within the trees. The night air had a crisp edge to it that gave her a strange sense of excitement inside. Autumn would arrive in a couple of months, and with it, the last fire festivals of the year. She paused when she remembered that her people would likely not be celebrating as publicly as they had before she had been imprisoned.

No, the Tuatha were slowly fading from these lands. Fading from the watchful armies of the Milesians, as they drove them further and further away. She clenched her fists at her sides, picking up her stride as she trudged up the trail, back to the place she would sleep. Sleep sounded like the best thing at the moment. The last few days had caught up with her physically and mentally.

The events of the evening at the river had taken a toll on

the sense of peace she had felt moments before her silence was disturbed. She had almost felt like her body was moving of its own accord as she had navigated the encounter with the Tuatha male. The fear that shone in his eyes told her that she had made her point—he was not welcome in her presence, and he should tread more carefully around those he felt he had a right to spy on. But she had taken it a step further. She wanted to make him hurt, and, at the same time, she wanted to move closer to him. She wanted to understand more about what emboldened him, what made him so brave as to approach with no thought for his own safety whatsoever.

She grumbled to herself as she thought of the infuriating way that he had just . . . *stared* at her. He might as well have been holding his mouth agape, the way he seemed almost dumbstruck by her naked form. Not that she cared, she had been in her natural state in front of men before. Hells . . . living with Hedrek had stripped her of any modesty she might have had left. She shuddered again, gritting her teeth, her hands in fists, swaying this way and that as she stomped back up the slight incline of the path. "Next time, it will be more than just an illusion. I'll truly carve his heart out," she mumbled to herself as she approached her outstretched cloak, making her campsite.

"Will you now?" She heard a deep and jovial voice call out from above. She jumped back a step as she looked around, trying to determine where the voice was coming from.

A man's sturdy form hopped down from the tree branch he had been sitting upon moments before. The Tuatha male from the river was standing directly in front of Aine, towering over her small form with a smirk on his face. She quickly reached into her boot to grab her dagger, but just as she retrieved it from its holster, a strong wind blew over her left shoulder, blowing it from her grasp to land several paces away on the forest floor.

"That wasn't very nice, you know." He stepped closer, smiling down at her with a curious look on his face, "What you did . . . I know fully grown males who would have to change their breeches if they'd seen a creature as terrifying as you, holding their heart in those hands . . . or claws . . . " He chucked to himself, glancing down to where her hands now fisted at her sides again.

"Would these grown males also have been watching a female bathing from afar, with no intention of making their presence known?" she countered, her face expressionless.

"Depends on the males." He chuckled, "You didn't seem to be in too big of a hurry to preserve any modesty, yourself."

She smiled sweetly, stepping closer with a look that took him a bit off-guard. A vine slithered down from the trunk of a nearby tree, wrapping around one of his ankles. In one fluid motion, the vine snapped taut, dangling the Tuatha male upside down in the air. His cloak and tunic fell off his muscular form and onto the ground below as his daggers, a coin purse filled with copper, and a quiver of arrows fell from his person, spilling in a heap onto the forest floor.

"How's that for modesty?" she sneered, turning, and gathering her own cloak from where it had been outstretched over the branches in a makeshift covering. She buttoned it in place, amusement painting her features as she witnessed the red-haired male struggling to move upright and free himself from the vines.

"That's fair, I suppose," he grunted out as he attempted to yank on the vines stubbornly binding his legs. "Wait—are you leaving?" he called out as she began to walk away. ". . . *Wait!*"

After she had walked several paces away from him, she paused. Not bothering to turn around, she snapped her fingers as the vines snapped away from his ankles, dropping him onto the ground with a huff. He brushed the dirt from his breeches and began to chase after her, not bothering to gather his belongings that lay strewn across the ground. He fumbled in the coin purse, retrieving something in his hands, before beginning to chase after her again.

"I don't seem to understand, I've made it quite clear that I would like you to leave me alone—" she began as he finally caught up to her.

"Here . . . " he called out, huffing as he extended his palm to her. She turned around, glancing down to see the fragment of a moonstone sapphire sitting in his palm.

Her eyes widened. "*Where* did you get that?" she demanded.

"Are you going to stop and let me speak now? Or will you try to cut out my tongue next?" he teased, replacing the stone in his pocket. Almost without her own consent, her eyes glanced over his bare chest as his muscles heaved with his increased work of breathing.

He grinned in response. She quickly averted her eyes to the ground, closing them as she gritted her teeth with her mounting frustration.

"The tongue part can be arranged. I will ask again. Where did you get that? Speak. Now," she insisted.

"From the same place the other fragments came from. And I can tell you where that is. I know the place you seek. The place your *companions* seek . . . " he added, Aine's eyes growing wider with each word.

"Come, let's make a fire, warm our bones, and I will tell you what you wish to know."

Aine and the Tuatha male sat by the fire, speaking for what felt like hours. She remained quietly contemplative, staring into the flames, as he told her of the quest of his scouting party and who he was.

He introduced himself as Dagda—son of the goddess Danu herself. Although, he admitted, his mother had not appeared in her physical form to her people in many years. She had reconciled her presence to remain on the other side of the Sidhe—or the land of light, separated from the comings and goings of the Tuatha on the continent of Éire by an impenetrable veil.

Dagda explained that his mother had lost her ability to connect and commune with her children—all the Tuatha people, as they had become more and more separated from their natural relationship with the earth. The land was mourning the loss of her people—that was clear. Famine, poor harvests, and weak livestock yields had told the tale of decreasing Tuatha populations. The Tuatha drew their draíocht from their deep communion with the forests and the sea. However, as they were forced from their ancestral lands more and more with each passing year, Danu also became less capable of leading her children.

Dagda explained that, as in times past, when the Tuatha people were in danger of losing their lands to the Famorians, Danu called forth an ancient divine feminine power to unite her peoples again. In truth, the source of this power was a culmination of her own mother-goddess energy, brought to fruition by a need for vindication for the injustices suffered by her children.

Her daughter—the Nichnevin.

The chosen queen of these lands, anointed by Danu. The one to unite the peoples of Éire and restore what was lost. One who held deep magic in her bones; magic that would call forth life back from the land and bring peace between the peoples of the continent.

In this case—Dagda's sister.

Aine sat silently as Dagda finished telling the tale of how he had scoured the lands of Éire for the last several months, searching for his sister—the long-lost queen. The one Aine and her companions searched for as well. Only, these revelations left Aine with more questions than answers.

"The last time I spoke with my mother, she told me where my sister had been left as a child," Dagda began. "She knew after her birth that she was the Nichnevin. The reincarnation of our queen, at a time when we had begun to need her the most. Tense relations with the Milesians were beginning to come to a head when she was born. Our people beyond the Land of Light needed her. But she had to be kept hidden. Warded. Safe, and living deep in the forest," he continued.

"She was to train with an elder of our draíocht each year, to learn all the facets of her magic—all four elements." He paused, looking down into the fire. "But when I arrived where my mother told me she would be waiting, all I found was ashes. Bodies, bones, and burnt texts strewn about the rubble of a crumbling cottage . . . and the *head* of that elder, impaled on a stake in a nearby village that had been destroyed."

Aine inhaled sharply. She remembered Rhia's stories of leaving her childhood home with Rowan, after losing her grandmother, losing everything.

"I began to track a set of hoofprints from that cottage within the forest. That lead me to where two traveling companions found you," he looked up to meet her gaze. She wasn't breathing. She exhaled slowly.

"You really are quite the spy, aren't you?" she said in disbelief.

"I prefer the term, *scout*. But yes," he continued, "I saw a fragment of the moonstone sapphire sitting upon the hilt of a Tuatha male's sword and on a necklace around the neck of the young woman traveling with him," Dagda paused. "I believe that young woman is my sister."

Aine's gaze shot to meet his. "But that would mean—"

"*Yes*. She is who we have been looking for. And we must do everything in our power to deliver her to the Hill of Tara . . . to Lia Fáil."

CHAPTER TWENTY-SIX

RHIA & ROWAN

The landscape of the coastline had taken on a rugged quality. The soft turns of green hills leading down to sprawling beaches had turned to more weathered cliffs with jagged edges jutting out to sea. Rowan and Rhia rode on, following the path ahead until they reached another turn in the road, leading to a forested area that turned back inland.

They had passed an area where the mouth of a river had led out into a delta, opening to the mouth of the sea. The delta had broken off into smaller streams like the one that lay ahead of them, winding back into the forest with the road ahead.

"At least we will have the cover of the trees and fresh water nearby tonight," Rowan remarked as they led the horses down the path into the tree line. Rhia smiled beside him as they ventured under the cover of the forest canopy, already shifting in color from green to bright yellow. Although the summer was still painting the landscape in warm sunshine, Lughnasadh would be upon them in several weeks, bringing with it cooler weather and the beginning of the season's fire festivals.

Rhia thought of Beatha and the sabbats they had celebrated together, just the two of them. Lughnasadh, Samhain, Beltane, Imbolc . . . her heart longed to see her grandmother again, if only she could speak with Beatha just one more time. She would give anything for just one more cup of tea with the woman. She'd never take her sage advice or the mischievous grin on her weathered face for granted ever again.

"What is it?" Rowan asked quietly from where he sat atop Seamus, riding next to her.

"Oh, nothing. I was just lost in thought," she replied, schooling her features and smiling over at him.

"Do you think I can't tell? I don't know if you've noticed or not, but we're bonded in more ways than one now . . . " he pointed between them. "I can feel when something is bothering you. I am not sure how, but I felt an inkling of what it was like to know your feelings soon after I met you—but now the feelings you have come forth even when I least expect it. I have no idea how to control it . . . I know you are missing your grandmother." He glanced down at the ground.

"Why didn't you say anything before?" she asked.

He huffed a laugh, "And risk being on the receiving end of that fire more so than I already was?"

"Fair," she chuckled. She glanced over at him, grinning for a long moment as a few minutes of silence passed between them. "I can feel it too." She marveled at how she had come to know his movements, his scent. She could detect subtle changes in the timbre of his voice, the tightness in his shoulders.

These feelings, this *bond*, had only heightened since they had come together as one.

His eyes met hers again as he curiously raised a brow. "Can you now?" he asked, amusement dancing in his eyes. "Then what, pray tell, is on my mind?"

A giggle escaped her lips, "Hmmm. Well, I can't say that I am shocked, but it involves you and I . . . alone . . . somewhere less conspicuous than this place. I think I would very much like to know more about what you have in mind—"

"Careful, Rhia," he smirked, his shoulders tensing. "The sun hasn't even set yet."

Memories flashed in her mind of Rowan's hands, his mouth, on every part of her body. She adjusted her seat in the saddle. As they rode ahead, she noticed that they could barely see the path in front of them. There was a noticeable drop in the temperature of the air around them.

A dense fog had descended into the forest and significantly obscured their view of the path ahead. Rhia began to feel uneasy yet again, as if they were being watched. Rowan was already tugging Seamus to the side, motioning her to follow. "I feel it too. We need to get off the path," he declared.

An ominous feeling had settled over his shoulders. They had remarked over the fire the previous night about their worries for Aine. Rhia pointed out that she was supposed to meet them a day ago. After seeing her destroy the Milesians in the forest that day, he knew the woman capable of defending herself. His brow was still etched with uneasiness as he pondered her whereabouts. He didn't like how tense it had made Rhia either—although he could see that she tried to hide it.

The fog seemed to be building as they led the horses to where the stream converged, then turned within a grove of tall trees. "Whatever happens, I swear to the gods Rhia, please just listen to me. Let me protect you," he pleaded, a warning in his eyes as they locked with hers, helping her down from the mare. His hands possessively lingered around her waist.

"Rowan, what do you think is happening?—"

A twig snapped behind them as two sets of footfalls approached from within the fog. The mist was so abundant, they could barely see their own hands in front of them. Rowan moved to grasp Rhia's hand, leading her to stand behind him, shielding her from where the noise was coming from. The hairs on the back of Rhia's neck stood at attention as she felt a strange familiarity in the pattern of the footsteps.

Suddenly, a strange light caught both of their eyes. A blue-hued glow was emanating from around the hilt of Faobhar and from Rhia's own necklace—the moonstone sapphires were *glowing*. As the footsteps grew closer, they could see another glowing blue orb floating through the air.

No, it wasn't floating. It was being held. By someone.

A tall, lean Tuatha male with long red hair stepped forward. The blue-tinged band of flesh on his left forearm was glowing in tandem with the moonstone sapphire he held in his extended palm. His bright blue eyes met Rhia's as she peered at him over Rowan's shoulder from her position behind him. She looked down at her own arm to see her Tuatha band glowing blue as well.

Rhia felt a strange tugging at her chest. A familiar feeling enveloped her body, like a warm embrace, the closer this male stepped.

"Do you know him, Rhia? Who is this?" Rowan whispered back to her.

"I am her brother. I am Dagda. And I have been looking for you for a very long time, Nichnevin," the male replied, a wide smile spreading across his face, tears building in the corners of his eyes.

Before Rhia knew what she was doing, she was running from her position behind Rowan. She bolted toward the Tuatha male who welcomed her into his arms with a firm embrace. "I do not remember your name, brother. But I remember *you*. I remember your spirit." She now had tears in her own eyes. She buried her face in his tunic, taking in his familiar scent—the scent of morning dew on the grass.

Rowan was speechless from his position behind her. He slowly stepped forward. "How did you find us? Are we being tracked?"

Dagda glanced up at Rowan's green-eyed stare. "I have been riding with a scouting party for several weeks now. I was sent by my mother," he looked down at Rhia. "*Our* mother. She sent me to find you. I've been tracking you two since you left the cottage in the woods." Rhia's eyes widened. "The time has come, sister. Our people need you."

"So, it is true . . . " she replied somberly. "But why *now*? I do not feel prepared. I do not know how to help. I have only just learned how to bring forth my fire draíocht," she glanced back at Rowan, blushing slightly.

"Your people are here to help you, Rhiannon. We are in your service. We will fight for you however we must, to restore you to your rightful place of power. You *are* our queen. Our liberator. I know you may not completely understand the full extent of your power and how it will restore our kingdom, but you must trust the plan of our Mother. It has been prophesied. As you step into the full strength of your magic, it will all begin to make sense."

She inhaled sharply as she stared ahead, into the misty forest.

"Destiny does not always allow us to choose the time in which She will call us to our true purpose . . . one does not always *feel* they are worthy, but that does not change the fact that they are," Dagda continued. He glanced up at Rowan, then down at Faobhar by his side.

"You have found your power through the bond. It seems that you have found your Dionadair," he smiled at Rowan. "It is incredible, is it not, how those we care for deeply can help us to draw our own power forth? A power that we may not even know or *believe* is there. They bring out our fire; the best in us." Rhia blushed again, meeting Rowan's gaze.

"This one brings a little light with her no matter where she goes," Rowan added, nodding to her glowing necklace and the light that seemed to now be emanating from her skin. "It makes sense now. She has never been able to leave well enough alone when it comes to helping others," he smirked. She rolled her eyes at the remark, smiling to herself.

"Well, I can attest that part is true," a lovely voice said, as a woman's form emerged from the mist.

"Aine!" Rhia beamed, running toward the woman, and throwing her arms around her neck. "When you didn't meet up with us by sunset yesterday, I thought the worst! I was beginning to worry—"

"Oh, not to worry about her. She was plenty busy stalking about the woods, torturing the souls of poor unsuspecting males—" Dagda began.

"*Stalking!?* You really have the nerve to accuse *me* of stalking?" Aine interrupted.

"Okay, wait. You two know each other?" Rowan interjected. "How does everyone here seem to know each other and what's going on except me?" he asked with an amused tone.

"Come, follow me but a short distance further, and I will explain everything," Dagda led them forward, toward a narrow path that emerged from the thinning fog around them.

CHAPTER
TWENTY-SEVEN
THE LAND OF LIGHT

As the mist around them thinned, Rhia noticed that the forest itself seemed to vanish as well. The trees dissipated around them, giving way to rays of bright, warm sunlight that shone upon a sprawling green meadow.

They could see the land rising into several small hills in front of them. As Rhia's eyes adjusted to the light, she could see what appeared to be a crowd of people ahead. They were standing on the hill, crowded behind the form of an old woman with greying wild hair and thick brows.

"Beatha!" Rhia cried out, pushing past the traveling party, and running ahead at full sprint. She cried out as she fell into the arms of her grandmother. Sobs escaped her lips as she pressed her rosy cheeks into the hem of Beatha's grey tunic, grasping the old woman desperately. "Why did you leave? I thought I'd never *see* you again!"

"Shhh . . . " she soothed, stroking Rhia's hair. "Child, I told you that I would find you again; that it was not the end of our journey. Your mother made it clear to me in a dream the night Elder Ecna was killed. The time had come. *Your* time had come."

The old woman met Rhia's gaze as she stroked the curves of her face with her thumb, tears running down her own cheeks "I wanted to return to you so many times. I did my best to guide you in any way that I could, but I needed to allow you to grow. To find your Dionadair." Rhia's suspicions that the owl was Beatha's presence watching over her were now confirmed in her mind. She smiled back at her grandmother.

Beatha glanced over her shoulder at Rowan standing next to Dagda and Aine, his eyes dancing with joy as he regarded their reunion. "All those trips into Baile, all those meetings with scouts from Tuatha outposts—all the while I was looking for him," she nodded toward Rowan as a confused look passed over his face.

Rhia peered up curiously at Beatha as the old woman laughed. "But I suppose the prophecy had to be fulfilled exactly as it was written: *Find her. Protect her. Restore what was lost.* I couldn't find your Dionadair because he was destined to find *you*."

Rowan stepped forward, leaning down onto one knee as he withdrew Faobhar from its sheath. He placed the flattened blade of the sword against his forehead as he knelt before Rhia, Beatha, and the hoard of Tuatha that now stood behind her. "I was raised a Milesian by a father who was Tuatha. A father who gave up everything to ensure I would one day fulfill my destiny. A destiny I now understand the importance of—one I'd give my life for. One I'd do *anything* to protect," he smiled at Rhia. "I know you said you didn't need me to pledge my sword to you." She chuckled, wiping a tear from her cheek as she smiled back at him from where she stood before him. "But it's yours just the same, Rhiannon," he continued. "As is my body, my heart, my very *life*. I don't ever want to know what this existence is like without you in it. I don't think I could bear waking each day now, without your smile, your wit, your *fire*."

Rhiannon walked forward, bending down to where he kneeled before her. She placed her hands in his, encircling the handle of Faobhar as he lowered the sword by his side. "The sword is nice," she chuckled as she glanced down at the moonstone sapphire that sparkled at its hilt, "but I'm more interested in the one who wields it," she added, taking his face in her hands. "You have my heart as well," she whispered for only him to hear. "I would do anything to protect you, as you would for me. Our destinies are now woven as one, intermingled, spun together like a finely woven tapestry. No matter what happens, you are a part of me now."

She brought his mouth to her own, slanting her lips over his and kissing him fiercely. A chorus of cheers and clapping erupted from behind them. They both stood, walking back to where Beatha stood. "What must we do?" Rhia asked.

"We must take you to the Kingmaker's stone. To Lia Fáil," Beatha smiled as she motioned to the valley below the hill on which they stood, "The stone will cry out under the sovereignty of the true ruler of these lands . . . but it must be made whole again."

The grass of the knoll they stood upon lay like a blanket of lush greenery over the land. Hills rose and fell in gentle waves around them from the sprawling village that sat like a mighty fortress on the hill. Beatha had told them that the ground on which they stood was the legendary Hill of Tara from the ancient Tuatha texts.

The veil of the Sidhe billowed all around them, like a sheer cloaking from the sky. It illuminated the sunlight that shone through it and—as Beatha had told her—shielded her people from the ever-watchful gaze of the Milesians. More powerful than a ward, the veil only lifted to those who possessed a shard of the moonstone sapphire. The legendary stone was chipped from the master stone—the large shining blue gem that sat atop the stone monolith of Lia Fáil.

As they approached the stone pillar that stood as a beacon in the surrounding rolling green hills, Rhia stopped to marvel at the sheer size and magnificence of it. The granite stone rose to a curved point, just a few feet taller than her *very* tall brother, but it was the moonstone sapphire that accounted for the rest of its gargantuan height.

In the light of the setting sun, she could see fragmented breaks within the stone from the way the light reflected upon places where the stone had been chipped off. Dagda moved forward, placing his fragment of the moonstone sapphire in her hand. She reached up, removing her necklace and grasping it in her other palm.

Rowan ran his hand over the hilt of Faobhar, rubbing the stone and remembering his father, fondly. His mind drifted back to the day he had discovered the stone in a box under his father's bed . . . the day they had welded it to the hilt of his family's ancestral sword . . . now here it still sat, finally returned to the place it was carved from.

To restore power to the one true queen of these lands, the one who held his hand *and* his heart. She had always been his destiny. He reached into his boot, retrieving his dagger, and used the blade to pry the stone loose from the hilt. He placed it in Rhia's palm, closing her fingers around it as he kissed them gently.

Rhia stepped forward, feeling the earth vibrating slightly beneath her feet. She lifted her palms as the stones floated in the air, high up toward the top of Lia Fáil, finally resting on the crest of the master stone. The ground began to vibrate more noticeably. Beatha bristled beside her. "Something is amiss," the old woman stated, peering up at the monolith. "The stone is not awakening."

Rhia's eyes adjusted to see that there was still a fragment missing from the stone's west-facing side . . . a very significant fragment. "I don't understand." The vibrations from the ground began to jostle the pebbles and rocks on the ground around them. This was no Tuatha spell working, no draíocht . . ."

Those were hoofbeats.

As Rowan drew his sword and Dagda withdrew his bow, knocking an arrow, they spun around to see an army of Milesians riding toward them at full speed. At their command, riding ahead, was a Milesian male with a shining crown atop his head, encrusted with rubies and emeralds. His face had been badly burned, almost disfigured from the thick bands of scars that could be seen running across his cheeks.

Aine shuddered as a cold chill ran up her spine. She felt sparks emanating from her palms, dark magic pulsating in her fingertips in his presence. *Impossible.*

It was none other than Prince Hedrek.

CHAPTER
TWENTY-EIGHT

Aine bellowed, an indecipherable sound escaping her lips—something between a scream and a shriek. Flames and fire burst forth from her palms as she began to stride forward, one step after another, heading straight for the army riding towards them.

"Are you *mad*, Aine?! *Stop*! We can hold them back, but you can't possibly face them all on your own!" Dagda shouted, running after her. Rhia knew that Dagda likely didn't know or understand Aine's deep-rooted history with the captain of the Milesian guard, but there was no time to explain now.

Rowan quickly moved to mount Seamus, reaching down for Rhia's hand as he helped her into the saddle in front of him. His arms flexed around her protectively as they rode forward. Hedrek was still riding toward them. *Fast*.

He held a stone above his head, clutched between his thumb and forefinger.

The missing piece of the moonstone sapphire.

The stone behind them, the monolith of Lia Fáil, began to pulsate in its presence. Rhia watched in amazement as the stone began to hover above Hedrek, floating on the air as if it were being summoned back to the rock from which it came from. She felt a deep pang in her chest, Rowan stiffened behind her—he felt it too, through their bond.

"We need to go the other way—we need to ride back to the monolith! We don't know what power will emerge from the stone once it is whole again," she called back to Rowan, her voice lifting above the chaos around them.

Rowan turned Seamus quickly, spurring the horse onward, as fast as he could run across the grassy hill, back to where Lia Fáil towered over the valley. As they approached the stone, Rowan helped Rhia dismount. She ran full speed toward the monolith, feeling the ground shaking beneath her feet. The floating fragment of the sapphire finally reached its mark, crashing into the gemstone with a sound as loud as thunder. Light poured out around them, flooding the valley in a white radiance.

Suddenly, a sound emerged from the stone, as if it was calling out from the depths of the earth itself. A loud cry pierced the air around them, silencing every noise in the atmosphere except the wailing that was coming from the stone itself.

Beatha stepped forward, placing her hands on Rhia's shoulders from where the young woman now knelt before the stone. She called out to the crowd of Tuatha and Milesian alike, gathering around them. "The ancient texts prophecy that the stone of Lia Fáil will cry out, will bellow from beneath the earth when the one true sovereign of Éire appears."

"That's very convenient indeed, seeing the situation I have found myself in, as of late," a deep voice called from behind them. The very hairs on Rhia's neck stood on end as she rose and turned to face Hedrek. She spied Aine on the other side of the crowd, Dagda standing protectively in front of her as she seethed at the man now facing Rhia.

Rowan rushed forward, stepping in between them. "I will say this only once. Step *away* from her," he spat at Hedrek, his features darkening, a voice like cold death.

"That's very lovely. The traitor to his own mother's people decides to finally embrace his own half-blooded *filth*. And from the looks of it, embrace the likes of hers as well," Hedrek seethed, wrinkling his nose as he looked down at Rhia and Beatha. "All this time I've spent, trying to cleanse our lands of these cursed Fae. All the blades I've pierced through their weakening bodies," he chuckled down as he glanced at Rowan's sword, his voice rising. "Blades that *you*, blacksmith, might have even forged *for* me. Have you told your little *whore* about that?"

Before Rhia could stop him, Rowan had already unsheathed Faobhar and pressed the sharpened end of the blade to Hedrek's throat. "Watch how you *fucking* speak about the sovereign of this land—" Rowan began.

"Which brings me to my second point," Hedrek continued, as he discreetly brought a closed fist in front of his own face. He opened his hand, blowing a fine powder into Rowan's face, eliciting a sharp inhale and cough from him, and from Beatha stood behind him.

Rowan felt a strong pull on his body, a heaviness, pulling his limbs down to the earth. An iron tang stung his eyes and tongue.

"*No!*" Aine screamed from behind, already recognizing the concoction at Hedrek's disposal.

Just then, the Milesian soldiers around them on horseback closed in, forming a circle around the Tuatha who were gathered nearby. They withdrew small vials from their own pockets, blowing a thick cloud of the powder, the heavy dust settling over the group of Tuatha. Coughs erupted from the crowd, chaos ensuing as Hedrek smiled at Rhia from where she stood behind Rowan.

Rowan could not fight the pull on his strength. For the first time, he cursed his father's blood running through his veins. Gasps and cries of pain began to resound from those around them, including Aine and Dagda who stood within the crowd of Tuatha.

"Stop it! Stop! . . . What do you want?!" Rhia cried, stepping forward, seemingly unaffected by the powder. *Strange*, she thought, *it is as if I am immune to its poison. But how?*

Fire surged at her fingertips, rage building deep inside of her. She held her hands with her palms skyward at her sides, flames dancing on the surface of her skin as the winds picked up around them and the sky darkened.

Hedrek sauntered menacingly toward Rhia. Rowan's body shook with rage from where he lay upon the ground, using every ounce of strength to beg Rhia through their bond to *stop*, as she continued walking toward Hedrek.

"The stone of Lia Fáil cried out before the true sovereign of Éire . . . just as the prophecy foretold," he bellowed, his disfigured face gleaming in the reflection of the stone's glow in front of him. Rhia squared her jaw as she stared up at him. Thunder bellowed in the distance as a bright streak of lightning shot across the sky, its light reflecting in Rhia's cold blue eyes.

"I will be frank with you, Nichnevin. My brother is dead. I am now the sole heir to the crown of the Milesian people. And I am in need of a queen," Hedrek said plainly. "The land has called out to you, chosen *you* as its ruler. Its sovereign. But we could rule the continent *together*. Finally uniting our peoples under one unified crown."

"*No!*" Rowan roared from nearby, his muscled arms fighting to lift his form from the ground, struggling against the poison pulsating through his body.

"Look at your people, Nichnevin. Look around you," Hedrek motioned behind him, where his men stood with bows and swords drawn, ready and willing to butcher the last of her people—weakened by the poison on the air.

She looked at Beatha's slumped form behind her, as the old woman shook, trembling under the effects of the poison.

She looked out to the crowd, at Dagda attempting to lift Aine into a seated position as she grasped her head in her hands. She was rocking back and forth, screaming a succession of *no*'s.

And then she looked to Rowan.

Her Dionadair.

Her protector.

His eyes met hers as tears began to freefall down her cheeks. *I love you,* she mouthed to him silently. She offered him an expression on her face that he had once given her

. . . weeks ago at the inn when his plan had almost gotten both of them killed. He recognized it immediately.

Trust me.

"You can protect them. You can be the queen that they need," Hedrek continued. "You can unify the land and *stop* this bloodshed once and for all. Come with me, rule by my side, share this power with my crown. And I vow to you that I will not harm them any further. I will withdraw my soldiers. Your lands will be safe, once again."

Rhia straightened her shoulders again and raised her chin as she looked Hedrek dead in the eyes, fire and flames flaring in her own.

She stepped closer.

"Say it again. Place your hand on the kingmaker's stone and say it again. *Vow* it," she motioned to the monolith behind her.

Hedrek stepped forward, placing his scarred hands onto the stone. Rhia could feel Rowan's anguish, his rage, his fury vibrating through their bond, his voice in her head screaming.

No. No. No. *No.*

"Come with me, Nichnevin. Unite with my crown as the Milesian queen and rule these lands by my side. Your people will be safe once again, your lands will be secured."

A long pause of silence passed between them as the stone pulsated like a heartbeat, sending static waves through Rhia's entire body.

She closed her eyes and breathed deeply.

She opened them again and turned to look at Hedrek, meeting his gaze with cold, calculated ferocity.

"I accept."

Lightning flashed across the sky again, illuminating the land in a blinding white light as a loud thunderhead brought the rains.

Heavy drops fell from the sky, pelting the ground around them, like tears soaking into the earth.

As if the very continent of Éire herself was weeping.

To Be Continued . . .

THE STORY CONTINUES . . .

A Destiny Spun in Silver

Book Two of the Chronicles of the Tuatha

Coming April 2024 - Pre-order available now with the link below.

Subscribe to my email newsletter by visiting my website to unlock an exclusive first look at Chapter One of Book Two: **A Destiny Spun in Silver**.

www.authorjessicaleigh.com

AUTHOR'S NOTE

This book really presented itself to me in a very unconventional way. What began with senseless daydreaming, slowly unfolded into a story with characters that developed into an intricate world if their own.

Part fiction, part history, and a whole lot of folklore, this trilogy contains themes based heavily on Celtic and Scottish mythology. I have been a lifelong lover of all things legend and lore. From the time I was a small child, I clung to everything from Arthurian legends to Grimm's fairy tales. I will never forget the feeling I had when I discovered that these fairy tales were often based on mythology that had been passed down through oral tradition throughout the world.

I have been enthralled with the tales of the Tuatha Dé Danann for many years. I wanted to tell a story with an original cast of characters that were based on the themes of who these mythical people were, as well as the values they stood for in the lore: respecting the earth, communing with nature, and working with elemental magic.

As I dove even deeper into their tales, I began to see incredible correlations between their symbolism and the characters that were presenting themselves within my work. The process of writing this novel was an incredible spectrum of feelings to experience. At times, I felt as if the characters had a mind of their own!

I feel so very fortunate to have worked with a wonderful editor from Ireland who had a deep understanding of the language, lore, and context of the speech that is delivered within the book. The gods and goddesses discussed within the series are very near and dear to my heart. There is a deep magic that I believe still exists in that part of the world and it permeates from the mythology. I wanted to do justice to the culture and the lore of ancient Ireland and avoid any themes that could be perceived as cultural appropriation. My editor was wonderful to partner with in the process of developing this work from a first-draft manuscript to what you are reading today. I am so grateful to her and look forward to collaborating with her throughout the entire trilogy.

After careful contemplation, there are a few creative liberties and variations of the lore that I took into account in constructing the plot of the story and the motives of the characters that I will discuss now. In Scottish mythology, the Nichnevin was a symbolic goddess that, in many cases, represented the dark elements of the feminine psyche. She was later contrived to be a goddess of winter, of witches, or an evil entity. Some consider her to be a derivative of Hecate from the Greek myths.

However, when you look at her lore on a deeper level, she is symbolic of the shadow that exists in all of us. As women, our shadow may not always be perceived as acceptable to those around us. Nevertheless, the shadow self is an important aspect of the divine feminine - she is beautiful, she is powerful, and she is terrifying. This is ultimately why I chose the theme of this goddess as the redeemer of the Tuatha, even though she does not specifically present as part of their folklore cycle in the recorded texts.

There are several characters from various cycles of the ancient Celtic pantheon whose symbolism is explored within the series. The Morrigan presents herself strongly within the work with the coming of battles and as an ominous foreshadowing of death. Her encounter with Dagda at the river is reminiscent to an encounter told in the *Book of Invasions* where she imparts prophetic knowledge to *the* Dadga through the sacred symbolism of copulation.

Lugh is described as the first Dionadair - a concept contrived for the purposes of the story - to tie his symbolism to Rowan's character. There is foreshadowing in the victory of Lugh in defeating Balor, as Rhia discovers in reading the ancient texts. The battle that occurs at Maig Tuireadh where Balor is slain by Lugh is a recorded account in the lore of the Tuatha Dé Danann. His banishment to the sea by the Nichnevin is an event that I included to weave her mythology into this particular cycle of invasions.

As for the landmarks in the book, specifically Lia Fáil and the Hill of Tara, these locations still exist to this day in Ireland. These ancient sites date back to around 3000 BC and are beautiful reminders of an ancient culture steeped in magic and mystery. Lia Fáil, or the king maker's stone, was revered as a sacred site for thousands of years, although its origins are still an enigma.

I encourage you to do your own research and read more about the fascinating culture, lore, and legends of ancient Éire. I know you will fall in love with the magic held within those shores, just as much as I have!

ABOUT THE AUTHOR

Jessica Leigh is an emerging author of fantasy romance. She has been an avid book lover since childhood, reading everything in sight from J.R.R. Tolkien and Marion Zimmer Bradley to Sylvia Plath and Aldous Huxley.

She lives in North Carolina with her husband and two fur babies. She holds a Master's degree and has worked in healthcare for eight years. When she isn't writing you can likely find her hiking, reading, or daydreaming about the next mythical world she would like to create and the enchanted characters that inhabit it.

This is Jessica's debut novel.

instagram.com/authorjessleigh

ACKNOWLEDGMENTS

I could not have completed this labor of love without the support and unending encouragement of *my* love, my husband. Justin, I love you endlessly.

Thank you to my family and friends for their constant love and support. I am humbled to have so many wonderful people in my corner, it's an incredible feeling!

I'd like to thank my lovely editor Sarah Giblin - thank you for your hard work and incredible feedback, for your attention to detail, and for working with the time difference between the U.S. and Ireland. You provided incredible insight into Irish culture and language. What a treasure you are!

To my incredible beta reader and amazing friend Cate Bleuel - thank you for always being my hype girl and support person throughout this process. You're one in a million, love.

To my wonderful friend and writing mentor Jillian Wray - thank you for your encouragement, feedback, and support! Your mentorship and your friendship are so precious to me.

To my ARC reader team - THANK YOU for taking a chance on an indie author and being a part of releasing my debut novel! I am so appreciative of your feedback and support!

I would also like to give a special thank you to the

following people for their support during my writing process:

Macy Greenway

Kluane Spake

Lisa Harris

Emily Barnett

Most importantly, **thank you to my readers**! There are so many indie authors out there just like myself, pouring our hearts into our work every day and putting it out there for the world to see. Of all of the books out there, you decided to pick up mine, that's an incredible honor! I cannot wait to share the rest of this trilogy with all of you!

www.ingramcontent.com/pod-product-compliance
Ingram Content Group UK Ltd.
Pitfield, Milton Keynes, MK11 3LW, UK
UKHW042004190726
13854UKWH00005B/2160

9 798218 248208